Shallow End Gals

"CATAHOULA"

Book One

BY

VICKI GRAYBOSCH
LINDA MCGREGOR
TERESA DUNCAN
KIMBERLY TROUTMAN

Copyright © Vicki Graybosch 2013
All rights reserved
Printed in the United States of America
Copyrighted Material

ISBN: 1493770756
ISBN 13: 9781493770755

Library of Congress Control Number: 2013921050
CreateSpace Independent Publishing Platform
North Charleston, South Carolina

Edited by, Erika Canter
Cover photography, Jennifer Unger
Cover model, Tim Wilson

List of characters at end of book

CATAHOULA

The Shallow End Gals

Teresa Duncan

Vicki Graybosch

Linda McGregor

Kimberly Troutman

Previous books:

Shallow End Gals Trilogy

"Alcohol Was Not Involved" Book One

"Extreme Heat Warning" Book Two

"Silent Crickets" Book Three

From the authors.........

Over our years of friendship we have discovered that we each have a unique opinion on the afterlife. We do agree that it is a comforting thought that angels may be among us. If so, it seems only logical there may be a learning curve in passing. We are hopeful that, as flawed mortals, new angels are given a great deal of patient training. This premise is a humorous secondary story line in our books.

CHAPTER 1

onday late afternoon...
Izzy slammed the brakes on her bike and stared at the tall grass in the ditch. She was sure she had seen a glint of metal. She lowered her kickstand and noticed her shoelace had broken again. It was already knotted in three places and difficult to tie. Her stringy brown hair fell across her young face as she crouched down and dug in the grass for the shiny object. She found it. It was round and thin, but packed in mud. She pulled a small rag from her bicycle basket and spit on the corner. Her brow furrowed as she feverishly scrubbed through the mud. The sunlight burst from the shiny edge and Izzy squealed. It was a quarter!

She dug into her pocket and found the small red velveteen bag that Gram had given her. Her tiny fingers gently loosened the string tie and she dropped the quarter in to join her other treasures. Izzy gently pulled on the string until the bag was securely closed. She stuffed the bag back into her pocket and pedaled toward Gram's. The hardest part of her trip was just ahead: making it past Otis's store.

Her bike slowed as she watched people leave the store with paper bags full of groceries. Her stomach fisted in hunger and her mouth watered up so fast she had to swallow twice. In her basket was a paper bag with an orange and a package of crackers she had earned from sweeping sidewalks for Ms. Nelson. Izzy had hidden the bag under some rags. Gram would love the orange. Oranges had vitamins.

Izzy's bike slowed to a stop at the door to Otis's store. She smelled fried chicken. Her eyes scanned the signs taped to the front window looking for the price of that chicken. Maybe she could buy Gram just one piece.

Izzy put her kickstand down and placed her bike in front of the big window. She retrieved her paper bag from her basket, took a deep breath and walked into the store. Her chin held up high, she walked to the glass case where Otis stood talking to a customer. The customer paid for his food with paper money, lifted his sack and waved goodbye.

Otis glanced at Izzy. "What can I get for ya, little miss?"

Izzy frowned at his calling her little miss.

She cleared her throat and said, "I'd like to buy a very small piece of your cooked chicken." The aroma from the chicken was so strong Izzy thought she might be able to lick the air and taste it.

While Izzy waited for Otis to give her a price, she noticed he also sold shoelaces. She leaned closer to the display to read the price tag. Ninety-nine cents! He must be crazy!

Izzy frowned at Otis, "If you charge ninety-nine cents for shoelaces, then your chicken must cost a million dollars! I have probably used up my money already just smellin' the air in here!"

Izzy had one fist on her hip and her paper bag clenched tight in her other hand.

Otis tried hard not to smile. "I don't charge for smellin'. Why don't you tell me how much you want to spend and we will figure out what size piece of chicken you can get?"

"I want that senior discount thing the door says." Izzy had her shoulders back and tried to look like a serious negotiator.

Otis chuckled, "Senior discount be for old people. You're what...ten?"

"This is for my Gram and she is real old."

Izzy pulled her red pouch from her pocket and put it on top of the counter. "I have almost a dollar."

Otis noticed her worn clothing and her knotted shoelaces. Her little fingers were white from clutching her paper bag. "What you got in the paper bag?"

Izzy whipped the bag behind her back and said, "I earned these sweepin'. I got Gram a whole package of crackers...and an *orange*. Can't leave 'em in my basket lest someone steal 'em." Her eyes sparkled when she said orange and Otis nodded his head.

Otis reached in an oven door and pulled out two large chicken breasts, placed them in a box, and put them on the counter in front of Izzy. Izzy's eyes opened wide, she swallowed and said, "I don't want to spend the whole dollar. I only need one piece."

Otis nodded. "It be buy one, get one free day. You're gonna have to take both." Otis smiled at her expression and added, "If you can impress me with your smarts, I'll throw in the shoelaces."

Izzy smiled from ear to ear. "I can do my alphabet backwards!"

Otis started laughing, "Why did you learn them backwards?"

Izzy grinned, "Case someday I gotta prove I'm smart!"

She stood as straight as a soldier and said her alphabet forward and back. Otis put the shoelaces in her bag. He gave her back sixty cents from her three quarters and told her to stop back anytime. The bells on the door jingled as she left the store. Izzy hid her treasures in her basket and pedaled as fast as she could to Gram's.

Izzy frowned at the mail on the porch floor. That darn mailbox fell off the wall again. She noticed most of the letters were pink. Gram always said once they turn pink, best be doing somethin' about 'em. Izzy shook her head in worry. She had to figure a way to earn some real money. Maybe just for today she would put the mail where Gram couldn't see it. Gram looked sad this morning and Izzy didn't want anything to spoil tonight's feast.

Her key turned hard in the lock and she twisted her bike to rest it in the foyer against the old plaster wall. She hid the mail in her basket, grabbed her paper sack with the crackers, chicken and the orange. She called out "Surprise!" as she ran for Gram's room.

Izzy stood at the end of Gram's bed, silent. Gram didn't look so good. Her lips were blue and her skin ashen. Izzy dropped her sack on the floor and cupped Gram's foot in her hands. She gave it a little wiggle. "Gram?" The silence in the room was deafening and Izzy could hear herself choking back sobs. She crawled on the bed and kissed Gram's cold cheek. Gram was her whole world, and now she was gone.

* * *

Early Tuesday morning....

Cat's direct line was ringing. He glanced at his watch. The office wouldn't open for another twenty minutes. The files on his desk had shifted and he had to unbury the receiver.

"Sabastian." Cat rolled his neck as he waited for the caller to identify themselves. After a moment he repeated, "Sabastian, can I help you?" It was another breathing call. He hung up.

His secretary, Martha, frowned in the do orway. "Was that another hang up call?" Her fierce protective side was showing.

"Technically, I'm the one hanging up." Cat rolled his chair away from the desk and tossed a paper wad across the room to the waste basket. He looked up and grinned, "Got anything fun for me to do in the next hour? I have court at nine."

Martha pretended a scowl as she placed a stack of files on his desk. "I don't know what kind of fun you expect as a prosecutor for the U.S. Attorney General's office." Martha noticed a slight stoop to his shoulders. "You've been putting in some hellish hours. Are you taking care of yourself?"

Cat rolled his chair back to the desk and started scanning file covers. "I'm just fine, but thanks for asking." He glanced up quickly and winked. Martha shook her head, left the room and repositioned herself at her desk. She was well aware that the rest of the office called it the hawk's perch.

A moment later he heard Martha raise her voice to someone. "You need to schedule an appointment like anyone else." Martha leaned back in her chair and turned to face Cat's office window. She mouthed, "Reporter", and shrugged her shoulders.

Cat smiled and motioned for her to transfer the call. Martha pointed down to indicate the reporter was in the building. Cat snickered at Martha's expression. She hated reporters. Cat's intercom buzzed. Martha must have put the reporter on hold. "He says it's important and he can only talk to you."

"Then send him in. I could use some entertainment."

About ten minutes had passed when a young man from the Times-Picayune softly knocked on Cat's open door. "Mr. Delacroix? Thank you for seeing me."

Cat stood and shook the young reporter's hand. "And your name is?"

"Reuben Florey, sir."

"Just call me Cat." Cat motioned for Reuben to take a seat and Cat returned to his. "What's so important?"

The young reporter looked very nervous and pulled out a small notebook. He quickly flipped a few pages and took a deep breath. He looked at Cat very seriously and said, "A man has been unfairly charged with murder. He has proof of his innocence and a lead on the real murderer. He wants me to pass the information to you directly. Not the cops…..just you."

Cat frowned. He was a prosecutor, not a detective. "Why me?"

Reuben answered, "He said he only trusts the prosecutor the press calls Catahoula."

Cat smiled at his memory of the first time that nickname had appeared in the newspaper years ago. The Catahoula is a Louisiana leopard dog that is known for its sharp instincts and cunning attack skills. The nickname had stuck and Catahoula had been shortened to 'Cat' by most people who knew him.

Cat tapped his pen on his stack of files. "Okay, then, why you? What's this guy's name?"

Reuben leaned forward and practically whispered, "Edward J. Meyer."

Cat sat back. He knew the name well. His mind began extracting fragments of information from his memory. He began reorganizing the details of the murder case that shook New Orleans to its core eight years ago. Satisfied he was ready to hear more, Cat leaned forward, brow furrowed, "He's dead."

"He's alive." Reuben shifted his position in the chair, took a deep breath and exhaled "He's my father."

* * *

Professor Thomas Hadley woke early and gingerly walked the pitch black perimeter of the camp site. Sleep had been sparse, interrupted by swamp noises both real and imagined. He had literally drawn the short straw for this assignment. The thick, humid swamp air stunk of rot and methane gas. His team of scientists had arrived last night to monitor the activity of the now thirty acre Assumption Parish sinkhole.

He could actually see the lazy whirlpool of the swamp waters mysteriously tease the land masses and trees at the sinkhole edge. Without warning huge hunks of earth and hundred year old cypress trees dropped silently below the water line - sucked into the unknown depths below.

What used to be marsh lands above the world's largest brine dome had been reborn into a living, breathing monster of unknown proportions. The dome had been abandoned and capped until accidently penetrated by a drilling team. The scientific community blamed this breach of the dome's shell as the catalyst of its collapse.

Swamp waters had rushed in to fill the insatiable void. Pressure from water above and gravity below crushed against the dome's compromised shell and accelerated its disintegration. Thomas had been stunned when the government acknowledged that within the dome was over fifty abandoned caverns that had been used for the storage of hazardous materials. He wondered how much money had traded hands to pull off that brilliant idea. One such storage cavern housed highly explosive butane gas byproduct.

Immeasurable pressures within the shifting dome were causing dangerous pockets of crude oil and natural gases to escape. These pressure vents were also accelerating the damage to the brine shell. Geologists nicknamed these vents 'bubble spots' for laymen and the media. Twenty new 'bubble' sites had been located in just the last two weeks. All that was needed now for an unprecedented catastrophe was an ignition source. One could only guess what greater dangers might lay beneath the giant dome.

To date the government's reaction had been to order the evacuation of the area's five hundred homeowners. Thomas shook his head. If this wasn't so damn serious, it would be laughable.

Thomas trained his night vision binoculars to the eastern sky where he heard the rhythmic warp of helicopter rotors approaching. The helicopter flew over the sinkhole center and circled back around. It would be sunrise in less than twenty minutes. Thomas wondered what possible purpose there was in doing an observation flight in the dark.

His jaw dropped in shock as a screaming man fell from the helicopter into the center of the sinkhole vortex. The helicopter banked and flew away. The screaming had stopped. It was as if nothing had happened.

* * *

Stone Carson could have become many things. Striking good looks and a brilliant mind were assets he had no intention of wasting. Many entities had vied for his favor over the years. Stone had been amused at their pitiful attempts to persuade him.

They would never come close to the offer he had accepted. Anything he ever asked for, for the rest of his life. He could pick his assignments and would be provided anything he needed. He wasn't the only one, but in the last ten years, he had become the best. His employer only had one requirement: clean results.

The result he wanted this early morning was for Senator Dalton's body to be sucked to the bottom of the Assumption Parish sinkhole. Stone studied the control panel of the Bell 429 helicopter and engaged the night vision beam. He looked to his copilot and yelled, "Get his ass on the edge." The copilot moved to the passenger bay, removed the cuffs from the terrified man and ripped the duct tape from his mouth.

"You'll never get away with this! What do you want? I can get you anything! Why are you doing this?"

Stone yelled back, "Wait a minute! I see movement down there. Let me circle around."

Stone circled, determined everything was clear, and yelled, "Now."

The copilot pried the Senator's hands from the door and kicked the center of his back sending the flailing man screaming into the center of the black whirlpool below.

Stone signaled for the copilot to take over and pointed back east where Stone was going to parachute from the copter back to his car. Stone checked the emergency gear on the chute, located his landing flare in the distance, signaled his exit and jumped.

He glided to a silent landing within fifty yards of his rental car. He removed the chute and turned off the battery flare in front of the car. Stone lit the chute with a lighter and stretched his neck. The forties didn't feel as good as the thirties had. Just before starting the engine to leave, he pointed his detonator toward the fading sound of the helicopter rotors. He watched as the sky exploded into a bright yellow ball of fire. Clean results.

* * *

Cat walked over to his office door and closed it. He twisted the rod to close the blinds and stood leaning against his file cabinet. There would be plenty of time later to ask questions. Right now he wanted to listen to Rueben. Cat looked at his watch, "You have fifteen minutes. Write down your contact information and start talking. I have to be in court."

Martha chewed on the end of her pen and saw the red light come on Cat's phone line. That meant do not disturb. This was only the second time she had seen him use it in eight years. Whatever that young man was saying was mighty important. Martha thrust her shoulders back and glared at anyone who even appeared to be heading toward Cat's office. The hawk was in her perch.

Reuben quickly wrote his private cell number on the back of his card and reached in his jacket pocket. Cat noticed a slight shake in Reuben's hand as he produced a flash drive and placed it on the desk.

Reuben focused his gaze on Cat and asked, "Can we watch this first?"

Cat sat in his chair and inserted the flash drive into his computer. He turned his monitor so Reuben could narrate. The picture was decent quality, if not slightly grainy. A well-dressed man was leaning against a brick wall in a narrow alley smoking a cigarette. Cat thought the man did look like his memory of Ed Meyer. It was obviously night and the green and red lights from an adjoining bar sign reflected on the wet pavement. A dumpster could be seen a few yards farther down the alley. A car abruptly pulled into the alley forcing the man to retreat backwards toward the dumpster. The headlights of the car clearly blinded Edward as he raised his forearms to shield his eyes.

The car door opened and a man walked over to where Ed was standing. Ed put his hands up in a defensive move. The attacking man slugged Ed and did something to his neck.

Reuben broke the silence, "Hit stop. I have blown up this portion and I believe he is injecting dad's neck with a needle. You'll see him put something in the dumpster in a minute."

Cat hit the play button and watched as Ed was dragged back to the car and shoved in the driver's seat. The attacking man appeared to be doing something to Ed and then he kicked the car door shut. The man removed gloves from his hands and appeared to be clutching some stained rags. He threw them in the dumpster, walked back to the car and leaned against the trunk as he made a call on his cell phone. Cat didn't recognize the man's face.

For nearly five minutes it looked as if he was guarding the car. Suddenly he abruptly turned his head and walked quickly out of frame. A swarm of police and flashing lights began to fill the alley from both directions and the man in the car was dragged out, slapped around, handcuffed and taken away.

Cat hit the stop button. "This was your dad's arrest?"

Reuben's eyes had filled with tears and he nodded. "Will you help us?"

Cat removed the flash drive and put it in his pocket. "I don't want you coming back here." Cat looked at his watch, "I have to leave. I'll call you. Soon."

Reuben stood and shook Cat's hand. Martha noticed Reuben quickly wipe his eyes as he left Cat's office. Cat's door reopened a few minutes later. He announced he was late for court and left. Martha twisted in her chair as she watched him wait for the elevator door to close. Her eyes instinctively narrowed. She could read his body language like a book. Something real big was real wrong.

CHAPTER 2

cer watched Stone's parachute glide off to the right and waited until Stone was halfway to his landing. He activated the helicopter's 3 AIX autopilot, put on his chute and jumped. If his timing was right, then Stone would land about the time that Acer's chute would be concealed by tree cover a few miles away.

Acer's feet hit the ground the instant the helicopter exploded. He smiled. Figured Stone would leave clean. Acer unclasped his harness and walked toward the motorcycle he had left outside of the small town of Crawsville. It was about a thirty minute walk. Just enough for him to have a little planning time. He had the advantage now. Stone will report the mission clean. Acer will prove it wasn't. Until then, Stone won't be worried about consequences and he certainly won't be worried about Acer.

Yeah, Stone was good. But he was better.

* * *

Officer Dante had pulled his patrol car off the main road for a nap. He had his sunglasses on so no one driving by would see that his eyes were closed. Not that anyone would be out this early. Sun wasn't even up yet. The static from the dispatch radio startled him awake.

"Dante! Got old Clyde Perrine out at his place, says a helicopter just dumped some screaming guy into the sinkhole. Copy."

Dante removed his sunglasses, rubbed his hands over his eyes and grabbed his radio. "That drunken fool ain't supposed to be out there! Been evacuated! Copy."

The dispatcher answered, "I know. Don't think he's drunk now though. Got a call about five minutes after his. Some geologist sayin' the same thing. Best you get over there. Copy."

What the hell? Dante started the car's engine, turned on his police lights and sped toward the Assumption Parish sinkhole. He suddenly realized he didn't know exactly where he was going. That whole area had been sanctioned off as dangerous and he had no idea where this geologist had set up camp.

Dante grabbed his radio, "Where in the hell is this geologist? Copy."

The static on the radio answered, "He doesn't know. Says he'll turn on some kind of special spotlight."

"Tell him to send up some flares. Copy."

"Did that. He says flares might cause the whole damn lake to explode. Copy."

"Shit!"

16

* * *

Reuben logged into his computer at the Times-Picayune and quickly glanced around the large room at the bustling people scrambling to meet deadline. His editor, Walter Trayer, had his door open and was screaming at someone on the phone. Reuben still felt shaken from his meeting with Catahoula. So much was riding on Catahoula helping them.

Trayer yelled from his office, "Reuben! Get your ass in here!"

Reuben grabbed his notebook and pen and stuck his head into Trayer's office.

"Get over to Assumption Parish. Cops got a call that some guy was dropped out of a helicopter into the sinkhole."

Reuben's involuntary response was to say "What?" even though he had heard perfectly. Trayer raised an eyebrow at him indicating he wasn't about to repeat himself.

Reuben dialed his dad on the ride over. He couldn't help but worry every time something strange happened that his dad was involved. "Dad? You okay?" Edward answered he was fine and Reuben added, "I gave Catahoula the flash drive. I think he's going to help us."

* * *

Ed returned his phone to his pocket and noticed his split nails. He winced at his reflection in the storefront window next to him. It seemed he was staring at a complete stranger. Where had he gone? Who was this staring back at him in the glass? His clothes were filthy, his hair a mass of dirty brown tufts. Working the docks at night, for cash, had been the only work he could do. Eight years of hell. Each dreadful day carved deep into his now leathery skin. His mind shot back to life before Katrina, when he had manicured nails, fine clothing and styled hair. When he had a name.

All of that ended that terrible summer. First his freedom. Then his identity.

Ed ran his fingers through his hair in an attempt to tame it. He was tired - of everything. Most of all, he was tired of being invisible. He missed talking to people. He missed laughing. He missed people asking for and respecting his opinions. Ed realized tears were running down his cheeks. My God, was he crying? Ed wiped his face with his sleeve and straightened his shoulders. His heart was pounding and the street sounds were blurred and contorted. Ed took a long, deep breath and forced himself to calm. He hadn't survived the last eight years to end up a blubbering idiot on the streets.

Reuben had shown the video to Catahoula. There was no going back now. This was real. Reuben's call had stirred something in his soul that he hadn't felt for a very long time. Hope.

Soon, he told himself. Soon I won't be invisible anymore.

* * *

Izzy woke as the first ray of sunlight breached through the cream colored lace curtain. Gram's cold body lay as Izzy remembered. It hadn't been a nightmare after all. Izzy tried to imagine what Gram would tell her to do. She would have to call an adult, so Gram was taken care of properly. Adults would want to make her a ward of the state. That's what Gram said happens. Izzy thought of her friend Tina, Gram said Tina turned into a ward of the state. The police came and Tina disappeared. Izzy never saw her again.

Izzy peeled the orange she had brought for Gram and slowly began to eat it. She decided she didn't want to disappear. She would need vitamins if she was going to raise herself. Gram would say she needed a plan. Izzy found Gram's key to their house and put it in her treasure bag. It wouldn't hurt to have two keys. She unlocked the bathroom window in case she had to crawl in later tonight. The police will want to take her away and they might put a special lock on the door. She will have to be careful.

Izzy took a bath, changed into clean clothes and packed her few clothes into her school backpack. There were only two days of school left before summer break. Best not go back. If, for some reason she couldn't come home tonight, then at least she had clean clothes. Gram always said, "Many reasons people be poor. No good reason people be dirty. You can clean up at lots of places for free." Izzy decided to put a small bar of soap and her pink washcloth in her backpack, too. She re-laced her shoes with her new shoelaces and sighed.

Izzy's gaze wandered over to Gram's closet door. Gram had a little tin box in her closet she told Izzy would be hers someday. Izzy dragged a chair from the kitchen, stood on her tiptoes and pulled the box down from the top shelf. She sat on the bed next to Gram and pried open the lid.

A small worn Bible was the first thing Izzy saw. She carefully lifted it toward the sunlight and opened the leather cover. Inside was a list of Izzy's family's names. Her eyes swelled up with tears as she read: *Joanne Dubois, Izzy's mother, died in childbirth.* Izzy leaned over and kissed Gram's cheek. "Thank you, Gram."

Izzy laid the Bible next to her on the bed as she pulled out a beautiful locket on a chain of gold. Izzy remembered seeing the locket years ago. Gram had told her she was too young for it then. Izzy's tiny fingernails sprung the latch to reveal the treasure inside. On the left side of the locket was a tiny picture of Gram and on the right side was Izzy's mom. They both looked beautiful.

Izzy lifted the chain above her head and watched as the golden locket dropped in front of her eyes to rest on her shirt. She pressed her hand against it and cried as she looked at Gram. This was all that was left of where she came from. What if someone stole it? Izzy dropped the locket behind her shirt and felt the cold metal against her skin. She vowed to wear it always.

Hidden in an envelope in the tin box were fifteen twenty dollars bills. Izzy gasped. She had never seen so much paper money all at once in her whole life. How had Gram saved this? Why hadn't Gram used this money for her medicine? Izzy felt a wave of panic. How could she keep this money safe? She decided to put one twenty in her pocket and divide the rest to put in her socks under her feet.

Gram looked like she was sleeping. Izzy knew Gram was in Heaven now. Gram would watch over her. She had promised. Izzy picked up the cell phone the state had given Gram. She dialed and waited for someone to answer.

A man came on the line and said, "911. What's your emergency?"

Izzy took a deep breath. Her throat tightened and her voice choked. "My Gram died last night and needs a proper burial. She is at 42 South Mission Street. I'll leave the door unlocked." Izzy hung up and cried. She already knew she wasn't going to like being invisible.

* * *

Officer Dante could see the eerie light of the beacon in the distant dark sky. He searched for a road that was still passable. The static of the car radio broke through Dante's cursing as he came upon another roadblock. He listened as his face contorted in a scowl, backing up the patrol car yet again.

"While you're out there, we got a helicopter or small plane crash 'bout ten miles east of you. Copy."

"Jesus! Ain't there anybody else workin' today? Copy."

Acer's screaming motorcycle whipped past Officer Dante doing at least fifty miles an hour over the speed limit. "Son of a bitch!" Dante knew he was losing the darkness to daybreak and the beacon would be of no use if he didn't hurry to the camp site.

He slammed his palm against the steering wheel and answered dispatch, "Call the FAA or whoever it is ya call when a plane goes down. I'll get to it when I get to it. Assumin' I don't get sucked into that damn sinkhole!"

* * *

Cat walked the large marble rotunda and waited for the bailiff to announce court was ready. The north wall of the huge hall was covered with portraits of prestigious men who had served the court. In a position of prominence was the portrait of William A. Javis, Prosecutor, and former Director of the Eastern Division of the U.S. Attorney General's office in New Orleans. Cat's eyes rose to concentrate on William's image. Even his portrait projected a man of strength and honor.

Cat felt a hand rest on his shoulder. He turned and acknowledged his boss, Theodore 'Ted' Dupre. Cat looked back to the portrait, "Still can't picture him putting a gun to his head." William Jarvis had committed suicide two weeks after Molly, his wife of forty years, had been murdered.

Ted took a moment and added, "He and Molly had one of those Hollywood movie type marriages. After her murder, well.....you know the rest."

Cat couldn't seem to find the time to date regularly, let alone sustain a serious relationship. William had managed to have it all. Cat lifted his court brief up and smiled, "I'm here for this. Why are you here?"

"This isn't public yet, but some people think I should run for Governor. Thought I would swing in and gauge my support."

"Governor? Congratulations." Cat wasn't surprised. The U.S. Attorney General's office was the favored stepping stone for state politics. Cat suspected Ted had postured himself for this from the day he took over William's position.

Cat allowed his gaze to rest a moment too long on Ted before he spoke. Cat sensed that Ted wanted Cat's reaction away from the office. Cat raised an eyebrow, "Can't help but notice the timing."

New Orleans was under a federally mandated consent decree to reorganize the entire justice system in New Orleans. Corruption and incompetence were systemic and reorganization promised to be a long and dirty battle. Cat expected his case load to explode any day.

Ted chuckled, "That was a consideration." Ted lost his smile, "I also wanted to tell you that if you want my job, it's yours."

"No, thanks."

"I expected you would say no. I'm actually glad. I can't imagine what would happen if we didn't have you in litigation." Ted gave Cat's shoulder a politician's pat.

Cat appreciated the compliment, but realized he was heading for some rough waters. "At least requisition some new bodies for this consent decree before you hit the campaign trail."

Ted nodded, "I'll take care of that today. Anything you want. Just ask." Cat knew Ted meant what he said.

The bailiff announced that court was ready. Ted joined a small group of men in the center of the hall and began eagerly shaking hands. Cat looked at the file in his hand. A political corruption case he was well prepared to nail. No big story, sadly a mere commentary on an established system. He heard an eruption of loud laughter from Ted's group and wondered who his new boss was going to be. Not that it mattered.

Cat glanced back at the picture of William. Very few men had earned that level of respect. Cat felt a sense of duty and dread as he fingered the flash drive in his pocket.

Cat came to New Orleans directly after Katrina. Just weeks after Molly's murder, the arrest of her killer and William's suicide. Cat witnessed the relentless dedication Ted and his team poured into the case. Before they could go to trial, Katrina hit and Molly's killer was one of the convicts that had drowned during the Katrina prisoner transfer. His body had eventually surfaced in the putrid sludge and his identity confirmed as Edward J. Meyer.

CHAPTER 3

Sasha poked her head through the heavy, red velvet cloth covering the door to Spicey's crystal ball room. Spicey sat flipping through her big tattered book titled 'Truth Seeker'.

"You know you got peoples lined up clear 'round the corner?"

Spicey looked up and scowled. "Beyond me why people wanna be famous! Look what it gets ya! I ain't even had breakfast yet." Spicey frowned at her reflection in the small mirror on the wall next to her and began smoothing her hair. "Ever since Mambo hooked me up with real spirits, we been havin' to put on disguises just to go to dinner."

Sasha chuckled, "Don't look like we missed too many dinners." She smoothed her flowered skirt over her hips. "You want me to go out and sort that crowd a little? Send the squirrely ones home?"

Spicey smiled, "Good idea girlfriend. Most them folks be glad to leave if they knew I still be learnin'." Spicey frowned at the words on the page in front of her. Mambo had given her this book six months ago, along with some real potions. Problem was most of the book was very hard to understand. There were special chants you had to do in special order. Spicey shook her head and made a 'tsk tsk' sound. Pure luck she hadn't turned some unsuspectin' soul into a toad by now.

Sasha flipped on the neon House of Voodoo sign and unlocked one of the doors to the sidewalk. It was a corner shop with doors to each street - prime real estate in the French Quarter. Sasha walked down the line of people explaining that Ms. Spicey couldn't possibly see them all today. Most of the people in line were gracious and stated their business could wait a day or two. One lady toward the end of the line just stared straight ahead as Sasha walked toward her.

Sasha cleared her throat, "What be your business with Ms. Spicey today?"

The woman's huge black eyes looked as if they were seated in the back of her skull. Her face had a spider web tattoo that crept from one side of her face to the other with a dangling spider hanging from the corner of one eye. She had long, stringy black hair and porcelain white skin. Her black lipstick had been applied narrower than her lip line, and her nose piercing held a small skull. Her nails were at least ten inches long, twisted at the ends and painted black. Around her neck she wore several scarves even though the temperature was already in the eighties and humid.

Her large black eyes fixed on Sasha and she answered in a low, raspy voice, "Ms. Spicey will see me."

Sasha straightened up, "Okay then." She could tell this lady was not going to leave. "You gotta wait your turn. There still be four people ahead of you."

Sasha turned and walked casually down the sidewalk and back into the store. She ran from the door, through the red curtain and stood panting in front of Spicey.

"You got one mean lookin' spooky lady that ain't gonna leave no how. She be about thirty somethin' and all Goth."

Spicey laughed at Sasha's expression. It didn't take much to send Sasha off on a tangent.

"You let her in first and we'll get it over with. Girl, you must be goin' soft on me. Since when is a *spooky* lookin' lady in Nawlens somethin' special?"

Sasha gave her a neck waggle and snap, "We'll just see 'bout that."

A few moments later Sasha pushed the red velvet cloth to her side and held her arm out to gesture the lady to take a seat with Spicey.

"Here ya go. You two have fun now." Sasha's eyebrows were raised in defiance. She nearly laughed at Spicey's weak attempt to mask her shock at the lady's appearance.

Spicey swallowed as Goth lady slowly lowered herself to sit. Her huge eyes practically glowed in the dimly lit room. Spicey watched her slowly un-wrap the scarves from her neck exposing deep ragged marks and purple bruising.

The lady placed her hands on the table near the crystal ball. The long, contorted nails began drumming as the black pools of her eyes darted about the small room. She suddenly focused on Spicey and leaned forward.

"I want *proof* you speak to the spirits."

Spicey's crystal ball began to cloud and a blue mist began to fill the room. Spicey was drawn to the crystal ball like a moth to a porch light. Her Spirit Advisor appeared in a white gown in the center of the ball. Spicey placed her palms on the ball and the Spirit said, "She is Dakin, a Hoodoo princess. She survived evil that buried her." The ball unclouded and the mist cleared.

Spicey peeked over the top of the ball. "Hear tell you be a Hoodoo princess named Dakin. Been killed and buried by evil."

A loud thunk confirmed Sasha had been outside the curtain listening and had fainted.

Dakin slowly leaned forward, "Your Spirits speak the truth." Dakin focused her large, black eyes on Spicey. She pointed her index finger at Spicey's eyes and made circular motions with her long black nail. The corners of Dakin's mouth twitched as she curled them up in a faint smile. "We will combine our powers. You shall help me obtain revenge."

* * *

The 1969 Chevy pickup used to be red. The parts not rusted through now boasted a variety of colors from spray cans left in the streets by graffiti artists. Claude had traded two goats and a block of frozen squirrel meat for it five years ago. The rope tailgate supported a salvaged sign piece that fit snugly in the bed concealing his often illegal cargo. Claude figured it was part of some old billboard, since it was the first half of a bikini lady lying on her side smiling. He had artistically added an extended middle finger to her hand. He also wrote Betty Sue next to her face in honor of his deceased wife. A somewhat ironic tribute considering he had killed her.

Earl gingerly opened the moaning truck door and hefted his oversized torso into the passenger seat. He carefully placed his feet on the hump in the middle of the floorboard since his side was gone. He scowled at Claude, "What the hell Mason want us to do now?"

Claude gave the truck some gas and waited for the delayed jolt forward. The fact that he had four different size tires on the truck, two of which were sized for small cars, and the muffler was wired too loose, made for a noisy and erratic ride.

"He's all pissed! Said we should have left that witchy lady in the cemetery after killin' her."

Earl rubbed his temples, "If she hadn't seen what we be doing we wouldn't be in this mess. It's Mason's fault - wantin' those bodies hid in crypts." Earl looked out the window, "So what are we doing now then?" Earl was worried about Mason being mad. He was counting on that money to keep coming in.

"Wants us to dig her up and take her to the swamp. Says we can't risk going back in town in daylight."

"Told you, weren't no good buryin' her out at Pete's place. Hell the swamp only a stone's throw from where she be." Earl lit a cigar and crossed his ankles on the floorboard hump. "Won't take but a few minutes no how. Best be careful nobody at the rental place sees us though." Earl snorted as he laughed, "Hate to 'splain how we know a body be in their back yard!"

Claude turned the truck down a dirt lane that announced Pete's Swamp Boat Rentals. A narrow drive off to the left led to a storage barn. In the distance they could see activity at the swamp boat docks.

Earl sat up straight and pointed, "Park over yonder in the shrubs. We'll take the shovels, drag her back here. This damn thing makin' too much noise."

Claude pulled the truck into a row of shrub trees and shut off the engine. Earl watched the people at the docks. Nobody turned to look their way so he was pretty sure they hadn't been heard. They walked the long narrow drive, all the while looking toward the docks.

Behind the storage barn they stood leaning on their shovels looking at a large earthen hole.

Claude spoke first. "Ain't this where we put her?" His head swung around surveying the ground.

"Yup."

"Think some damn animals dug her up already? Don't seem like they'd take the whole damn body."

Claude scratched his head, "Don't see no blood." Claude's eyes opened wide and his face froze. "What if she came back to life?"

The longer Earl looked at the hole, the spookier it felt. "Looky there." Earl pointed the tip of his shovel to long scratch marks in the dirt, all along the sides of the hole. "She done dug herself out. She *is* a witch!"

Claude quickly started walking back toward the truck. Earl caught up to him wheezing and choking back coughs. "What the hell we do now?"

Claude didn't answer until they were both in the truck and the engine started. Claude pointed the truck back toward town and looked at Earl. "Pert near got no choice but to kill 'er again."

* * *

Jackson flipped through the receipts on his desk looking for the one Abram said he had left right on top of the pile. Not there. Jackson pushed his chair back to look at the floor a second time and pushed all of the papers on the desk into one big pile. He flipped the entire pile over and began to pull each piece of paper up and wave it in the air before he examined it and put it to his right.

One of them was goin' crazy. He was betting on Abram. Just then he noticed an invoice stuck to the back of a report. Jackson peeled them apart and saw sticky fingerprints all down the side of the missing invoice. Ah ha! Abram been snackin' again and left his sticky mess on Jackson's desk.

Abram popped his head in the door, sporting a grin from ear to ear. "Got a party of six goin' out in 'bout twenty. You comin'?"

Jackson dangled the sticky invoice in the air, "See what I found? A sticky ass invoice! I wasted a bunch of time here messin' on this."

Abram displayed a toothy smile, "I do all the hard work around here. Man gotta eat!"

Jackson and Abram had each been given reward money for helping the FBI last fall. They had decided to use some of the money to go into business together. It wasn't easy staying on the right side of the law when you didn't have any money. This was a shot at a second chance. They bought out Pete's Swamp Boat Tours, mostly because it was so far out of town and away from the hood. After doing some much needed repair on the office building, they also invested in three new boats. They now had a fleet of five boats for rentals and one big boat for swamp tours.

Business had been better than they had expected. All of law enforcement and many of the locals recommended them as local heroes. Now that it was spring, the tourist trade was picking up and they were already showing profits. Only one obstacle remained. They were both terrified of the swamp.

Jackson pointed to the TV and turned up the volume, "You hear this yet? News guy says some helicopter dumped a screaming man into the middle of that big sinkhole in Assumption Parish."

Abram listened for a minute and shook his head. "Now that be a pretty efficient way to get rid of a person, ain't it? Hope this catches on. Might slow down the number of bodies floatin' in the swamp."

* * *

Mathew Core walked into the gym and saw Zack sitting on a wooden bench wiping his neck with a towel. The gym pulsated with the rhythmic drumming of the punching bags and the clangs of the free weights. The grunts from the fighters on the mats were interrupted by frequent shouts of their trainers. This wasn't a social gym. This was a serious business that had one customer: the federal government.

Mathew saw FBI agent Jeanne Manigat on the far side of the room grab a gym bag from a bench and drink from the fountain against the wall. She pushed the double doors open to the outside as she gave a brief wave to Core and held up three fingers.

Core nodded, knowing she was referring to their three o'clock date with the New Orleans SWAT team. He had heard rumors she was more lethal than she was beautiful. He looked at Zack, "Did I tell you she was assigned to help me evaluate SWAT progress in self-defense training?"

Zack rolled his neck and took a big gulp from his bottled water. Zack was every bit as well trained and muscular as Core. Ex-Special Forces, ex-ATF, owner of the gym and part time employee of Core's security company. Zack often chose Core as a work-out partner. Zack tilted his head and looked up at Core. "That chick is *spooky* strong. And skilled. She just beat the shit out of me."

Mathew Core watched Zack roll his shoulders and stand. Zack started walking away and Core noticed a slight limp. Zack stopped and looked back, "And she was holding back."

* * *

The Director of the FBI watched out the jet window as the stripes on the runway flashed by. He thumbed through the report he had just received from the Department of Justice. New Orleans remained a hotbed of criminal activity and corruption. The DOJ made it quite clear that the FBI would shoulder the responsibility of supervising the mandated consent decree transition.

The Director's phone flashed an alert that Louisiana Senator Dalton was missing and presumed in danger. Baton Rouge FBI field agents found the

Senator's pilot dead in his personal car at the airport. All of the pilot's identification was missing, and surveillance cameras showed the Senator boarding a helicopter scheduled to arrive in New Orleans.

A second alert: agents were heading toward the site of a reported helicopter crash near the Assumption Parish sinkhole.

Third alert: local police had eyewitness reports of a man pushed from a helicopter over the deadly whirlpool.

The Director looked back out his window as he felt the jet leave the runway and take to the air. He had no doubt of the Senator's whereabouts.

The New Orleans field office headed by SSA Dan Thor was already overworked and understaffed. The reorganization required by the consent decree had the FBI assisting the local police in both law enforcement and training. This had originally been planned as a multi-agency effort. Now it had been dumped entirely on the FBI. There was no way the New Orleans field office could take on the additional murder investigation of a Senator.

The Director exhaled as he dialed Supervisory Special Agent Roger Dance. He knew Roger was taking a long overdue vacation, but would not refuse him. "Roger? Any chance I can talk you into heading back to New Orleans?"

CHAPTER 4

Roger handed Kim a bucket filled with peat moss and sat on the ground next to her to finish planting the last four tomato plants. She had seen Roger take a call when he was standing by the wheelbarrow. Kim raised an eyebrow as she held out her dirty hand for another plant. "Let me guess. Your vacation is over." She glanced at Roger and smiled.

Roger put a plant in her hand and smiled back. In spite of the bizarre circumstances of their meeting and the connection they both had to Kim's mother and her friends that are now angels, Roger knew he would spend the rest of his life with Kim. He had hidden an engagement ring in his desk drawer in the house. Tonight he had planned to propose.

"I need to leave for New Orleans, right away."

Kim still had nightmares about Roger in New Orleans from six months ago. "Just you?"

Roger stood and held Kim's hand to help her up. "I'm going to call Paul and probably try to put our team back together." Roger knew Kim would understand the implication of him wanting the entire team.

"This is a big problem then?"

Roger nodded. His face broke out in a boyish grin, "Maybe our angels will give us a hand?"

Kim kissed his cheek and whispered, "I'll ask Mom to watch over you."

* * *

Supervisory Special Agent Dan Thor sat at his desk in the New Orleans field office and tried to reorganize the duty roster. He didn't have nearly enough agents to cover the mountain of active cases. As it was, he was trying to keep up with reports and do field work. His intercom buzzed and Thor hit the button, "Yeah?"

The voice on the other end said, "SSA Roger Dance is on line three for you."

Thor pushed the line three, "I want your first sentence to be: I'm coming to New Orleans."

Roger laughed, "The whole team is coming to New Orleans."

* * *

Tuesday 12:00 pm

Catahoula pulled Reuben's card from his shirt pocket and dialed. Reuben answered on the first ring. "Yes, sir?"

Cat shut his car door and started his engine. Court had gone quicker than he had thought. "I have about an hour, right now, if we could meet somewhere."

Reuben stopped breathing for a moment, his mind went blank. "I...I can't think where..."

Cat interrupted, "I'm not too far from Loyola University. How about the park?"

Reuben sputtered, "Yes, sir." and heard the phone line go dead. He glanced at his half-finished report on his monitor, hit save and closed it down. He was nearly finished with his sinkhole story and had just started working on the helicopter crash. Reuben looked at his watch. There was no way he would finish by deadline. His eyes scanned the newsroom and landed on Marla, his favorite columnist. He quickly dialed her extension and watched her pick up.

"Swear to God, you have to help me!"

Marla turned and looked at Reuben with her brow furrowed. "What do you want?"

"I have a story I need finished by 12:30 deadline and I have to leave. You have to make it sound like me or Trayer will have my ass."

"Means I have to use bad grammar, lots of typos..."

Reuben interrupted, he was nearly in tears. "Please? I will pay you back somehow. This is really life or death."

Marla hung up her phone and walked over to Reuben. "What's your passcode?" She could see his hands shaking as he wrote it on a blank page of his notebook.

"He can't know." Reuben had tilted his head toward Trayer's door.

"Got it." Marla waltzed back to her desk and Reuben ran for the elevator.

Marla glanced at her watch again. She had less than twenty minutes to make sense out of Reuben's shorthand and finish his column. She made a quick call to the police that had responded to the sinkhole call and she did a quick phone interview with a representative from the FAA on the helicopter. She figured she could probably write the story better than Reuben just from what she had found out on the phone.

Marla flipped a few pages into the notebook and saw where Reuben had scratched, *Catahoula / today / Take proof.* Catahoula? Her curiosity peaked, she flipped a few more pages. Nothing. Reuben had certainly been upset and in a hurry. Her gut told her he was working on a big story. Catahoula was not a name you casually tossed around. While Marla still had his passcode she searched his recent computer activity. She saw where he made a copy of a video file and retrieved its file number. She walked over to her desk, grabbed a blank flash drive and returned to Reuben's desk. After making a copy of the file, she finished Reuben's story and sent it to the deadline desk.

Marla dropped the flash drive in her pocket and returned to her own story. She barely got it submitted by deadline. Reuben said he owed her. Maybe he would let her help with his big story. This could finally get her into something juicy.

* * *

Izzy crouched down by a bush and watched Gram's house from across the street. A police car and a coroner wagon had their lights flashing. Neighbors stood on the sidewalk talking and soon two men came out of the door with a bed on wheels and a sheet over a body. That was her Gram. Izzy wiped her eyes with the back of her hands and watched the coroner van pull away.

A male voice boomed behind her, "Isn't that your grandma's house?" Ed had seen the activity from his living room window and noticed Izzy standing by his front bush.

Izzy jumped. She hopped on her bike and sped away as fast as she could. Sure wasn't easy being invisible.

* * *

Stone walked into the casino lobby and walked over to the reception desk. A bright eyed blonde pushed her chest out and asked, "May I help you?"

Stone smiled. "I'd like a room for a couple of days." He winked. "Make it a nice one."

The girl blushed and quickly hit a few keys on her computer. "I have a VIP suite available for tonight and tomorrow?"

"That will be fine." Stone laid a charge card from an alias on the desk. "Use this and process checkout now. I don't want to have to stop back."

"Yes, sir, Mr. Williamson."

Stone winked and slipped the room key in his pocket. He grabbed a drink from a passing hostess and surveyed the game floor. He was feeling lucky.

* * *

Acer had placed a message with his contact requesting a face-to-face. That kind of request had better be important or you just arranged your own death. He waited at the outdoor café and skimmed a newspaper left by an earlier diner. His contact joined him.

"This is most interesting. It was only hours ago that I was informed of your tragic and unexpected death."

Acer had his confirmation now, too. He could read it in his contact's eyes. His days with the machine were numbered. He knew he hadn't failed at any of his assignments, so why did they want him dead? He knew it was fruitless to get an honest answer. One person may be willing to tell him, Stone.

* * *

Reuben saw Cat sitting on a bench under a large oak tree and joined him. Cat spoke first, "Tell me what else you have."

Reuben gave a nervous nod, "That video was from a hidden camera at a store across from the alley. Over on Mission Street. Otis Grocery?" Reuben waited for some sign of recognition from Cat and then continued. "Otis never trusted the city cams and had his own installed. Still has them. His habit is to take the video home each night for safe keeping. Man never throws anything away."

Cat looked impatient and Reuben started talking faster. "Since all the police had been over there, Otis watched the whole video after he got home. He knew Dad. Liked him. Otis wasn't sure who to trust and didn't know about me. Mom remarried when I was young and gave me my stepdad's name."

"After Katrina we had a small memorial service for Dad, since they said he was dead. Otis was the only person, not family, that was there. Everyone thought Dad was a murderer. That's when we met and he told me he had something for me to see." Reuben leaned in and lowered his voice, "He also gave me the stuff that guy put in the dumpster. Bloody rags, needle, and gloves that might have fingerprints."

Cat said, "Go on."

Reuben swallowed, "I thought Dad was dead, remember, and I was scared. I didn't know what to do.

Then one day, about four years ago, Otis calls and tells me to come to his store. In the back room sits my Dad."

Reuben inhaled quickly, "Dad said the prisoner transfers were a joke. At first the Sherriff wasn't even going to move the prisoners. He was forced to evacuate the jail, so it wasn't very organized. Did you know there are still fourteen convicted prisoners missing? When the prisoner boat turned over in the storm, Dad just swam for safety. Anyway, Dad gave his shirt to some guy that lost his in the floods. Prisoner shirts have ID numbers stamped on them. Went up in some dead guy's attic and was rescued by the National Guard, flown to Baton Rouge. Apparently the guy that got dad's shirt died."

Cat asked, "Why did your dad come back?"

"He wants his life back. He has spent the last years tracking down the man in the video and following him around. The guy in that video is a cop. Mason Dooley. Bad dude with bad friends."

Reuben handed Cat a file folder. "Pretty much everything Dad has found out is in here."

Cat glanced in the folder and saw documents and photos paper clipped together. It looked fairly thin for eight years of detective work. Cat stared at Reuben. "Your dad is taking a big chance coming to me. If I don't believe in his innocence, I'll go after him with everything I have. William and Molly Jarvis deserve no less."

"That is exactly what Dad said you'd say."

* * *

Cat spent the next two hours at the office review-ing the Jarvis file and the prosecution notes. Martha stuck her head in the office door, "I'm going to the cafeteria if you want anything?"

Cat shook his head and kept reading. He sensed Martha was still there. She was. Martha asked, "I thought you had court at three?"

Cat looked at his watch, "Damn. I do!" Cat closed down his monitor, grabbed his briefcase and rushed past Martha. He was halfway to the elevator when he yelled back, "Thanks."

Tuesday 3:00 pm

Roger had caught the first charter available from South Bend, Indiana to New Orleans. Paul Casey, often partnered with Roger on cases, agreed to take an FBI jet from Cancun immediately. Roger chuck-led to himself that Paul was going to give him some grief for pulling him off vacation. Pablo Manigat and Todd Nelson were also on their way to New Orleans. They had been members of Roger's team in New Orleans six months ago. Agents had come to calling them the 'dream team'.

Roger had spent the flight reviewing everything the FBI had on Senator Dalton. What was remark-able to Roger was that it didn't appear there was anything very interesting about Senator Dalton. Usually there was a glaring political motive. Senator Dalton had run a grass roots campaign and for the most part had been one of the few Senators willing to cross party lines on the big issues. His reputation was clean and the Bureau didn't have any personal notes that suggested anything different.

Roger's cab delivered him to the side door of the New Orleans field office. The mid-day heat and humidity took Roger's breath away. The New Orleans heat was not a fond memory. Roger entered the building and headed for SSA Dan Thor's office. Thor had assumed the senior position for the office six months ago. Roger had brought Thor to New Orleans as part of his 'dream team' at that time and Thor had stayed. Roger had heard that Thor and Jeanne Manigat, another member of the team, were now a couple.

The intake agent warned Roger that Thor was in a foul mood. Roger expected as much. Thor was a bulldog of an agent; strong, aggressive and fearless. He was definitely not suited for the delicate politics of an administrative position. Roger knew Thor only accepted the position so he could stay in New Orleans with Jeanne.

Roger knocked on Thor's open door. Thor looked up and smiled. "Damn, I'm glad to see you! I'm dying here!" Thor had stood and reached his hand across the desk to greet Roger.

Roger chuckled, "You might not be so happy when I tell you why we're here."

Thor frowned. He gestured Roger to take a seat. "I figured there was a catch. What's up?"

Roger leaned back in his chair, "We believe Louisiana Senator Dalton was dumped in the Assumption Parish sinkhole about six hours ago. I'm expecting the field reports from Baton Rouge any minute."

Thor moaned. "I saw the alert that he was missing. Didn't know about the sinkhole. Damn, that will make for some headlines."

Roger continued, "That's not all. The Director said the DOJ has officially dumped the entire consent decree on this office. The Director has asked me to lead the Senator case. The Bureau has requisitioned more agents for this office and has offered to bring Frank Mass back to do administrative. That would put you back in the field with me, if you want."

"HELL YES!" Thor's expression made Roger chuckle.

Before Roger could even say anything, the intake agent knocked on the door. Thor looked up at the ceiling, "Yeah?"

"Got that Voodoo lady here, says she has to talk to you."

Thor threw his head back and laughed as he looked at Roger, "Just like the old days. The minute you get here, shit starts. You want to join me?"

Roger stood, "Sure. Might as well jump right in."

* * *

Spicey crossed her legs and folded her hands neatly in her lap. She glanced around the stark room, then uncrossed her legs, crossed her ankles and placed her hands on her handbag. She cupped her hand in front of her mouth and huffed out some breath. Satisfied, she tossed her head and gave her hair a quick flip. Her fidgeting had moved her hair extension to the side of her face and a long pink feather now pointed straight toward her mouth. She blew at the feather from the side of her mouth a couple of times and then yanked the entire piece from her head.

Spicey crammed the hairpiece in her purse, leaned forward and shook her shoulders until her amulets hung neatly in her cleavage. She started drumming her nails on the table top. What the hell was takin' them so long?

Thor and Roger watched from the observation room. Thor looked at Roger, "We actually get good information from her from time to time. Jeanne says she really has Voodoo powers or some damn shit. We better go listen to her before she explodes in there."

Roger smiled and followed Thor into the room. After introductions, Thor placed a notepad in front of him and began writing. He looked up at Spicey's frowning face. "The intake agent said you claim to have some knowledge about a murder?"

Spicey sat up straight, her eyes narrowed and she said, "Murders. You got dead people all over the cemetery."

Thor raised an eyebrow and asked, "Where would you rather they be?"

Spicey looked at Roger. "This one thinks he's funny." She had pointed to Thor. "I mean you got extrees. Been stacked on top who supposed to be there, in them damn crypts in the City of the Dead."

Roger curled his index finger around his chin and asked, "Is this information from a 'vision'? How do you know this?"

Spicey leaned forward, "I know from a lady that got killed, almost. She wants to stay secret, but she be wantin' some bad revenge. She be Hoodoo, they don't mess around. I'm thinkin' if you catch the killers first, we save us some bad Mojo." Spicey started nodding her head to some music only she could hear. "I also got some information from my Spirits that might help some."

Thor eyes flashed over to Roger and then back down to his notebook. "What did the Spirits say?" He positioned himself to take notes even though he was trying to keep from laughing.

Spicey waved her finger at him. "You ain't gonna think this so funny when you start crowbarin' them crypts open! My Spirits say these all be missin' people of some importance." Spicey smoothed her skirt and looked at Roger, "You need to find a rainbow truck and a big headed lady named Betty Sue. Oh yeah, Betty Sue got an attitude." Spicey pointed her middle finger in the air for effect. "Them be your killers. There be two of 'em."

CHAPTER 5

Mathew Core leaned against the wall in the large gymnasium and watched the janitorial staff unroll the huge mats. Jeanne came through the far door and walked over to him. Her long, black hair was twisted in a braid that fell midway down her back. She wore a khaki t-shirt that failed to hide her ample bosom and her athletic stride confirmed that she was a warrior at heart. Core noticed the men working had stopped and were mesmerized by her as she passed them. She was not just a beauty, she was stunning. Core could tell Jeanne did not let her beauty define her.

Core spent two decades as a contractor for the U.S. government. Often the line defining the right and wrong side of the law was blurred. Last fall Core had fully severed his ties to the dark side and as a reward had been re-established by the FBI as a security consultant. Jeanne and Core had a history from last fall. Jeanne actually rescued Core's wife and daughter from a drug cartel. They now had a mutual respect for each other that had been earned under the worst of circumstances.

Jeanne nodded at Core and looked at her watch. "Have they all been through level four yet?" There were ten levels of self-defense expertise and the FBI's goal was to have the entire SWAT team at level six.

Jeanne was referring to the members of the New Orleans SWAT team that were expected to arrive in minutes. She and Core were to evaluate their progress in their self-defense training. The New Orleans officers had been working with trainers at the FBI gym for months. These men would be the core of the New Orleans Police Department when they were done.

"Got most of them through level five now. One or two hot shots may be level six." Core shrugged. "How do you want to do this? I think we have twenty seven scheduled for today. We are also supposed to give our recommendations for the top two."

Jeanne shrugged, "I'm fine with you laying the ground rules. Just remind them this is training, we don't want to get hurt and we don't want them hurting each other."

Core nodded his head as the first group of noisy men filtered into the room and dropped towels and gym bags on the bleachers. More men followed and soon all twenty seven were there.

Core looked at Jeanne with a boyish grin on his face. "Want to start with a scramble? Quick way to weed them out."

Jeanne smiled.

Core blew his whistle and walked to the center of the mats. The men all stood at attention and waited for Core to speak. Jeanne noticed that the most intimidating of the men stood at the opposite ends of the line. They probably were the alpha males with their loyal packs.

Core held his hand up and pointed to Jeanne, "We have Special Agent Jeanne Manigat from the local FBI field office helping us today. For those of you who have not met me, my name is Mathew Core. I own Core Security and have been commissioned by the FBI to assist in your training evaluations."

Jeanne noticed some of the men whispering among themselves. She was quite sure they were disappointed to see a woman doing their evaluations. She was used to this attitude and had found it rarely to be a problem once they realized she was skilled.

Core looked at Jeanne, "I'll go first." Jeanne nodded.

Core wiggled his fingers at the men on the sidelines. "Come and get it. Twelve from the left. We'll do this in halves. This is training, so don't hurt me. I'll try not to hurt you."

One of the alpha men yelled over, "You want all twelve of us to attack you?"

Core answered, "Single file, keep it moving. Humor me."

The men started walking onto the mats and approaching Core. He systematically tossed them as they came. One by one they got back up and attacked more aggressively. Core pointed to one alpha. "Training!" The alpha attacked again, but with less anger and more concentration on skill. Core had all of them down on the mats and blew his whistle. Core signaled for the remaining men to attack.

"Come on! We don't have all day." After contact with each one at least twice, Core blew his whistle again.

He wiped his brow and said, "Good work. A lot of you have made real progress since last month." Core stepped off the mat. "Take a ten minute break and we'll go again."

Core walked over to Jeanne. "What did you see?"

Jeanne tilted her head toward the group of men slowly standing after Core's demonstration. "You've got at least two alphas that want top spot. They are both good, but may have control issues."

Core agreed and said, "Hot shot in the red sweat-shirt wants my ass now. He's not going to want to play with a woman."

Jeanne watched the men a moment and said, "I think he's okay. You just didn't leave his ego any room. He's got his boys watching, remember. I think the one in the black shirt will be our problem."

Core said, "You may be right. Let's give them a demo while they cool down and then you can have a turn."

Jeanne smiled, "Sure you're ready?"

Core shook his head. "Not really. Zack said you beat the shit out of him today. Don't hurt me."

Jeanne chuckled and walked with Core to the center of the mat. Core called for everyone's attention. "Bet you think I'm copping out fighting a woman?" Nobody said anything. Core pointed at Jeanne, "She's the bad ass." One of the men snickered behind his hand. Core added, "Never underestimate your opponent. Agent Manigat holds the

FBI record in blades and trained with FBI SWAT for weapons. She is sniper certified and holds the agency's highest level in self-defense."

A wave of respectful faces appeared on the men.

"Agent Manigat and I are going to demonstrate for you some of the countermoves if you encounter a level nine or above attacker."

After an impressive five minute demonstration of skills, Core raised his hand to stop. Jeanne immediately lowered her leg that was positioned to kick. Core stepped off the mats and yelled, "Go get some. Single file. Keep it comin'."

The men gingerly approached Jeanne. She waited for them to get within attack range and took command of each one. Red sweatshirt approached her from the side. Jeanne turned, stopped his punch and twisted his arm behind him as she propelled him behind her. He immediately got back up and charged from the back. Jeanne twirled on her heel and kicked his mid-section. She dove on his side as he fell and placed her forearm against his neck. She leaned down and whispered, "This is training. Control yourself. It's all about control."

Red sweatshirt got back up and attacked again. This time turning in time to cause Jeanne to miss a kick and grabbing her leg.

Jeanne smiled. "Very good."

Red sweatshirt nodded. He was beaming. Mathew blew the whistle.

The second group approached Jeanne very aggressively. Mathew yelled "Training" a couple of times. Jeanne held her own, but sensed the aggression of this second batch of men. Mathew blew his whistle to stop the attack.

Black shirt came at Jeanne from the side. He must not have heard the whistle. Jeanne saw his heel coming in from the side and spun. She crouched below his airborne leg, grabbed and twisted it with her left hand as her right arm struck the back of his neck. She knew he felt her blow, but she had controlled herself. He lay on the mat moaning and Jeanne stood over him and offered her hand.

He pushed himself up from the mat ignoring her hand. Jeanne tried to offer him a face saving moment. "You are very strong and very good. But this is about self-defense. Not aggressive attack. Didn't you hear the whistle?"

Black shirt flexed his hands, "Guess I missed that."

Core reminded everyone there would be another evaluation in two weeks and dismissed them. Jeanne asked, "What's that one's name?"

Core checked his sheet. "Mason Dooley."

* * *

It had been hard for Ed to finally fall asleep. He was exhausted from working the docks all night, but knowing that Catahoula knew he was alive had his mind in overdrive. His fitful sleep was broken by a loud pounding on his door. Ed glanced out the window and saw a patrol officer on his porch. Had Catahoula discovered where he lived already? The officer pounded on the door again. Ed decided to face his fate, whatever it was.

He opened the door, "Can I help you, officer?"

The officer pointed across the street. "Lady that rented over there died yesterday. We're lookin' for her granddaughter. Have you seen the little girl around?" Ed paused not sure what to say. Before he could answer, the officer continued, "We need to find her. Can't have her livin' on the streets of Nawlens." He pushed a card to Edward, "Call this number if you see her." The card was for Child Protective Services. The officer turned and left. Ed watched him walk to the neighbor's house and repeat his speech.

Ed remembered how startled the little girl had been when he spoke to her this morning. He knew that look. She was hiding. She, too, had gone invisible.

* * *

After court, and back in his office, Cat attached the flash drive to his office computer. He entered the security pass code and began his search into the Edward Meyer case file, again. It was Cat's practice to 'map' a case and code each section based on relevance. What he was looking at was clearly the work of Ted's entire team saving data as they each saw fit. The case had not gone to court, which explained some of the random naming of the folders. This was going to be a big job.

Cat went to the background data on Edward Meyer and saw a file labeled 'press'. He opened the file and saw notes from Steven Marks, Senior Assistant Attorney General. Marks had a reputation for being a detail guy. He still worked out of the New Orleans office, but had transferred to the fraud division before Cat had come to New Orleans.

Cat scrolled past the first few pages Marks had scanned to the folder. A few headline stories after Meyer's arrest described Ed as a conspiracy theory nut and a crazy professor.

Marks's Note: Press release 7-4-2005 / Two days before murdering Molly Jarvis / Evidence of Meyer's mindset about establishment/

Times-Picayune article: interview of Loyola University Political Science professor Edward J. Meyer:

Interviewer: What response do you have for the comments made by Molly Jarvis yesterday on Meet the Press? She claimed it was evident from your ranting that you should not be in a position of molding young minds.

Edward Meyer: She has to say things like that. Look who she's married to. I like Molly, we have a friendly agreement to disagree on some topics.

Interviewer: The rumor is that the University has taken her suggestion seriously. Does that concern you?

Edward Meyer: Does it concern me that a private citizen can suggest to an institute of higher learning that a professor may need to be censored? What do you think? Have you offered to let her censor your articles?

Interviewer: You have given your permission for this paper to print your manifesto. In light of these criticisms, are you still comfortable with that?

Edward Meyer: That brief statement suggesting there is a design and plan that controls everything but the weather could hardly be called a manifesto. People who read it and think I'm a nut have either chosen not to think for themselves or have a stake in the design. Why should I care what they think?

Marks's Note: Manifesto is evidence of Ed Meyer's ability to construct devious schemes. A physiological analysis of underlying character issues is recommended prior to trial.

Cat scrolled down the page and found a reprint of the so-called manifesto:

If I represented the richest interests in the world, namely oil, and I wanted to ensure that no politics or people would get in my way, I would do the following: First, I would obtain full control of the U.S. Armed Forces. (I would own the Secretary of Defense) No way around it. I would need a hawkish political party in charge of defense and I would want to control the spin and quality of the 'intelligence' given to the people in power. (namely the President) I would ensure only my men were appointed to the top positions at the CIA and NSA.

I would want to foster a fear mentality in the American people, so when I said we were being threatened, everyone would climb on my bandwagon and be less likely to object to an unfounded war.

I would cripple the effectiveness of law enforcement through legislation (ATF dismantle policy) and I would do nothing to slow the flow of illegals into the U.S. After all, they are the workers for my drug business. I would lay the economic foundation for a society that is dependent on the government, uneducated and without hope of changing their circumstances. They will be easier to manipulate for future use. Simply threaten their entitlements.

I would get the Supreme Court to reinstate the opportunities for my businesses to contribute unlimited monies to my favorite political agendas and spend billions promoting the premise that 'clean energies' are too expensive. I can afford to spend millions for decades discouraging any energy source that isn't mine to control. Like the sun. Imagine an entire world that looks up and sees the sun every day has been taught to believe it is better to drill our earth. The advertising of 'clean coal' being a perfect example of absurd thinking that sells.

I would look at an aging boomer population and promote their use of prescription drugs to the point of dependency. I would confuse the health care system to the point that only the wealthy have adequate care, the rest is all business profit. I would brainwash them with as many commercials for drugs as fast food and then slowly introduce adequate poisons in the pharmaceuticals to ensure large numbers of shortened life spans. (Census shows declining life expectancies already.) This will substantially reduce the threat that Social Security and other social program costs actually start to risk the sacred budgets of my military. (Notice the conversations about reducing SS benefits only got serious when defense spending cuts hit the table.)

I would make sure that my news agencies never reported that the gun manufacturing companies are the only entities currently protected by Congress from any kind of liability litigation and coincidently account for ninety percent of the contributions that fund the NRA. (Contrary to the grass roots propaganda the NRA spouts.)

I could easily accomplish all of this by decades of carefully hand- picked politicians, long term special appointments and legislation that is virtually ineffective. As insurance, I would carefully insert just enough fringe personality types into Congress to ensure a perpetual stalemate. My interests are best served if nothing happens and I have the money to make sure those are the people elected.

Alas, there is only one threat to my design. Free Speech. If I could just find a way to silence those people who challenge conventional wisdom. Thankfully, they seem to do this to each other.

Cat finished reading the manifesto for the second time. Edward Meyer certainly left no one out of his tirade. Cat could see why Molly Jarvis may have found his opinions too hardened for young minds.

Cat marked every file he found for copy to his flash drive. He scanned the documents and photos Reuben had given him into a folder, transferred that to his flash drive and deleted the file from his hard drive. Until he had a chance to review them in private, he wanted to keep them secret. Cat dropped the flash drive into his briefcase to rest next to Reuben's file and the flash drive of Edward's arrest. He had no sooner zipped his briefcase closed when Ted knocked on his office door as he opened it.

"Got a minute?" Ted was already taking a seat across from Cat and held a stapled pile of papers in his hands. Cat nodded and Ted continued, "I have six attorneys being assigned to this office effective immediately." Ted pushed the papers over to Cat to review. "I think you'll be impressed with who I was able to get for you."

Cat scanned the names, his eyebrows raised. "How did you get these guys? This is great!"

Ted smiled, "I'm glad you're pleased. I feel bad leaving you in the middle of this consent decree mess. I know your case load is already heavy."

Ted shuffled in his seat and said, "I took the liberty of making some case assignment changes there on page two. Anything you don't like, change. I figured you might appreciate clearing your desk some before the tide rises."

Cat glanced over Ted's changes. The people coming in would have no problems picking up these cases and taking them to finish. Cat's workload had virtually disappeared, if only until the expected storm hit from enforcing the consent decree cases.

Cat exhaled, "Much appreciated. We're going to miss you once you're Governor."

Ted stood to leave and waved his hand in the air, "Hopefully these guys know what they're talking about. I about crapped when I heard how much money we have to raise."

Cat pulled out his money clip, "I've got a couple of twenties you can have."

Ted shook his head and looked at the briefcase on the desk, "You going back to court this late?"

"Taking some work home." Cat was tempted to ask Ted a couple of questions about Molly's case and then changed his mind. He really needed to do more research before he began asking questions.

"Has Martha seen these?" Cat had held up the papers Ted had given him.

Ted chuckled, "You know how much she enjoys changes. I thought I'd let you have that pleasure."

CHAPTER 6

We had been told to wait for Ellen in the park at Transition College in Heaven. Mary and Linda got there first. Teresa had attempted to train me on our GPS watches, but I kept getting lost. This part of my angel training has not gone well. As a mortal, I was considered transportation challenged. Can't see at night, won't turn left without a traffic light, no driving on snow. Since we are graded as a group, everyone is doing their part to bring me up to speed.

Mary looked at Teresa, "Well? Where'd you finally find her?"

"Iraq."

Linda frowned at me, "Why did you go to Iraq?"

Teresa interrupted, "I told her it was *time to head back*."

Mary started laughing. "And you heard...?"

I frowned at Mary, "*Time* you to Iraq. I never flew so fast in my life!" In my defense, I have hearing issues.

Teresa sighed, "I turned around and she was speeding off in the wrong direction." Now she looked at me, "By the way, why did you keep going back and forth there at the end?"

"I always get Iraq and Iran confused."

Ellen appeared on a bench across from us and started laughing. "Boy, that last little bit was a riot to watch. Okay, gals, we have to talk about your next assignment."

Linda raised her hand, "Don't we have to do more training now? I thought Betty said we still had two classes to finish."

Betty was one of our angel trainers that Heaven had assigned us. She looked and acted just like Betty White. Ellen was our other angel trainer that looked and acted like Ellen DeGeneres. Heaven decided to allow us to keep a portion of our mortal thinking processes. This is supposed to assist in our assignments helping mortals. Our thinking like mortals and angels at the same time has proven to be a challenge for all involved. Since as mortals, we all loved Betty White and Ellen DeGeneres, Heaven felt it would be comforting for our trainers to appear as them.

Ellen smiled, "You do have more classes to finish, but Vicki's daughter, Kim, has asked if we could help Roger again. The FBI is sending his whole team back to New Orleans."

Ellen looked at me, "I know you're happy to hear Kim will be helping us again." Ellen was right, Kim had been the only mortal Heaven allowed to see and hear us. Whenever we helped Roger, I got to visit Kim.

Teresa asked Ellen, "What kind of help does Roger need?"

Ellen answered, "Right now I only know about a Senator that was dropped into a sinkhole."

Linda and Mary looked at each other. Mary gulped, "Uh oh."

Ellen slapped her knee and laughed. She had read Mary's mind. "I don't think you have to go into the sinkhole. Of course things might change…" Oh goody.

Ellen said she was going to let Roger know that we were available to help. She told us to look up Spicey and Sasha at the Voodoo shop.

"Spicey has a little project that will probably involve Roger a little later today. This way we can have a head start."

Linda raised her hand. "Betty said we can show ourselves to people like Spicey now. Is that right?"

Ellen answered, "You can show yourselves to mortals that have been chosen by spirits. Not just anyone. You can show yourself to Spicey. She can only hear you in her crystal ball. Keep in mind she is still new to all of this and fairly fragile."

I remembered Spicey and Sasha from our last trip to New Orleans. They are too much fun. This could be a hoot.

Ellen frowned at me, "You keep forgetting we can read your mind." I don't forget. I just haven't figured out how to hide it yet.

* * *

Marla watched the video from Reuben's file on her monitor at work. What the hell just happened to that man? Who is he? Holy shit! Why does Reuben have this? What does it have to do with Catahoula? Marla nervously glanced toward Reuben's desk. He looked up at that moment and saw her. She bent her head down and cleared her screen pretending to work.

Reuben knew something was wrong. Marla looked guilty. Reuben sent a message to her screen. "What?"

Marla answered, "Nothing."

Reuben messaged back. "BS."

Reuben checked his activity log on his computer and saw where Marla had finished his article and sent it to the deadline desk. Then he saw where she had copied a file. Reuben paled when he realized which file she had copied.

He messaged her, "We need to talk. NOW."

* * *

Cat sat clicking his pen as he reviewed archived news articles on Molly Jarvis. He was impressed with the number of community groups that Molly actively supported. He saw photos of her at the food banks, the homeless shelter, and front and center in several public demonstrations. Cat smiled to himself that William probably had his hands full with her. She looked to be in her early fifties but Cat knew she was actually a year older than William's sixty two.

If Ed Meyer didn't kill Molly than who did? Cat kept scrolling stories and stopped. Headline: Jarvis v. Boggs, Righteous to clean up Raunchy? The article detailed the relentless war Molly had waged against the strip clubs in the Quarter and surrounding area. She had organized a citizens group of community leaders from the churches, education, and a few political supporters to circulate a petition to limit the activities of the clubs. The petitions had gained enough signatures to be placed on the next ballot.

In addition, she had pressured city officials to enforce penalties against the owners of those establishments for building and conduct violations. Molly had volunteers that provided videos of offenders and offences. She demanded local city officials diligently prosecute and fine the violators whenever warranted, and went public when she believed injustices escaped penalty.

Cat was impressed with the passion Molly brought to her causes. Her comments criticizing Ed Meyer certainly paled to those she made of Dillard Boggs. Boggs, according to the Times-Picayune was the owner of five establishments Molly had vowed to shut down. Cat made a quick note on his pad. A search of court records disclosed that Boggs was no stranger to the New Orleans courts. He also was a named defendant in a class action suit Molly had filed a week before her death. Mr. Boggs had a motive.

Cat was certainly interested in meeting Boggs. Cat ordered a background check and financials and returned to his online search on Molly. A woman this vocal may have angered more than one person enough to wish her dead. The more Cat searched, the longer his list of suspects grew.

Cat knew that dropping the charges against Ed didn't mean he had to find Molly's killer. It could be years, or never, for that to happen. Detectives would reopen the files and do exactly what he was doing now. Cat felt almost a sixth sense about this case now. Something was driving him to keep digging.

* * *

Tuesday 5:00 pm

Roger and Thor were reviewing the city maps of the cemeteries when SSA Paul Casey stuck his head in the room. "Nobody's going to welcome me back to New Orleans?"

Roger stood and patted Paul's back. Roger and Paul were often a team. Thor called them Batman and Robin when they weren't around to hear. Roger stood back and gave Paul a 'once over' glance, "Good to see you. Looks like you got a nice tan on your vacation."

Paul grinned and shook Thor's hand, "Best vacation in years. Mexican beach, bikinis, and booze."

Paul looked at Roger, "Then you called." Paul was such a handsome man the FBI actually had his picture on their recruiting brochures. He had the looks of a young Robert Redford. Aside from being handsome, Paul's accomplishments with the agency were nearly as impressive as Roger's. If Paul had a weakness, it was probably his reluctance to commit to a serious relationship with a woman. He claimed there were far too many to choose from.

Roger chuckled, "Pablo and Nelson are due any minute."

Pablo appeared in the doorway, "Already here boss."

Roger told Pablo to gather everyone in the conference room for a briefing about Senator Dalton's murder.

Thor added, "Don't forget the field trip to the cemetery."

* * *

Acer knew Stone's habits like he knew his own. Stone's rental car was at the casino in New Orleans. It only took Acer a few seconds to determine Stone's overnight bag was not in the trunk. Stone would be gambling for a day or two: celebrating another job well done. Stone would stay near so he could watch the local news feed. Stone's ego was his vulnerability.

Acer took a seat in the casino lobby. He used his phone to hack into the hotel's system and then the registration records. There it was, one of Stone's aliases, Michael Williamson, Room 427.

Acer rode the elevator to the fourth floor, located Room 427 and unlocked the door with his electronic device. Stone's open bag rested on the credenza. There was evidence that he had showered. Acer fished the Senator's ID from his pocket, wiped it clean and dropped it into Stone's bag. He thumbed through the pictures on his phone, selected two and attached them to a message: Stone Carson, alias Michael Williamson, Room 427 casino. Last to see Senator Dalton alive.

The message had been sent to the New Orleans FBI office. Acer's New Orleans contact would regret ever placing a hit on him. This was just the beginning. Acer knew the moment he was told he would 'partner' with Stone, they wanted him dead. Acer now knew his days with the company were over. Stone would find the FBI a credible nuisance is all. The company would soon tell Stone that Acer had survived, if they hadn't already. Stone's ego would put him on the road to revenge. Acer would be waiting.

Acer picked up a newspaper in the lobby, grabbed a cocktail from a hostess and sat in an oversized chair with a full view of the door. He wanted to see what the local agents looked like. This was going to be fun.

* * *

Izzy let her bike rest in the tall grass and bushes at the back of Gram's house. The neighborhood looked pretty quiet. It was supper time. She pushed two cement blocks that had held a planter over to rest under the bathroom window. Gram's favorite lilac bush concealed her as she pushed the window up, tossed in her bag of treasures and crawled through the opening.

It was so nice to be home again. Her legs were tired from riding her bike all day. She didn't know where to stop. She didn't have anywhere to go that felt safe anymore. Otis had given her a funny look when she paid for her piece of chicken with a twenty dollar bill. She told him it was a birthday present. It felt terrible to lie to Otis, but she didn't want him to think she had stolen it.

Izzy walked around inside the house and noticed all of the small signs of intruders. She realized the police and medical people had not been real careful. Dirty footprints were on the floor and Gram's furniture moved some. Probably because of that metal bed they used to take Gram away. Izzy could see the big padlock on the front door from the window. The back door had one, too. Gram's bed was empty. Izzy sat on the corner of the bed and ate her piece of chicken. She assumed Gram could still hear her, so she told Gram about her adventures of the day.

Izzy took a bath and changed into clean clothes. She decided to nap for a while and then make a plan for tomorrow. The money Gram left her wouldn't last forever. She needed a job. The sounds from the street became distant and Izzy fell into a deep sleep.

* * *

Jeanne reported back to the field office after she finished at the gym. She heard familiar voices from the conference room and ran toward them. Pablo jumped up from his chair and hugged her the moment she entered the room. They were twins and hadn't seen each other for six months. Roger, Paul and Nelson stood in a line for their hugs, too.

"Wow! This is almost the whole team." Jeanne took a seat at the table and smiled at Roger. After some brief catching up, Roger signaled he wanted to get on with business.

Roger asked Jeanne, "How did the SWAT evaluations go?"

Jeanne answered, "They are doing better than expected. Some of them are already very good."

Roger told Jeanne that Thor would brief her on what was known about the Senator's disappearance and possible murder. Until more information came in from Baton Rouge office and the NSA, they were going to concentrate on other issues.

Roger looked at the group and asked, "How many of you remember the Voodoo lady, Spicey?"

Agent Todd Nelson rolled his eyes, "She's kind of hard to forget. Does this have something to do with our field trip to a cemetery?"

Pablo looked at Jeanne, "Cool." They had grown up in New Orleans, were half-Haitian and both declared Voodoo as their religion. Jeanne was unique in that she had brilliant blue eyes. A blue-eyed Haitian was very rare. Voodoo believers professed them to be chosen by the spirits.

The intake agent popped his head in the door and pointed to Thor. Thor smiled as he pointed at Roger, "New boss."

The intake agent moved his urgent stare to Roger, "Got a video text you need to see. Just came over the main line. I can put it on the big screen there." He was pointing across the room.

Roger nodded, "Do it."

The team all rose from their seats and gathered around the large black screen. The text came first: Stone Carson, alias Michael Williamson, Room 427 casino. Last to see Senator Dalton alive.

Roger glanced at Paul, then back to the screen.

The first photo loaded. It was a man handcuffed to a metal support with duct tape on his mouth. Roger cringed. He recognized the man as Senator Dalton. The second photo was a very good looking man that Roger assumed was Stone Carson.

Roger turned to the intake agent. "Send that last photo to all agent phones, now. Forward the entire text to cyber forensics."

Roger turned to the group. "We have to assume this is legit and move on it." Roger stood and began checking his weapon. The others did the same.

Paul asked, "How do you want to do this?"

Roger looked at Thor, "You and Jeanne go civilian. When you get in position, we'll come in. Assume this guy is trained to spot trouble. Let us do the take down. The rest of us will wear vests and body cams.

Someone is setting this guy up and I'll bet he wants to watch."

Roger addressed the intake agent, "Send a few guys to the casino in street clothes with full video tech. I want every person there on film before this goes down."

Thor looked at Jeanne who was smiling.

Jeanne volunteered, "I have a sexy little outfit in my locker. Maybe I can distract him."

Roger nodded, "That might help. Thanks." Jeanne left the room, undressing as she ran.

The room became silent. Every man there looked at Thor.

Thor shrugged, "She's good at distraction."

* * *

CHAPTER 7

R euben was pacing next to his car waiting for Marla to meet him. He felt sick to his stomach by her betrayal. How could she copy one of his files? They were friends. He knew she had watched the video, he could tell from her guilty expression.

Marla's voice broke through his thoughts. "I am so sorry, Reuben."

Reuben saw she was crying. He didn't care. "Get in the car."

Reuben rested his forehead on his steering wheel. He wanted to collect his thoughts before he said something he would regret later. He looked over at Marla. She looked a wreck. Her hair was in strange clumps and her eyeliner had run down her cheeks.

Reuben couldn't help himself, he starting laughing. He couldn't stop. Marla's facial expression looked as if she had been shocked with a bolt of electricity. Then she looked concerned, like maybe Reuben had gone mad. Every time her expression changed, it made Reuben laugh even harder. Reuben shook his head and figured it had to be the stress he had been under. He knew it was also a sign of the ultimate trust he still had in Marla.

"I'm sorry." Reuben wiped his eyes.

Marla was concerned and confused. "You're sorry? What the hell is going on, Reuben?"

Reuben asked, "Can I trust you?"

Marla started crying again, "I don't know. I don't know why I copied that file. I just wanted in on your big story. I saw the note you made about meeting Catahoula."

Reuben remembered that he had left her his notebook. "It's not just a big story. It's much more than that to me."

Marla was dabbing her eyes with a tissue she found on Reuben's console. "I can tell you this for sure, if you want me to forget everything that happened today, it's done." She sniffled and said, "Maybe you shouldn't tell me anything. I don't want anything to hurt our friendship. If I mess up somehow…"

Reuben told her the whole story.

Marla practically held her breath the entire time. When Reuben finished, he asked her for her thoughts.

Marla barely whispered, "Holy crap."

* * *

Mason Dooley was not happy. Not only did he have to take this self-defense crap with the FBI, but he just found out he would have to re-qualify for his weapon. This was his tenth year on the force. This mandated consent decree was a pain in the ass. Half of his fellow officers had been kicked off the force. Another dozen or so feared prosecution for past deeds.

Working for the police department wasn't Dooley's real income. He made far more money doing the dirty work for people of power. Hell, he didn't even know who he worked for. He had one contact and just did what he was told. Whoever these people were, they had power. Mason had never had to pay the consequences for anything they had asked him to do.

A joint account with his mother held his special money. He would inherit all of it anyway. Dooley pulled a short list from his uniform pocket. Four names and three were already scratched off. Once he got rid of this last one, he would be paid twenty thousand dollars. Cash. Dooley took a pen from his pocket and crossed off Judge Ingle's name. Done.

The Chief had told them at morning role call that the FBI was bringing in additional agents. A lot of them. Dooley spit out the patrol car window. Damn Feds. He saw a small gang of young men turn the corner. He flashed his lights and let out a siren chirp. The gang quickly turned and left. Last thing he needed was a bunch of punks hanging around.

Mason heard the clanging of a muffler dragging and the low rumble of a tired motor. He looked in his rearview mirror and saw Claude's pickup truck pull up and park behind him. The truck sighed with such finality that Dooley worried it wouldn't restart.

Claude walked up to Dooley's window, "Where it be?"

Dooley pointed to the vacant lot across the street. "Drive down the alley in the back and load it up. Take care of it tonight." Dooley frowned, "Try not to be seen, okay? This might be the last one for a while. Things are heatin' up."

Claude scratched his armpit, "When we gettin' paid?"

"When I call you. Now move it! I'm supposed to be on the other side of town. I'll keep everyone away 'til you leave. Take it to the cemetery tonight about ten. I'll guard the corner like usual."

Claude got back in the truck and started it. He looked at Earl, "Dooley says this be the last one for a while. Things gettin' hot."

Earl moaned, "Damn it all. I got bills needin' paid." They drove around back to the alley, tossed the lifeless body in the back of the truck and covered it with a blue tarp.

"You see the suit this guy be wearin'? That be a five hundred dollar suit I bet. Dooley done ruined the jacket. Put two holes in it."

Judge Ingle had made the mistake of handing down too many tough sentences on the wrong people. He had ignored warnings and paid the price tonight. His vacation was to have started in the morning. The fact that he had no family meant he wouldn't be missed for two weeks.

Earl looked out the back window of the truck to the large tarp in the back. "Reckon we could sell them pants right easy."

Claude belched and pointed ahead, "That there is the bar I was tellin' ya about. Real good jambalaya. Let's stop and get us some. This guy ain't goin' nowhere."

* * *

Tuesday 6:30 pm

The cluster of bells at each door announced even more customers were heading into the Voodoo shop. Sasha raised her eyebrows at Spicey and tilted her head toward the door. Sasha had been ringing up sales at a feverish pace all afternoon. Spicey had just walked into the storefront from a nap.

Spicey yawned, smiled at an elderly couple holding hands and asked, "Anything special you be lookin' for, you just ask. You just want to browse, that be okay, too." Spicey waved her arm in the air and then smoothed her long, flowing silk dress as she pretended to dust a few objects.

The elderly woman remarked, "My, what a beautiful woman you are! The brilliant colors on your gown and headpiece look like a magazine cover."

Spicey blushed as she fluffed her hair. Spicey looked over to make sure Sasha had heard. Sasha rolled her eyes. Spicey smiled and the old lady crooked her finger for Spicey to move in close.

The old lady whispered, "We would like to purchase a love potion. LOTS of it. Everyone in the Quarter says you're the real deal." She looked at the old man and giggled.

Spicey tilted her head and whispered back, "You mean to *fall* in love or so you *get* some love?"

The old man was hanging on to the corner of the counter to steady himself. He grinned, "To get some." The old lady winked.

Spicey walked back behind the counter and squeezed herself between Sasha and the rows of potions. She whispered behind Sasha's back, "Got us a couple of live ones." She picked up the potion jar for love and saw it was almost empty. Spicey held up her index finger to excuse herself, went behind her velvet curtain and placed the near empty potion jar next to her crystal ball. She sat down, put her hands on the ball and concentrated on calling her Spiritual Advisor. Soon, she saw the Spirit within a mist in the center of the ball. Spicey said, "I'm almost out of love potion and I don't know how to get more."

The Spirits image disappeared and Spicey sat up straight. "Huh." She looked over and the potion jar was full. "Damn if this shit ain't spooky as hell." She went back to the counter where the old couple was patiently waiting. Most of the remaining customers had checked out and left.

Spicey took a small spoon and carefully scooped out a spoonful that she dropped into a small envelope. She heard the old lady clear her throat and Spicey looked over. The old lady tilted her head indicating she wanted more. Spicey slowly scooped out another spoonful and placed it in the envelope. She glanced at the old lady who smiled. "Dear, I think we might just buy the whole jar."

Spicey and Sasha looked at each other. Spicey tried to choose her words carefully, "This here potion be the real deal. You only have to sprinkle a little pinch to get the job done." Spicey waited for the old man to stop coughing up his lungs. "Don't want to kill nobody."

The old lady and man started laughing and nudging each other with their elbows. "Oh honey, ain't just for us. We be on the organizing committee for an event."

Sasha's head went back, "What kind of event you need a whole jar of love potion?" She was getting a very disturbing mental image.

The old man straightened up and answered, "We're having a Woodstock reunion next week over in Jefferson Parish. Got people comin' from all over the world. Even got some of the bands comin' back! Been hoardin' our meds for over a year now."

Spicey's jaw dropped.

Sasha nodded her head, "Okay. Got it. Think one jar be enough?"

* * *

Jeanne and Thor walked into the main gaming room at the casino. Jeanne quickly glanced around the room and spotted Stone Carson purchasing chips at a half empty blackjack table. Jeanne turned her back to Stone and looked at Thor, "Got him at 10 o'clock. Give me some money and you go to the slots on the right."

Thor made a show of digging his money clip from his pocket and waving a handful of bills at Jeanne. "I get this back, right?"

Jeanne smiled and turned from him. She slowly took in the whole room and stopped her gaze on Stone. He had noticed her. Jeanne walked to his table and took a seat next to him. She put Thor's money on the table for chips and smiled at Stone.

Stone smiled back, "I don't pay for it."

Jeanne opened her hand that held her FBI badge, "I don't sell it."

Stone started to lean back in his chair and felt cold steel on the back of his neck. Thor dangled cuffs in front of Stone's face. Stone smiled at the dealer, "I guess I'll pass this hand."

Roger and Paul had flanked Jeanne and Thor. Stone and Roger locked in a cold stare. Roger looked at Thor, "Have Nelson and Pablo assist in transport. Paul and I will finish up here."

Paul glanced at Roger as they watched Jeanne and Thor lead Stone from the casino. "That was easy."

Roger was watching the casino crowd, "Yeah."

Ten plainclothes agents were mixed in the crowd taking videos. Roger and Paul approached the registration desk and requested the key for Room 427.

In the elevator on the way to the fourth floor, Roger called the Director and reported the text tip and the arrest of Stone. The Director had seen the text and the photos just minutes before Roger had called. The Director and Roger had a unique relationship since Roger's last assignment in New Orleans. The Director had met Ellen and knew about the angels and the role they played in helping the FBI six months ago.

The Director asked, "That picture of the Senator was obviously taken by someone inside the helicopter. We know there were both a pilot and a copilot that left the airport with the Senator. Could we have one of them turning against the other?"

Roger answered, "I agree the photo came from inside the helicopter. We need to prove Stone Carson was one of the pilots. I haven't drawn any conclusions yet, sir. I'll keep you posted."

Paul held the elevator door for Roger and said, "The forensic people are in the building, should be here any minute."

Roger slid the key through the lock and opened the door to Room 427. Ellen had manifested herself as a black cat and sprang toward Roger as he opened the door. Roger and Paul stumbled backwards as Ellen closed the door and vanished. A thunderous blast from the room blew the door from its hinges and sent fiery debris flying from the opening. Flames shot past the debris and quickly retreated back into the room. The contact blast explosive was designed to concentrate damage in one direction and then consume oxygen and extinguish itself.

Roger notified the hotel staff to disarm the sprinkler system and evacuate the guests. The bomb was a smoldering heap of debris, no longer a fire threat, but Roger feared there may be more than one. Paul notified the forensics staff to wait until the bomb squad finished.

Paul straightened his jacket, stepped over some smoking debris in the hall and smiled at Roger, "Guess Ellen's back."

When Roger and Paul first met Ellen, she had decided to appear as a black cat and communicate with them through winks. In order to explain her presence, Roger had passed her off as his pet. He paid the price to his reputation. He was now known as being eccentric when it came to cats. Heaven had unique rules about mortal and angel interaction. Roger and Paul were still learning. Kim was the only mortal that could actually see and talk to Ellen and the gals.

Roger and Paul made an inventory list of what had been in Stone Carson's room, including the Senate ID of Senator Dalton. Roger pointed to the bed, "Stone didn't even sit on the bed. Nothing is disturbed. He checked into the room forty five minutes ago, took a shower and went to the gaming floor." Roger's gut told him a key element was missing. "Unless he sent the text incriminating himself, he didn't know we were coming. He didn't set the bomb."

Paul stared at the bomb remains near the door and the bag on the credenza. "Why plant evidence to trap someone and then risk blowing it up before it's found?"

"The design of this blast was targeted for the door. There was no intention of damaging evidence. Or whoever set the bomb wasn't aware of the evidence. I think Stone has two problems. Someone wants him to take the fall for the Senator and someone else, who didn't know about the setup, wants him dead." Roger's eyebrows went up, "Unless the bomb was for us."

Paul answered, "He's going to lawyer up and we're going to have to turn him loose. We've got nothing."

Roger and Paul made their way back to their car and headed for the field office. Roger moaned, "God, I hate to do this but I think we need Mathew Core. He can find out who knows this guy."

Core owned a security company the FBI contracted with for a variety of services. A tight leash was on Core in light of his history. He knew all of the wrong people. Roger had helped him re-establish himself with the government and put his family back together. Asking Core to help might put him in the gray area of the law again.

Paul responded, "Core can get us information we would have to wait days for if we go through the proper channels." Paul understood Roger's reluctance. "You know the rest of them do it."

Roger was sure the Director would assist them if the other agencies complained. "The techs reported that Stone's alias, Michael Williamson, is a registered DBA. That makes it legal for business purposes. What little there is of a bio says he is a Harvard graduate living off inherited money. Pays taxes, spends his time traveling." Roger glanced at Paul. "You're right. We have nothing. Except proof he was set up."

When they reached the field office Roger excused himself to call Core. He sent him what they had and asked him to search every database available to find out something on Stone. Core had answered, "I have to admit that I'm a little worried to hear you are back in New Orleans. You seem to find smoke and fire before the match is struck. I still have codes to enter NSA and CIA. I also have a buddy at DOJ. How much do you want?"

Roger answered, "I know you have access left from the old days. Don't go there. We have to be very careful about what lines we might cross. I will stand with you, but I have to trust your judgment." Roger exhaled, "I mean this Mathew, if you feel like you are risking your future with Lisa and Jamie, don't do it. There are always ways to catch guys like this. Understood?"

Mathew Core glanced toward his living room where Lisa and Jamie were putting the finishing touches on their redecorating project. They had Mathew moving the furniture around for an hour trying to make a larger craft corner.

Mathew answered, "I'm in full agreement. I'll not risk what I have ever again. Give me an hour or so to come up with something. I'll call."

Roger replaced his phone in his pocket and answered Paul's inquisitive stare. "He'll help and he's going to be careful."

Paul had gotten them each a cup of coffee and sat across from Roger at the desk. "Stone Carson is in an interrogation room. Hasn't asked for a lawyer yet."

Roger twisted slowly in his chair, "He won't until he hears what we have." Roger sighed, "We can hold him seventy two hours, but I think I'd rather not. I think we tell him he has two enemies: one that wants to frame him for the Senator and one that wants him dead. We'll watch what he does. We can offer him protection, which he'll refuse."

"So we wish him well and send him on his way?"

"I want to chat first, but yeah."

* * *

Mathew Core rinsed out his glass and walked in the living room. "If you two divas are finished torturing me, I'm going to run in to work for a while."

Lisa tilted her head, "You haven't gone back to work at night in quite a while." Lisa patted Jamie on the head and walked over to Mathew.

"Roger's in town and needs me to get him some information."

Lisa smiled as she pointed her finger at Mathew, "You tell Roger I expect him to keep you safe."

Jamie yelled over from her new craft corner, "Dad? Can you remember to bring me home some more paper?"

"You got it."

Jamie looked up, "Dad? I'm thinking I should learn to play the violin. I think if you would pay for my lessons it would be good for my cognitive thinking. You know, improve memory function." Jamie looked back to her drawing.

Mathew looked at Lisa and raised his eyebrows. He whispered, "Cognitive thinking? Where does she get this stuff? She's seven years old."

Jamie answered, "Internet Dad. You really need to read more."

Lisa chuckled at Mathew's expression and kissed him goodbye. She gave his hand a little squeeze. He knew she worried he would slip back to his old life of espionage and government secrets. It would take time to earn her trust back completely.

Mathew stood next to Jamie, "Do I get a hug?"

Jamie's face expanded with a toothy smile, "I always have hugs for you. If the violin lessons are too expensive I have other ideas."

Mathew smiled, "I'm sure you do."

Mathew Core arrived at his office, located in the heart of the French Quarter, and started booting up his servers. He entered the data from the phone transmission Roger had sent earlier and stared at the face of Stone Carson.

"Let's find out who you really are."

* * *

Cat placed a call to the establishment 'Dirty Secrets' and asked to speak to Dillard Boggs. The girl who answered sounded like a teenager and claimed Mr. Boggs wasn't taking calls. Cat asked if Mr. Boggs was actually there. The girl answered with a snicker, "Oh he's here alright. Just not a good time to talk on the phone, if you know what I mean?"

Cat assured her he understood and hung up. He looked up the address for the bar and saw it was in the Quarter, on Bourbon Street. Few people that live in New Orleans bother with the Quarter. It is designed to give tourists the shocking, vile, drunken experience vacation they paid for. Cat grabbed his briefcase, said goodnight to Martha, and headed for the French Quarter. If he was lucky, Boggs would be available to talk to by the time he got there.

On the way he tried to piece together a scenario that would fit his evidence. Whoever did kill Molly also had to know Mason Dooley, the cop in Ed's video. It was also possible that Dooley shot Molly. It wouldn't be surprising if Dooley and Boggs might be acquainted.

Cat searched for ten minutes to find a parking spot within reasonable walking distance. With his briefcase and jacket locked in his car, he maneuvered his way through the crowd to Dirty Secrets. The posters on the front windows boasted promises of the pleasures that lie within. It was definitely a raunchy establishment. Cat wasn't a prude but he had never understood the popularity of such places.

Cat stood inside the door for a moment so his eyes could adjust to the darkness. The music was grinding, gritty and blaring. His senses were being attacked by odors of food, booze and bodies. Cat was acutely aware his white shirt and tie was not standard attire. He smirked as several patrons headed out a back exit after spotting him. He knew he looked like the law.

A tall blonde stepped in close to him, her voice raspy and flirtatious. "Honey, I can get you the best table in the house, you just wait a minute."

Cat considered this wasn't a woman. "I want to speak with Dillard Boggs. Is he here?"

The blonde leaned back and looked him over, "You sure you don't want a special table first?" A big toothy smile revealed at least four missing teeth.

"Mr. Boggs please. Tell him I'd prefer not to wait." Cat gave the blond his card which had the DOJ gold seal over his name. That worked. The blonde sputtered and told Cat to sit over in the corner, where a large overstuffed booth with a reserved sign waited.

Cat caught himself scanning the seat for a clean spot. He sat with his back to the corner and with full view of the activities and people within. As Cat glanced around the room, he chuckled to himself that there was a whole world out there he had insulated himself from. It was one thing to read about different lifestyles on court papers and quite another to see them firsthand. He watched the stripper on stage perform for a row of fat, drunken men.

Cat thought the girl looked very young, and strangely detached. He wondered what she was really thinking as the men jeered and the music throbbed. She may be a single mom, thinking about what she would feed the kids. Maybe she was a law student, paying her way through college. One thing was clear. Dillard Boggs wouldn't know her story, or care. She was making him money, and that was the name of the game.

A short, fat, red faced man walked from behind a curtain and straight over to Cat's booth. He held out his hand to shake and Cat reluctantly shook hands with him. Dillard Boggs had beady little blue eyes that darted about the room and rarely focused on who he was speaking to. Boggs was staring at the stage and asked, "So what does the law want with me now?"

Cat answered, "I want to know where you were the night Molly Jarvis was murdered."

Boggs practically choked on the drink he was sipping. "Molly Jarvis? Hell, how long ago was that? I don't know what I was doing last Friday? Do you?"

Cat found Dillard Boggs repulsive. Glancing around the establishment Cat could easily see why Molly had felt so passionate about closing it down. Even the Quarter should have some limits. If Boggs wanted Molly dead, he need not search any farther than his own clientele to find someone to hire for the dirty deed.

Cat asked, "Is there anything in your financials or your personal background you want to explain before I review them?"

Boggs paled. "Why you lookin' to me on this? You guys got your man years ago. Done. End of story. Ain't there enough crime in New Orleans to keep you busy?"

Cat answered, "Molly Jarvis was determined to close you down."

"Who isn't? Look around, Mr. Delacroix. These fine patrons will always find a place to go, and hopefully, I'll own it. She was a nuisance all right, but not worth goin' to jail for." Boggs pointed to a young woman on the stage that was nearly completely stripped. "Now, that's *almost* worth goin' to jail for."

Boggs had no alibi he could remember but promised to look back in his old records. Boggs claimed the government had taught him to keep track of every time he took a piss. He was sure he would come up with something.

Cat left 'Dirty Secrets' and walked back to his car. The last time he had been in the Quarter was last year when Jacqueline had been in town on business. They had dated on and off for a couple of years and finally gave up. They cared for each other but never had the time to see if it could become more. She also had a demanding career that required constant international travel. It just seemed too much work.

Cat smiled at his memory of their night in the Quarter. Jacqueline had twisted her mouth and asked, "How can you live in such a vile place?" They had spent the next two days in his house and she returned to Paris. Months ago he received a birthday greeting from her. His birthday was still a month away.

CHAPTER 8

Cat unlocked the door to his townhouse, tossed his briefcase on the table and walked into the kitchen. He washed his hands and forearms twice after spending time at Dirty Secrets. He opened his fridge door and stared at the empty shelves. He thought he had bought some groceries a while ago. Guess not. Cat promised himself to make an effort to get a real life soon. At forty two he wasn't getting any younger.

He poured a splash of scotch over a couple of ice cubes and stood by his recliner. As he looked around the room, it struck him how sterile it looked. A staged model home had more personality. He saw no proof he lived here. But he did.

His eyes moved over to his briefcase. His mind began telling the story of Pandora's Box. He took a sip of scotch and walked over to the table. He would work an hour or so, get a sandwich somewhere and find that alley. He wanted to see for himself where Edward Meyer stood that night. He wanted to see the street cam over Otis Grocery.

Somebody shot Molly Jarvis three times when she answered the door eight years ago. Somebody scooped the heart and will to live from William Jarvis that night, too. Cat unzipped his briefcase and pulled the folder Reuben had given him to the center of the table. Cat held up the first picture in Reuben's file. Mason Dooley, the cop, talking to someone in a black sedan. The next photo showed the same scene, but from a different angle. The license plate identified the car as belonging to the government. Mason Dooley was in uniform. The third photo showed the same sedan parked at the Justice building in a spot reserved for William Jarvis.

Cat finished the scotch and wiped his mouth with the back of his hand. There was seldom anything he was sure about in the beginning of a case. In this case, there was one glaring absolute; it was going to get ugly.

* * *

Claude and Earl started their second bowls of jambalaya just as a guy walked in the door hysterically laughing. He pointed at them, "Who in their right mind would steal that piece of shit truck you two drive?" The guy grabbed the corner of the bar and held his forearm against his stomach as he bent over laughing.

Claude and Earl just watched him with their spoons frozen in the air and their mouths open.

The guy continued after he caught his breath, "Couple o' punks just took that truck of yours. Be bouncing down the road pert near regular speed considerin' them tires you ride."

Claude and Earl jumped up and ran for the door. Sure as shit, the truck was gone. Claude's face froze in a look of terror. Earl pulled his phone out of his pocket. "Mason? Uh, got us a problem. Gonna need your help, quick."

* * *

Tuesday 8:00 pm

Ellen had told us to visit Spicey and help with whatever project she was involved in. When we arrived at the Voodoo shop, Sasha was locking the doors and Spicey was counting the money in the register.

Teresa pointed to a flyer lying on the counter near Spicey. It was a colorful announcement that the Woodstock Reunion was next week. Teresa looked at Mary, "Do you think we are supposed to help with this Woodstock thing?"

Mary started singing Hendrix's 'Foxy Lady'. I was in shock. Show tunes? Yes. Mary had them all covered. Jimi Hendrix?

Linda pointed at me, "Look at Vicki's face."

Mary stopped singing. "What? You think I don't know about Woodstock? I'll be in charge of music."

Just then Sasha said, "You best get some more love potion mixed up for Woodstock. I bet they decide to get more."

Spicey laughed as she put the register money in her bank bag. "If all them peoples gonna be as old as those two we be needin' a lot of port a potties."

Sasha giggled, "Or diapers!"

Teresa looked at Linda, "I don't think this is what Ellen wants us doing."

Just then Mary screamed.

Dakin had pressed her face to the window and was tapping on the glass with her long fingernails.

Sasha put her hand on her chest, "You best tell your new little friend there to quit scarin' the bejesus out of me!"

Spicey grabbed the front door keys and let Dakin in.

Teresa's eyebrows went up and she looked at Mary who was hiding behind a rack of long dresses.

Linda said, "Mary, they can't see us, get back over here."

I thought Mary had a good idea.

Dakin pointed her long black fingernail at Spicey, "I want you two with me at the cemetery tonight. I have a ritual to draw the evil into the open."

Sasha put her hands on her hips. "First, I don't like the sounds of invitin' evil to join us. Second, any ritual you want to do, we can do right here. No need disturbin' the dead. Ain't that right Spicey?"

Spicey was in total agreement with Sasha and added, "Dakin, I said I'd do what I could to help you. Let's just say that the 'evil' you be wantin' to show up, really does. Then what? I got nothin' but healin' potions."

Dakin looked thoughtful. "I know the Spirits look out for you. If you are in danger from evil, they might come to help."

Spicey straightened up her shoulders and pointed back at Dakin. "That's your plan? Put me in danger with evil and *hope* my Spirits show up?"

Teresa looked at us and said, "I bet this is our assignment. Somehow we have to let Spicey know we are here and that we can help."

Talk about bad plans. I sputtered, "Whoa there, sister. I don't know about you, but I haven't had any class on fighting evil yet." I looked at Linda. She usually recognized when I was making a good point.

Linda glanced at Mary who was shaking her head in micro movements so Teresa wouldn't see. Linda looked at Teresa and then back at us. Uh, oh. I know what's coming next.

Linda said, "We aren't here on vacation. Ellen did say we would be helping Spicey, so I think Teresa is right." Dang.

Teresa rubbed her hands together. "Yes! Okay, how do we let Spicey know we are here? Ellen said she can see us if we will it."

"Wait!" This was me. "Ellen also said Spicey is fragile, so we shouldn't shock her." Too late. Teresa had concentrated so hard on Spicey seeing us, it happened.

101

Spicey grabbed the Woodstock flyer and started fanning herself while she stepped backwards to sit on Sasha's stool. We were sort of floating near the ceiling over the door and Spicey pointed to us. Dakin and Sasha both whipped around and looked. They couldn't see anything. I grabbed a dress from the rack and threw it over me so they could see. Sasha fainted.

Mary frowned at me, "That wasn't your best idea."

* * *

Mason Dooley listened to Earl explain how their truck, with a dead judge in the back, was stolen while they stopped for jambalaya. Mason couldn't believe what he was hearing. He happened to be standing at a homicide scene with three other police units and the coroner on the way. He couldn't leave a murder scene to chase down a stolen truck. He couldn't report it stolen.

Mason hissed through clenched teeth, "You get that truck back now. I don't care how. I can't help you." Mason wiped his forehead straight back leaving his hair standing straight up. He walked over to his patrol car and saw his reflection in the window glass. These idiots were driving him mad. Mason combed his hair back down and tried to control his anger. "Did anyone see who took it?"

Earl answered, "Yeah. Couple of punks."

Mason rolled his eyes. "Doesn't really narrow it down, does it?"

Earl made a face at Claude who had been listening as much as possible. Earl offered, "Why don't we borrow a car from somebody and hunt 'em down?"

Mason scowled, "You do that. Keep me posted." He ended the call and his mind raced with possibilities of what might come from this. None of them were good.

* * *

Izzy was startled awake by the sounds of glass breaking. She sat up, grabbed her bag and listened. Two male voices were talking outside the front window.

"You be sure nobody live here?"

"Hell yes. Died yesterday. Watched 'em take the old lady this mornin'. I'm tellin' ya we can stay here at least a week before the city boys show up."

Izzy realized these men planned to live in her house. She ran for the bathroom and climbed out the window. After loading her bag in her bike basket, she quietly pushed her bike to the neighbors and then pedaled as fast as she could to get out of there. She stopped a few houses down the street and watched as the light in Gram's room went on and shadows moved around the house.

She felt violated. That house was hers and Gram's. These were bad people to break Grams' window and live where they didn't belong. Izzy was so mad that tears streamed down her cheeks. Ms. Nelson's dog, Patches, came up to the chain link fence and whined at her. Patches was kind of a medium sized mutt, mostly white with black patches. Gram had said Patches was a good old dog, kept strangers away from Ms. Nelson. Izzy stuck her fingers through the fence and scratched his chin and then the top of his head. Izzy saw his dog house in the long grass in the corner of the yard and got an idea.

She bent down and whispered to Patches, "If I find you something to eat, can I stay at your house tonight? I'm kind of afraid of the dark."

Patches let out a soft little bark as if he knew they were keeping a secret. Izzy told him she would be right back as she headed for the dumpster by Otis's store. Surely between a bar and a grocery store there would be some food in the dumpster.

* * *

Tuesday 9:00 pm

Cat had been reading the official files for over three hours. He was starving. He wrote down the address of Otis Grocery and grabbed his car keys. Seems there was a bar nearby he could grab some dinner and then check out that alley. He thought about calling Reuben to join him, but changed his mind. He still had a lot of research to do and well researched questions often answered themselves.

His GPS directed him right to Otis Grocery on Mission Street. He sat in his car a few minutes to take in the neighborhood. He was one of the few prosecutors that didn't carry a weapon. He had never justified the inconvenience until now. While there were people on the sidewalks and some traffic, he was surprised at how vacant it felt. Almost other-worldly compared to his side of town. He imagined eight years ago there had been more commerce and fewer signs of decay and neglect.

Otis Grocery seemed the one bright spot in the neighborhood with relatively clean windows, good lighting and signs that bragged 'Nalwens' Best Family Store'. Cat looked at his watch, 9:00 pm. His stomach growled as he twisted in his seat to watch the bar patrons come and go. Two men left the bar and walked down the sidewalk toward him. Cat put his window down and listened to them talk. No grounds for concern, working men, talking sports and local news.

Cat crossed the street, entered the bar and sat on a stool at the far end. The bartender walked down to him and wiped the counter with a rag he had been wearing on his shoulder.

"What can I get ya?"

Cat looked around for a menu. "Do you serve food this late?"

The bartender smiled, "For a dude in a suit, you're damn right we do." He reached under the bar and handed Cat a menu. "Must be a cop or something?"

Cat smiled, "Not a cop."

The bartender's eyebrows went up, "If you're not a cop, then you're lost. Ain't nothin' in this neighborhood that calls for wearing a suit. Just sayin'. You be careful when you leave here, got gangs roamin' this street at dark."

Cat thanked him for the warning, ordered two cheeseburgers and asked, "Do you know the guy that owns the grocery across the street?"

The bartender held out his hand to shake, "My name is Toby, Otis is my brother-in-law. Good guy. Why you askin' about him?"

Cat immediately regretted he had. "I have a friend doing a story on New Orleans neighborhoods and how much they have changed since Katrina. Otis's store looks like it's been here a while."

Toby nodded, "Over thirty years now. Got the best fried chicken this side of town." Toby gave a toothy grin and left to turn in Cat's order. Cat felt the eyes of a man farther down the bar looking at him. Cat turned his head to face the man and lifted his beer as a hello. The man finished his beer in one long gulp and moved down to sit next to Cat.

The man's breath nearly caused Cat to gag. He had obviously been at the bar a while. "You a cop?"

Cat shook his head. "Nope. Just wearing a suit."

The man leaned back to take in more of a view of Cat. "Somebody die?"

Cat had enough. His piercing ice blue eyes glared at the man, "Not *yet.*"

The man nearly jumped and backed away. He left a few bills on the bar and Cat heard him mumble something about bad attitudes.

Toby walked back over with a napkin holder and condiments for Cat. "Thanks. I've been tryin' to get him to go home for two hours."

Cat smiled, "I guess my social skills are rusty."

Toby delivered Cat's cheeseburgers and they quickly disappeared. Cat asked for his tab. "Those were the best burgers I've had in years."

Toby smiled, "Get all our meat from Otis. Farm fresh daily deliveries. Makes a difference."

Cat stepped outside and walked to the edge of the building. The alley looked the same tonight as it must have eight years ago. Even the dumpster was still in the middle. Cat faced Otis Grocery and saw the camera in the lettering of the store sign. He thought back to the video and remembered the car pulling in the alley only about twenty feet. Cat saw why. There was a concrete drain line that extended about four feet into the alley. Mason Dooley knew it was there or he would have pulled in further.

The street lighting was good in this block, but the alley itself was very dark. Had that car been pulled in farther the camera would never have caught Mason's face or the license plate. Cat decided there wasn't much more to see and started walking back to the street. A group of four young men turned into the alley. Before Cat could react, they jumped him. A bat landed squarely on the back of Cat's skull. He felt more blows from the bat on his body and the alley began to spin. It seemed thousands of feet were kicking his body. He tried to fight back but was too injured.

He felt them searching his pockets. His face was on the damp cobblestones of the alley. He heard himself moaning. He heard one of them yell, "Shit. This dude is a cop or somethin'. He got a badge in this wallet." He felt his body being pulled behind the dumpster. He knew he was out of view of anyone that could help.

Soon the voices were gone. Cat felt a tiny hand on his forehead. A soft cloth began gently rubbing his face. A little girl's tiny voice asked, "You okay, mister? You look pretty hurt. I think some bad people hurt you."

Cat's eyes fluttered open for a brief moment and he saw a little girl kneeling over him. Blood was running into his eyes. She looked very worried. Cat tried to sit up and fell back on his elbow. He saw a pink bicycle lying in the alley next to them.

The little girl took a long look at Cat's face. "I need an adult to help you, I'm only ten years old." Izzy worried about leaving him alone. "I'll be just a minute and I'll come right back. I promise."

Cat tried to talk. He didn't know if she had heard him or not or even if he had really said anything. The next thing he knew, there was a crowd of people around him. He saw the blue and red flashing lights of a police car. He realized he was being loaded into an ambulance.

Toby stuck his head in the ambulance, "You'll be okay, man. Come back, but don't wear no suit."

Cat tried to ask him about the little girl, but the ambulance attendant pushed him back down. All Cat could think of was that little girl on her bike, alone at night, on the streets of New Orleans.

CHAPTER 9

Back at the field office, Jeanne had changed into her khakis and t-shirt. She waited for the rest of the team in the conference room. Pablo and Nelson walked in together with four large pizza boxes.

Pablo pulled out a piece and took a huge bite. Jeanne smiled as Pablo tried to say "Starving" with a mouthful.

Nelson looked at Jeanne, "Gotta tell ya, every guy in that casino fell in love when you walked in. Lookin' good there, Agent Manigat." Nelson winked and gave her his best smile.

Pablo realized Nelson didn't know about Thor and Jeanne being a couple. "Uh, Nelson, my man, little sis here is livin' with Thor."

Nelson sputtered, "I'm sorry. Shit. I didn't know."

Jeanne chuckled, "Hey, no problem. Thanks for the compliment." Suddenly her eyes lit up, "Do you think we can still go to the cemetery?"

Pablo almost choked on his pizza. He started laughing and looked at Nelson, "She *wants* to go."

Thor walked in the room with a handful of drawings, laid them in the center of the table and grabbed a piece of pizza. "These are rough plot plans of the cemetery. Roger and Paul are going to stay here and visit with our Mr. Carson while we wait for someone to give us something to hold him on."

Pablo looked angry, "An ID of a missing Senator in his hotel room and a bomb isn't enough?"

Thor shrugged, "Both those things seem more like the work of someone setting him up, doesn't it? What would you charge him with?"

Pablo took another bite of pizza and grabbed a drawing from the table.

Nelson walked over and took a copy also, "Cool. 'City of the Dead', the oldest above ground graveyard in New Orleans. Five square miles of creepy crypts. Shouldn't we do this in the daylight? These guys aren't going anywhere."

Thor nodded, "Roger wants us to check it out. He seems to think Spicey's Voodoo tips are legit. If we find something, CSI will need these bodies as fresh as we can get them. We'll rope it off and turn it over to them. Grab a crowbar. Local cops will meet us there."

Jeanne smiled at Nelson, "If Spicey says we've got 'extrees'…"

Nelson finished her quote, "Then we got 'extrees'."

* * *

Claude went back in the bar. "Who wants to earn some money helpin' Earl and me find Betty Sue?"

A guy at the end of the bar raised his hand, "I want paid up front. Fifty dollars."

Claude's jaw dropped, "Twenty dollars."

The man started walking over to Claude dangling his car keys in front of him, "Fifty dollars."

Claude reached in his overalls and pulled out a wad of bills. He counted off fifty dollars and shoved them at the man. "Damn. I been robbed twice and ain't even finished my dinner."

The bartended yelled, "You ain't paid for dinner yet, Claude."

Claude stomped his boot, "I'll get you tomorrow!"

Claude and Earl loaded themselves into the man's car. The man scrunched his face and asked, "Don't you boys ever shower?" They were about four blocks from the bar and the man stopped. "There you be."

Claude and Earl looked at him like he was crazy. Claude yelled, "What the hell you mean, 'there you be'?"

The man pointed out his driver's window to an old vacant house across the street. Just inside the tattered fence was Betty Sue's face peeking through the missing slats. Her extended middle finger was just visible above the fence.

"How the hell did you see that?" Earl squinted at the fence.

The man answered, "Saw 'em pull in and knew it be your truck. Waited a few and saw a couple punks runnin' away. Look like they be carryin' clothes or somethin'. Best check your shit's all there."

Claude slammed his fist on the dashboard. "You charged me fifty bucks and you knowed it only be four blocks away!"

Earl and Claude cussed as they walked back to the truck. Earl peeked under the tarp. "Yep, he be missin' his pants. Shoes gone, too."

* * *

Jackson and Abram had spent far too long on the last swamp tour of the day. The ride back had been dark and spooky. They had been on the boat with six tourist ladies, all beautiful, drinking booze. Jackson smiled, this was probably the best day of his life. Those gals were pretty, funny and loved their stories. They had totally lost track of the time. Jackson knew Abram was gonna talk about this 'til the season ends.

Jackson had used the majority of his reward money to buy a nice little two bedroom home for himself and his momma. He had also paid for her to have surgery on her eyes. She stood in the doorway now, watching for his car. Jackson talked out loud to himself, "Don't matter I be forty years old. Momma gonna want a report on why I be late."

Jackson pulled in the drive and heard his momma yellin' from the porch as he got out of the car. "You mind pickin' up some groceries? I done spoiled dinner. Let it burn." Her face looked like a child confessing.

Jackson yelled back, "No problem. What you want? Lots of places closed."

His momma was deep in thought. Finally Jackson offered, "How 'bout I go over to Dinky's and get us some crawfish. Already cooked, ready to eat."

Momma's face broke into a big smile. "That there sounds good. You be careful boy, that side of town got them gangs."

"Yes, momma."

Jackson pulled back out of the drive and headed for town. He knew his momma was right. There were a lot of places you didn't want to be in the dark. Over by the 'City of the Dead' was one of 'em.

* * *

Cat must have fallen asleep. When he opened his eyes, Martha was sitting next to his bed. He started to sit up. Searing pain shot through his head and forced him to collapse back on his pillow.

"Martha? What are you doing here?"

"Just where do you think you are?"

Cat looked around and saw he was in a hospital. It all came back to him. "Why...how...?"

Martha draped a sweater over her shoulders. "Why do you think they keep these damn places so cold?"

"Retards bacteria growth. How did you know I was here? What time is it?" Cat turned his head slowly to look for his watch.

Martha answered, "I'm your 'in-case-of-emergency' number. Remember? You, sir, have had an emergency."

Cat chuckled, "You should see the other guys." He winced, "Don't think I even got off a punch."

Martha was shaking her head. "I had patrol pick up your car and take it to your house. Here are your keys." She dropped them on his nightstand. "What in the world were you doing in that neighborhood at night?" Martha's eyes had narrowed and she was expecting an answer.

"I got a couple of hamburgers."

"Fine. Don't tell me. The doctor says you can go home in the morning if that skull of yours isn't any worse. You have a nasty bump on your head, a broken rib and a badly twisted wrist. Who knows how many bruises."

Cat looked at his left hand. That explained the bandage. "They had a bat."

Martha was clearly worried. "I saw where Ted moved your cases to the new guys comin' in." Cat hadn't told her yet and was surprised she knew. "Yeah, I know. Ted told me when I called to tell him about this." Martha had dramatically swept her arm down the length of Cat's bed.

"You can fire me if you want, or have me arrested, but I had your keys and went in your house. I knew the hospital would let you come home tomorrow and I suspected you didn't have any food. I was right. I filled your fridge with some healthy crap you probably won't like. I also donated one of my bottles of scotch. You'll need it." Martha stood, "I don't want to see you tomorrow at all. If there is something you can't live without, call me. The hospital will make sure you get home in the morning."

Cat reached out his hand. "You are my guardian angel. I'll be fine." He squeezed her hand and winked.

Martha laughed, "Look at you flirtin' already! Save it for the pretty nurses. I'm sure by now the word is out that you're here. You wink at them and get yourself a good woman. Lordy. The idea of you going to the hood for hamburgers."

Just then a beautiful, blonde nurse walked into the room. Martha was quite sure the nurse had forgotten to button the top two buttons of her uniform. "Mr. Delacroix? I'm your night nurse. Let's see if we can't get you more comfortable."

Martha shook her head, Cat shrugged and smiled.

After Martha left, Cat thought about the coincidence that he had been mugged by a youth gang just hours after vising Boggs. This was certainly a neighborhood that Boggs had influence; one of his clubs was only blocks away.

* * *

Acer had gotten a room at the hotel across from the casino. Close enough to walk over and gauge the FBI's progress without being too obvious. He had overheard a security man call into his radio that a bomb had exploded in Room 427. That was Stone's room. Stone didn't do it. He didn't do it. Could be he and Stone both needed new jobs.

* * *

Thor, Jeanne, Pablo and Nelson stood in front of the huge grave crypt of Marie Laveau.

Jeanne read from the inscription over the door, "In all times, in all worlds, for all people. The Voodoo Queen. Born 9-10-1801 died 6-15-1881."

Jeanne looked at Thor, "She gets more visitors than Elvis."

Thor glanced at the crypt and then back to Jeanne. "They probably know each other."

Pablo and Nelson walked up to join them, each carrying two crowbars. Pablo gave one to Jeanne and Nelson gave one to Thor.

Nelson looked around, shining his flashlight creating moving shadows all around them. "Where the hell do we start?"

Jeanne starting walking straight to the back of the cemetery. "If you were going to hide a body, wouldn't you pick a spot as far from the street as you could?"

Pablo flanked out to the right, "Look for crowbar marks on the doors." It wasn't long before even the movement of their flashlights disappeared. The cemetery had no lights and was poorly maintained. What should have been clear rows between crypts were overgrown with tall grass and low shrub trees.

The cemetery, St. Louis Cemetery #1, had city streets on three sides. On the north street, Mason Dooley waited in his patrol car for Claude and Earl to arrive. Mason would guard the corner keeping people out of that part of the cemetery. Mason could not see the street where Thor had parked.

In a cab two blocks away were Spicey, Sasha, Dakin and us. Spicey was trying to convince the cab driver to just wait an hour or so and come back. The cabby insisted she wasn't going to find a ride back at that hour in this neighborhood. "This here is probably the last ride this side of town. You stayin' or I be takin' you somewhere else? Ain't got all night." He kept looking at Dakin.

Spicey opened the door of the cab and we all got out.

Sasha shook her fist and yelled after him, "Our deaths will be on your hands tomorrow."

Spicey elbowed her, "Ain't nobody dyin' tonight."

* * *

Claude and Earl had arrived at the cemetery a little early. They just wanted to get rid of the judge's body and go home. Mason wasn't on the corner yet, so they drove into the cemetery from the opposite side where it was darker and lifted the judge from the back of the truck.

"He be getting' heavier every time we move him." Claude had to do the majority of the lifting since Earl was a smoker and downright fat.

Earl grabbed the crowbar from the back of the truck. "Let's just drag his ass over to a dark spot and lean him 'gainst somethin' 'til we get a crypt open."

"Brilliant idea. That's what we do every time, shithead." Claude hated the way Earl always stated the obvious.

Earl stopped and whipped his head around. "You hear that? There's people talkin' over yonder!"

Claude listened. He heard something, too. Claude hissed, "Set this dude against this here stone and we'll check it out. Maybe that witchy lady come back here."

They pulled the judge to rest against a crypt and took turns moving closer to the voices while hiding behind the larger crypts.

Suddenly the light from a flashlight passed across where they were hiding.

Claude started running for the truck. Earl was afraid to move, but he was also afraid to stay. He knew he couldn't run, so he started crawling. Fast. When he got to the truck, Claude was on the phone with Mason. "We got us a problem."

* * *

Spicey, Sasha and Dakin had just barely made their way into the dark part of the cemetery when they saw the back of a well-dressed man, sitting on a crypt stoop. Spicey put her finger over her lips, "Best be quiet. Got a man over there mournin'."

Dakin continued to walk ahead. She stopped when she got in front of him, stepped back and pointed. Spicey and Sasha crept up quietly from the side, Sasha had a death grip on the back of Spicey's skirt. Spicey and Sasha gasped at the sight of the two bullet wounds in his suit jacket and the dead stare on his face. Sasha shook Spicey's shoulders as she screamed and then took off running. Spicey and Dakin ran after her. Spicey yelled back at Dakin, "Where be his pants?"

* * *

Thor, Jeanne, Pablo and Nelson all heard Sasha's scream. Thor pulled his weapon and pointed north. "It came from over there."

All four of them ran into the blackness dodging debris and crypts. Shortly, they heard sounds of people running toward them. Thor yelled, "Light 'em up."

Four flashlights blazed into the eyes of Spicey, Sasha and Dakin.

Thor yelled, "Freeze! Hands in the air."

Sasha fainted. Dakin and Spicey threw their hands in the air and froze. Spicey dropped the bag of conjuring potions she had been holding.

Jeanne went over to Sasha who was now coming around. Jeanne holstered her gun and helped her stand, "This is Sasha. Spicey's friend."

Spicey said, "Spicey right here. Any chance you can move the light from my eyes?"

Sasha and Dakin squeezed next to Spicey. Jeanne asked, "What are you doing out here?"

Dakin answered, "We have a ritual to remove evil."

Nelson looked at Pablo who shrugged. Thor asked, "Who screamed?"

Sasha answered, "I screamed when I saw that man with no pants."

Thor twisted his head looking around, "We've got a guy out here with no pants?" Thor looked at Nelson, "Why don't you chase down the pervert while we finish this."

Spicey added, "He might be a pervert alright, but you ain't gonna have to chase 'im none. He be dead over there." Spicey was pointing behind her.

Sasha leaned toward Jeanne and whispered, "Got two bullet holes in a real fancy jacket."

* * *

Mason Dooley couldn't believe Claude and Earl had left the judge leaning against some tombstone. Dooley told them to just stay in the truck while he checked things out. A patrol car pulled up and parked behind his. It was the officer Jeanne had called red sweatshirt at the SWAT training. Nathan Cottard walked over. "I thought I was the only car sent over here."

Dooley didn't know what Cottard was talking about and tried to bluff, "I just lit up a car on a traffic. What's up?"

"Guess the FBI wants to pry open some crypts. They asked for a patrol to help. You might as well come, too." Cottard left his lights going and started walking toward the back of the cemetery. Dooley was a few steps behind him and saw flashlights waving up ahead.

Cottard pointed and said, "I think we found our guys." As Dooley and Cottard got closer they could see a crowd of people around a large tombstone. The flashlights were focused on a man sitting on the ground. Cottard identified himself to Thor and asked, "Wonder what happened to Judge Ingle's pants?"

* * *

CHAPTER 10

*T*uesday 10: pm
Roger and Paul had just sent Stone Carson on his way. Mathew Core had not found anything useful in the intelligence databases yet. The Director agreed with Roger that they may learn more from seeing what Stone did next.

Roger sat heavily in his chair and looked across the desk to Paul. "I'm beat."

"I started today on a Cancun beach." Paul looked at his watch, "About twelve hours ago."

Roger chuckled, "We can hardly call it a day when the rest of the team is at the cemetery. I'll call Thor and see if they are about done." Roger called Thor. Paul watched Roger's expressions. It was pretty obvious the day wasn't over. Roger finally said to Thor, "Paul and I will come over with some crowbars and give you guys a hand. I don't want the locals messing this up. I'll get our CSI over there and the coroner. See you in a few."

Roger smiled at Paul.

Paul rolled his neck, "Sounds like we have some more work to do. Voodoo lady must have been right?"

Roger answered, "Don't know. They haven't even opened any crypts yet. So far they found two live Voodoo ladies, a Hoodoo Princess and a half dressed dead judge."

Paul stood and dangled the car keys. "Welcome to New Orleans."

On the ride over Paul asked, "What is the difference between Hoodoo and Voodoo?"

Roger answered, "According to Jeanne, and I might get this wrong, Voodoo is a religion, tied closely to Catholicism in that they worship the same saints. Voodoo is all about protection and a close relationship to protective Spirits. Hoodoo is a folk practice that can range from herbal healing to trickery and black magic. Conjuring is the term I think. They each have their own potions, tokens, chants, and titles. I hope I got that right. You should probably ask Jeanne to get the real definitions."

Paul shook his head, "That's plenty right there buddy. I'll just go with what you said."

* * *

Dooley excused himself on the pretense to take a piss. He watched the four FBI agents and Nathan Cottard head toward the back of the cemetery. Shit, shit, shit! They had crowbars. How the hell did they find out? Dooley called Claude's phone,

"Get the hell out of here! There's FBI everywhere. Don't start up that truck. Push it a few blocks away first. Damn thing will bring the Feds on us like a swarm of hornets."

* * *

Thor told Spicey, Sasha and Dakin to go home and report to the FBI field office in the morning to give a statement. The three women practically ran from the center of the cemetery back to the street. Spicey held on to a light post and tried to catch her breath. She glared at Dakin, "Before I listen to your bright ideas again, we gonna visit Mambo. Gotta be an easier way to do this thing."

Sasha frowned, "I ain't going to Mambo's no how, no way."

Dakin's eyes lit up, "You would take me to meet Mambo?"

Sasha beamed with pride, "Spicey sees Mambo all the time. Best buddies, them two."

Dakin pressed her hand to her heart as a sign of admiration. Spicey shook her head and mumbled something about Hoodoo.

We had been flying around the cemetery watching everyone. It was pretty creepy seeing the judge just sitting there. Teresa thought we better hang around Spicey and make sure she got home safe and then go back to the cemetery. I really don't want to go back. I know we aren't mortal anymore, but hanging out at the cemetery is still very creepy. Mary kept stopping and reading the memorials. She is quite the historian at heart.

Mary said, "You guys are really missing out here. These memorial stones have a lot of rich history on them."

Linda reminded Mary that our job was to keep an eye on Spicey. Mary mumbled that nobody made time for culture anymore. Whatever.

We found Spicey, Sasha and Dakin standing under the street light.

Spicey yelled and pointed, "There goes Betty Sue!"

About a block away an old pickup truck was being pushed down the street. Under the street light you could clearly see Betty Sue flipping off the world as she crawled away.

Jackson had just picked up the crawfish dinners for himself and his mom. He turned the corner to head home and saw Spicey, Sasha and Dakin running down the center of the street toward him.

Spicey flagged him down and Sasha and Dakin plopped into his backseat. Spicey jumped into the front seat and said, "Thank God you came along, Jackson. Turn around and help us follow that truck. Those guys been killin' people!"

Jackson's eyes looked as if they would pop from their sockets. "Killin' people? Ms. Spicey, what happens when we catch 'em?"

Spicey thumped on the dash a couple of times, "Just hurry it up. They done got inside that ol' truck and started up the motor."

Sasha leaned up toward the front seat and tapped Spicey's shoulder. "I already be in this here back seat with a 'princess', so now you be thinkin' you some kind of 'Wonder Woman'? What you plan to do when we catch 'em?"

Spicey dug into her purse, pulled out a pistol, and waved it in the air. She looked to the back seat, "You ain't got to be no Wonder Woman if you be packin'."

Dakin added, "We left our bag of potions in the cemetery. We can't fight evil with that little pistol of yours. Heck, they're probably packin' too!"

Jackson pointed to the back seat, "You best listen to them two, Ms. Spicey. I ain't prepared to fight no evil. I'm half drunk, and my momma's waitin' on her dinner."

"Fine. We'll just follow 'em. See where they go."

* * *

Dillard Boggs waited for Mason Dooley to answer his phone. A cocktail waitress came over and wiggled her boobs in Dillard's face. He backhanded her face hard and sent her tray flying. She covered her face with her hand and tearfully apologized as she started to clean the mess.

Dooley finally answered. "Yes, Mr. Boggs?"

"What the hell's going on? I've got a federal prosecutor over here asking about Molly Jarvis."

"What?"

Dillard rolled his eyes, "Jarvis, you idiot. I'm supposed to call him back with my alibi. Sabastian Delacroix, do you know him?"

Dooley sure knew the name and knew it meant big trouble. "He's the one they call Catahoula."

"Oh crap!"

* * *

Virgil Holmes enjoyed all of the trappings his position provided. As Senior Assistant to the National Security Director, he only had to answer to the Solicitor General and the Department of Justice, Attorney General. Each of them having enough on their plates to ensure Virgil only met them at social functions.

Virgil had been groomed and mentored by the machine for decades. He was now one of their most powerful men. New Orleans had always been his pet project. There were unlimited opportunities for the machine if they controlled the ports. The foundation of a corrupt political base made infiltration easy.

After Katrina, the dollars flowing to the area were an unexpected boost and incentive for criminal entities. The recent declaration of a federally mandated consent decree to clean up the crime and corruption actually proved an opportunity to remove their enemies. Virgil had hand-picked his primary contact for the New Orleans office, right after Katrina. He afforded this contact a great deal of discretion in decision making. This morning's news suggested that decision may have been a poor one.

Virgil dialed his New Orleans contact. "You and I have a problem. NSA intercepted a transmission from Acer to the New Orleans office of the FBI. It was forwarded to me by an associate. This transmission contains photos of Senator Dalton's last moments and of Stone Carson's location. Stone obviously failed at his entire mission and Acer has gone rogue. The result of this transmission is that the FBI is bringing in a substantial number of agents to your district. Be on the alert. I need not remind you that we are approaching several sensitive deadlines. We did not need the FBI brought into this by Acer. " The line went dead.

The contact had listened carefully to the call and took special, personal note of the abrupt ending. When Acer proved Stone had failed at the mission, the contact decided to eliminate Stone as punishment. If the FBI was tipped by Acer that Stone was at the hotel and the bomb detonated, the FBI may assume the bomb was meant for them. Bombing FBI agents would not be viewed favorably by Holmes. The New Orleans office had just been put on notice. Amends would need to be made quickly.

* * *

Virgil placed a call to Stone Carson. "You are only to act on orders given by me. If the New Orleans contact calls you, I want you to report back to me. Is that understood?"

Stone answered, "I have trust issues. My hotel room door was wired to explode. I don't believe Acer did it. He wanted the FBI to find the evidence he had planted. I think the New Orleans contact ordered my door blast."

Virgil asked, "Who did open the hotel door?"

"FBI."

"Shit." Virgil paused, "You are the best we have Stone. From here on, I will personally take care of you."

Stone smiled, "I understand, sir."

Virgil hung up from the call and began pacing in his office. What the hell was wrong in New Orleans?

* * *

Zack locked the doors of the gym and promised himself he would hire another trainer by the end of the week. Working fourteen hour days was getting real old, real fast. Core had called and asked if he would stop in at their security headquarters. Zack's curiosity peaked.

Core buzzed Zack in the building and gestured for him to take a seat. "Got a mystery man Roger wants some info on. I'm hitting brick walls here."

Zack leaned closer to the desk, "Show me what we have." Zack stared at the pictures of Stone Carson and the man wearing duct tape. Zack tapped on the picture of the duct tape man, "Uh, heard Senator Dalton was missing, then I heard he was on a hunting trip. That's him."

Core stretched his neck to both sides and answered, "He's not missing anymore. Feds say he was dumped from a helicopter into the Assumption Parish sinkhole this morning."

Zack was holding the picture of Stone Carson and frowning. "I think I've seen this guy's photo." Zack laid the photo down and tapped it with his index finger, "ATF connected him with a hit of some Embassy guy last year. Couldn't make it stick." Zack's eyes narrowed, "Now I remember! Department of Justice took the case and buried it. A lot of pissed off people over that one. This guy has a friend at Justice."

Core twirled his pen, "Do you have any friends left at ATF?"

Zack smiled, "Just one big one."

* * *

Roger and Paul drove the perimeter of the cemetery before they saw the cluster of vehicles and officers in the far corner. There were two coroner wagons, which wasn't a good sign. They parked and walked over to where Thor was prying on a concrete door with a crowbar.

Just as Roger was going to volunteer to take over, the door popped open. The stench from inside sent everyone stumbling back. Thor pointed for the cemetery workers to check inside.

The worker held a mask over his face and worked his flashlight around the small room. "Got one that belongs and two that don't."

Thor threw his crowbar on the ground and motioned for the coroner's team. He looked at Roger, "So far we have seven 'extrees' as Spicey would say."

Paul glanced around at the unending rows of crypts. "How did you select which ones to open?"

Thor pointed to the front of the concrete door. "See down here? Whoever has been doing this hasn't been very careful. Only takes a glance to see their tool marks."

Thor looked at Roger, "I say we pick up from here in the morning. This might be all there is."

Roger nodded, "Long day, I agree."

Walking to their car, Roger commented, "I can't shake this feeling of dread."

Paul opened the passenger door to the car and said, "It's because we're in New Orleans. Every event is connected. Right now we only have a ball of loose threads."

Roger pulled away from the cemetery and let out a small chuckle. "I don't know where I'm driving to. Do you have a hotel yet? I can drop you off."

Paul shook his head, "I went straight to the field office from the airport."

Both their bags were at the field office. Roger fought back a yawn, "We can swing in, pick up our bags and see if we have any messages. How about that hotel across from the casino?"

Paul yawned, "Works for me."

* * *

Acer had sent a text message to Stone to meet him for drinks at 10:30 pm at Acer's hotel across from the casino. Stone would either talk or try to kill him. Acer sat at a corner table and watched the door. 10:45 pm, no Stone. Acer played with the rim of his glass with a small straw and decided he might as well leave. Stone had probably decided to kill him.

Just as Acer reached in his pocket for his money clip, Stone walked in the room. Stone walked to the bar, got a drink and walked over to sit across from Acer.

Stone took a sip of his drink and raised one eyebrow. "You're looking well for a dead man."

"I could say the same for you."

Stone glanced toward the door and then back to Acer. "Just spent a few hours with the FBI. You could have just sent me a text you were alive." Stone sat his glass on the table, "I don't get the bomb though. Why bother?"

Acer sat his glass down too, "I didn't do the bomb. That's why I thought we might talk."

Stone was silent.

Acer added, "I had a face-to-face this morning. I wanted them to know I survived. I also wanted to know if the 'machine' wanted me gone or you. I wasn't given another assignment, so I have my answer."

Stone shrugged, "So now you know. I wasn't too worried about you. Most people know I work alone. I figured you might take precautions. Just business, not personal."

Acer actually laughed, "Yeah, not personal. My first clue when they said I would be with you." Acer leaned back and actually relaxed some, "So, now the question is, why do they want you dead?"

Stone had been asking himself that question for the last three hours. "The timing is all wrong. Too much work in the pipeline."

Acer nodded, "Exactly."

Stone pointed his straw to the door, "FBI. Those two just wasted three hours of my life thanks to you."

Acer glanced over to the door and watched as Roger and Paul took stools at the far side of the bar. Seconds after sitting, Roger's eyes locked on Acer. Paul raised his phone and took pictures. Acer moaned, "Shit. How many hotels in New Orleans and they pick this one?"

Stone chuckled, "You're the one that invited them to play."

Roger walked over to their table, "Going to introduce me to your friend, Stone?"

Acer put his hand out, "John Smith. Your name?"

"Roger Dance." Roger ignored Acer's outstretched hand and took both of their glasses. "I'll send you fresh drinks."

Stone pushed his chair back and stood. "No, thanks, we're done."

Roger nodded, "Yes, you are."

* * *

Jeanne had tried to talk Pablo and Nelson into staying with her and Thor. Pablo had dismissed the offer, "No offense, Sis, but I think we can find more action in the Quarter."

Jeanne flipped Pablo's black hair from his face and gave him a kiss on the cheek. "Nice to have you home, big brother." He was five minutes older than Jeanne and nearly as good looking. Nelson had a Brad Pitt look going for him and Jeanne was sure the two of them would have no trouble finding ladies.

Thor and Jeanne drove home singing along to the music of Buddy Guy. Jeanne smiled, "I'm going to turn you into a Cajun yet." Thor shook his head as he chuckled.

Thor glanced at Jeanne as he parked the car in their driveway, "My gut says this cemetery mess is just the beginning."

Jeanne was sure of it. "The Spirits wouldn't come to Spicey unless there was a real danger."

Thor held the porch door open for her, "I noticed that one cop seemed to have a problem with you."

"Mason Dooley. He's SWAT. He has a dark aura." Jeanne freed her hair from its braid by running her fingers through it. She shook her hair and smiled at Thor's expression as he watched her. He was clearly mesmerized.

Thor shook his head as he laid his gun on the table and pulled off his boots, "Dark aura. Of course."

* * *

Jackson was glad to see Betty Sue pull into a dirt drive just outside of town. Maybe his momma's crawfish would still be warm when he got home after all. Jackson turned to Spicey, "I ain't drivin' down that path. Least now you know where 'evil' lives."

Spicey looked at Sasha and Dakin in the back seat, "You two okay if we go home now? Let Jackson here eat his dinner." Spicey tried to give Jackson some money. He waved her off.

"Ms. Spicey, I ain't takin' your money. You done put me on the righteous path last year. I still owe ya." Jackson had another thought, "Don't mean I'm willin' to go fight evil with ya though."

Jackson dropped them off at their homes and headed back to his momma. By now he was cold sober. After following Betty Sue for a few miles he was also a nervous wreck. Who knew evil drove a ratty old rainbow truck named Betty Sue?

CHAPTER 11

Wednesday 7:00 am

Roger made a pot of coffee in the break room and grabbed a carton of milk. He glanced at the glass dome over a pile of donuts and paused. Kim would tell him to grab a piece of fruit. He grabbed an orange and dropped it in his pocket. He had called her from the hotel late last night. Her mom, Vicki, had already told her about the cemetery. It had been easier than he would have thought having angels in his life. Kim was obsessed with why the judge didn't have any pants. Roger chuckled to himself. It would be nice if that were the only unanswered question.

Roger reached the door of the office Thor had assigned him. Someone had taped a sign, The Boss, on the door. Roger pulled the sign down and threw it in his basket. He suspected Thor had put it there to keep people away from his own office. Roger smiled to himself at Thor's often misunderstood humor.

Paul knocked on Roger's open door, holding a cup of coffee. "You taking visitors yet?"

Roger nodded and smiled, "You get enough sleep?"

Paul laughed, "No. Never do. You?"

Roger turned to his computer, "Nope. Let's see if Core found anything on Stone Carson."

Roger sent an email and was surprised to get an immediate answer back. Roger looked at Paul, "He's got something. Sending it now."

Roger called CSI to have them process the prints from the glasses he took from Stone and Acer and run them in the databases. Meanwhile, Roger was waiting for what Core might have found on Stone.

Paul pointed to Roger's monitor, "You got something."

Roger opened the document from Core. He clicked on a link Core had attached and began reading an ATF file on Stone Carson. Roger clicked print and handed the paper copies to Paul as they came off the printer. Roger kept reading the monitor. After about five minutes, Roger was finished and turned from the screen. Paul was finishing up the last page.

Roger peeled his orange and passed half over to Paul. Paul took a bite and said, "This smells bad." Roger looked at his orange. Paul waved the papers, "These."

Roger nodded agreement. "He's not verified in any government database. How does he get protection from someone at Justice?"

Paul leaned back in his chair, "Private contractor?"

"Too private. Nothing sticks to this guy, and he's off the grid. My money's on a dirty friend at Justice."

* * *

Ed Meyer walked home from working the docks all night and noticed the small pink bicycle lying in the grass outside his neighbor's fence. He slowed his pace down and saw a small shoe protruding from the door of the doghouse. That little girl had slept in there. Ed's heart melted.

Ed walked to the edge of the fence and said, "Little girl, I know you're in there." The little shoe disappeared into the dog house. Patches ran out barking. Ed raised his voice, "I know you're hiding. I don't care. I can keep your secret, but you can't sleep in a doghouse. I live in the white house across from your grandma's. Just knock on my door when you're ready for help. My name is Ed." Ed paused a moment and added, "This is our secret. I'm trying to be invisible, too."

Izzy watched Ed walk down the sidewalk through a crack in the doghouse. Gram had warned her there were bad men that wanted little girls. Ed sounded nice. Like Otis. She and Ed had a secret together now. They were both invisible.

Ed unlocked his door, washed up in the bathroom and went to his kitchen. He hoped Izzy would follow him home. In his fridge was a decent slab of ham and half a dozen eggs. He started browning the ham and heard a soft knock on his front door. He saw Izzy standing on his front porch. It looked as if she was ready to turn away.

Ed opened the door. He was whisking the eggs in a bowl and said, "I'm making ham and eggs if you want to help me eat them."

Izzy nodded her head as she looked down at her shoes. Ed said, "Look me in the eyes. You need to learn how to read people. Not all people are nice."

Izzy looked him in the eyes. "I see sad in your eyes." Her voice was tiny. "Did you do something wrong?" Her words rang with the kind of truth only heard from a child.

Ed was momentarily stunned. This child could read people just fine. Ed tilted his head toward the door, "You can bring your bike inside if you want. I'll get these eggs going. You like scrambled?"

Izzy's voice had a confident ring now, "I love them."

* * *

Spicey woke to the sound of hammering at her back door. She opened the door and walked into a huge turkey foot that had been wrapped in leather straps with feathers and a big clump of hair. It was hanging in the center of her doorway. Dakin popped her head from around the corner, "I'm not done yet. You weren't supposed to see it yet."

Spicey flicked the turkey foot with her index finger and sent it swaying. "What's this supposed to be?"

Dakin stopped the swinging foot and held it for Spicey to see up close. "Native Americans believe the turkey represents abundant harvest and wellbeing. It has been called the earth eagle for many centuries. These feathers represent courage, speed and pride. This is buffalo hair which represents stability, strength and power." Dakin's pride in her token was obvious. Spicey was touched.

Dakin continued, "A token made of these elements, gracing your home, will protect you anywhere. I used the largest foot I could find for you."

Spicey was overwhelmed and dabbed her eyes, "Come here you crazy lookin' Hoodoo girl." Spicey gave her a big hug. "Since you woke me anyway you want some tea? Sasha be here shortly."

"I need to finish putting this on your wall right so it doesn't hit you in the face." Dakin laughed. "I don't drink tea. You got Pepsi?"

Spicey chuckled in her kitchen. Some Hoodoo Princess. Don't do herbal tea. Hoodoo all about herbs, roots and conjurin'. Wants Pepsi!

* * *

Cat had taken a cab from the hospital home. His doctor told him to stay home a couple of days and not to drive. Cat dumped the pills they had given him into his wastebasket. They would make him drowsy and he figured he could stand the pain. It was his ego that might not recover. Cat saw the two cards in his hospital sack with nurses' phone numbers. He placed the cards on his counter and threw the rest of the bag in the trash. One of these days he had to start a social life again before he forgot how.

Cat looked in his fridge to see what Martha had brought. There was a plastic container with a masking tape label that said Martha's homemade vegetable soup. A gallon of milk, a half dozen fruit yogurts, a dozen eggs, a pound of bacon and a container of ready to microwave macaroni and cheese crowded his shelves. All his favorites. She had to be the best assistant in the world. An unopened bottle of scotch was on the counter with a note: Do not open unless you had a meal and are free of medication.

Cat grabbed the vegetable soup, spooned some in a large bowl, and put it in the microwave. Vegetable soup for breakfast made as much sense as anything else lately. He carried the soup over to his recliner as he balanced a glass of milk in his elbow. The local news reporter was standing in front of The City of the Dead cemetery. Cat turned up the volume.

"FBI sources have confirmed that the murdered body of Judge Ingle was found last night here in the City of the Dead. There are unconfirmed reports that as many as seven bodies were found in addition to the judge. These bodies had been hidden in already occupied crypts."

Cat's first thought was that he wondered how the FBI knew to look in crypts for hidden murder victims. His second thought was that with Judge Ingle's death, there were now only a handful of judges he felt were competent.

He took his empty soup bowl and glass over to the sink, rinsed them out and put them in his dishwasher. Cat decided to run the dishwasher since it appeared to have nearly every glass he owned in it. His mind went back to the images of the little girl that had saved him. Why was she out in the streets at night? Where were her parents?

Cat saw his reflection in the sliding door to his patio and peeled the bandage from his head. He chuckled to himself and wished he had a better story to tell at the office than being mugged by a group of kids.

The reporter had moved on to the local murder report and corruption investigations. Cat realized his desk wouldn't be empty for long. He glanced over to the table where his laptop and briefcase held Ed Meyer's future. That would be today's project.

* * *

Jackson arrived at work before Abram. After checking the boats, he went in the office to grab a cup of coffee. He had just turned on the small television when Abram came through the door. "Man does my head hurt today. I drank a lot more than you did last night." Abram's face erupted in an ear to ear smile,

"I think I dreamed about them girls all night long. Now *that* was a good day at work."

Abram poured himself a cup of coffee, still mumbling about the night before. Jackson turned up the volume to hear the news. The reporter was talking about seven dead bodies found in crypts last night, and a dead judge. In the City of the Dead.

Jackson's jaw dropped and he pointed at the TV. "I was there! Ms. Spicey had me chasing some ratty old truck with killers in it!"

Abram shook his head, "Say that again. You went to that cemetery last night with Ms. Spicey?"

Jackson waved to make Abram shut up. He wanted to hear the whole news story. When it was over, Abram stared at Jackson, "Holy crap."

* * *

Marla had thought about Reuben's situation all night. Now she understood why he was so private, even shy. She had just assumed he wasn't interested in her, that maybe he was gay. For two years she had tried every trick in the book to get close to him. Huh. She had come very close to ruining their friendship yesterday. She felt her guilt so heavily she was sure it was as visible as a purple coat, for all to see.

Reuben said the guy in the alley with his father was Mason Dooley, a cop. Marla had friends in this town and somebody would know something useful. This wasn't like doing a community entertainment article for the Sunday edition. She would have to be sneaky. Like an investigative reporter.

Marla called a friend that worked in dispatch at the police department. "Gayla! Girl, how have you been?"

Gayla replied, "Marla? My gosh, I haven't talked to you for ages. I'm good. What's up?"

Marla put her sneaky voice on, "I came across the cutest cop. I was hopin' you could tell me if he's worth my time or not?"

Gayla chuckled, "You give up on that reporter dude?"

Marla sighed, "He isn't ever going to go for me. I think he has someone else anyway."

Gayla sounded like she was whispering in her phone, "I don't want to talk here, ya know? Let's grab lunch at Scotties."

"Noon?"

"Noon."

Marla called her friend Sam that worked in the medical examiner's office. Sam answered, "Yeah?"

Marla scolded him. "Is that how you guys answer the phone there? Yeah?"

Sam laughed, "Hey, Marla. What can I do for ya?"

Marla carefully worded her question, "Have you ever declared someone dead and have them show up later alive?"

Sam laughed, "You mean like a zombie?"

Marla sighed, "No. Like a mistake. How sure are you guys when you identify somebody as dead?"

"Usually someone that knows them makes the identification. Why? Did we mess up?"

Marla paused, "I've been reading a fiction book and wanted to do some fact checking. The book claims to be mostly based in fact. Claims there were people declared dead during Katrina that really weren't."

Sam laughed, "Anything could've happened during Katrina. Who would know? I wasn't here then. Yeah, that part might not be fiction."

* * *

The plaque in the lobby listed the Office of Solicitor General as being in the building. There was no reference as to which floor it was on, simply the ominous statement that visitors would be escorted. The Solicitor General had just taken a call from the Director of the FBI on his private cell phone.

"I'm more than a little curious that you are calling at this hour, Jim. Good morning."

The Director of the FBI had known the Solicitor General for years, both privately and professionally. "This conversation is off the books, Dan. I'm sending a text to your cell phone now. I want to hear what you know about this."

The Solicitor General looked at the picture of a man with duct tape on his mouth and a second man's face and read the text. He responded, "What am I looking at?"

"Senator Dalton. He was kidnapped and dropped into the Assumption Parish sinkhole yesterday. The other man is Stone Carson. ATF claims someone at Justice let him take a walk last year on the hit of an Ambassador. This man has dirty friends at Justice. I'm telling you that my team will find out who they are. Can I count on your help?"

The Solicitor General leaned back in his chair and exhaled. Everyone in law enforcement knew that the FBI had some kind of 'special' team the Director used for his pet projects. They weren't just good. They were spooky good. "How sure are you that Dalton's dead? I heard he was on a hunting trip."

"He's dead. His regular pilot was murdered at the airport; there are eyewitness reports of a man dumped in the sinkhole and the Senator's helicopter crashed a few miles away. No bodies."

The Solicitor General sighed, "He was a key witness in a case we are bringing on a lobbyist next month."

"Start there. Stone Carson is implicated in two hits involving someone with the DOJ. We have this Ambassador from last year and now Dalton. Can I count on you?"

"Yes. Where is this Stone Carson now?"

The FBI Director answered, "Last night he was in New Orleans. We have NSA tracking him. ATF claimed it was someone at the National Security Division of your office that pulled the rug last year on that case. I know that doesn't narrow it down much, but it's a start. There was quite a stink."

"I'll get back to you."

The Solicitor General put his phone in his pocket and walked over to his office window. The morning sun blasted from every surface below. He was well aware that the machine had penetrated every office in Washington and dictated most policies. He had stopped dreaming years ago that he would ever expose them. Even the ones in Justice were ghosts. They were careful, well-funded and left few crumbs. It was rumored that they knew no limits. Rumors yet unproven.

Something about the Directors' voice gave him hope. Maybe this time could be different.

* * *

The Director of the FBI called Roger and told him that Senator Dalton was scheduled to testify as a surprise witness in a DOJ case against a lobby organization based in New Orleans. The lobbyist represented the oil interest of Lanitol Oil Company, the largest oil entity in the Gulf.

Roger stated, "Lanitol Oil was one of the entities we named last year in our racketeering case here in New Orleans."

The Director answered, "Yes, it was. Evidently the good Senator was willing to testify that specific individuals approached him. First with a bribe and later with threats."

"Regarding what?"

"A bill being presented to the Senate. My understanding is that Lanitol Oil is looking for substantial fine reductions, because of their oil leak, and a cap on liabilities. Senator Dalton was one of two Senate votes stopping that cap."

Roger asked, "The obvious question now is who is the other vote and when does this vote take place?"

"Senator Welsh is the second vote and the vote is Thursday." The Director continued, "Before you ask, Senator Welsh lives in New Orleans and I have notified him of Senator Dalton's true circumstance."

"Will he allow protection?"

The Director chuckled, "I just hung up from talking to him. He's begging for it."

CHAPTER 12

Wednesday 8:00 am

Mary, Teresa, Linda and I were all watching Dakin hammer the turkey foot on a strap to Spicey's Voodoo shop. Linda looked at Mary, "What are we supposed to do now? Just watch Spicey?"

Mary shook her head. "Ellen said we were supposed to help her with some problem. I think we should go check on those two guys in the truck. They seem to be the problem."

I offered, "We can go back to the cemetery, too. Roger will want to know about the dead guys. Once we find out their names, we can use our locators to find out more about them."

Teresa said, "I think you're both right. Where do we go first?"

Linda volunteered, "Let's get the names for Roger first. By now the bodies are at the Medical Examiner's office."

Oh goody. A room full of dead people. I offered what I thought was a good idea, "If we could hack into the medical examiner's computer, there's probably already a list."

Teresa was shaking her head, "I bet not. It's going to take them a long time to match a body to a name. They might not even know these people are missing."

Ellen appeared sitting on Spicey's door stoop. "Morning, gals. Teresa is right. The best way you can help is to go to the medical examiner's office and use your watches to do DNA tests. The mortal information will show on your watch monitors. This is how we are really going to help Roger in this assignment. Angel technology will get him information days faster than anything available to him now."

Cool. Mary had her face scrunched in a disgusted expression. "How do we do DNA tests?"

Ellen took Linda's hand and pointed to her watch. "See this little clasp here? Pull this out and Voila! Looks like a little blood meter right? Just poke some tissue and push the blue button. This should give you a full history on the person."

We were all sliding our little meters in and out. I think they add new shit to these watches when we aren't paying attention. I certainly have never seen this bar before.

Ellen frowned at me and continued, "Once you have identified them all, hit the green 'send' button and it will automatically text Roger to check his email. Piece of cake."

Mary was trying to poke herself. Even I knew we didn't have blood anymore. Ellen looked at Mary, "Stop it. You're getting like Vicki."

Hey.

Mary got an exaggerated look of terror on her face and then smiled at me. Funny.

Linda asked, "After we get these names, should we check out those men from the truck? Spicey seemed pretty sure they were dangerous."

Ellen nodded, "Oh, yes. They're dangerous. They plan to kill Dakin again."

Again?

* * *

Cat placed a call to the New Orleans FBI field office and asked for SSA Dan Thor. Cat had met Thor last year when he assumed the administrative position at the field office. Thor had shared with Cat that he hated the politics of his new position, and hated the upcoming consent decree mess. Thor had promised Cat that anything he needed from them was available.

"Sabastian Delacroix. I have a favor to ask."

"Shoot."

"The FBI has taken over the reorganization of the police department already, right?"

"Right."

"I would like the complete records of an officer named Mason Dooley sent to me." Cat added, "If you could keep this unofficial, I would appreciate it.

I'm at home today, so I am going to give you my personal email." Cat thought about the extensive data bases the FBI had at their disposal. "Could you also run a Dillard Boggs?"

Thor noted Mason Dooley was the dark aura guy from last night at the cemetery. "Dooley and Boggs sound like a perfect pair. Boggs is always in our crosshairs. File might be thick."

Cat answered, "That's okay. I need to go back at least to 2005 before Katrina."

Thor told Cat about their field trip to the cemetery. "In case you end up with these cases, it was easy to tell from the tool marks that the same people opened each of these crypts. Not that long ago either. I bet the oldest corpse was only a week."

Cat paused, "I saw the report on this morning's news. My first thought was the additional heat coming to town with FBI was causing someone to clean house."

Thor agreed, "That is exactly what I've been thinking. These people were either witnesses or snitches. Did you know Roger Dance is here?"

Cat smiled to himself, "That means you guys have stepped into something."

Thor laughed, "Yeah, usually does means that. I'll send you what I have on these two and we'll take a peek into archives and personal crap. Give me your email."

Cat gave Thor his contact information and asked, "Is Roger available to take a call?"

Roger's last memory of Cat was at the New Orleans Hospital when they had both been shot outside of the courthouse. Roger answered, "How's the leg?"

Cat laughed, "Best thing I have right now." Cat told Roger about his adventure in the alley. Roger scolded Cat for not having his weapon on him.

Cat asked, "I need your help on a case I have started. I think mostly your technology and databases."

Roger grabbed his pen and a notebook, "Give me your address, and Paul and I will bring you a lunch later."

* * *

Earl was having enough trouble trying to sleep with the damn rooster outside his window. Crazy thing was really making a racket this morning. Earl heard Claude's axe chop. Rooster kept crowing, so it wasn't for him. Earl cursed himself to have sold his place and moved in with Claude. Brother or not, the place was a hell hole.

Earl stumbled into the kitchen where Claude had a pile of chickens on the table. All of them had broken necks. Claude was chopping their heads off and throwing the bodies in the sink.

Earl protested, "Get a garbage can for the damn heads. You just throwin' 'em on the floor."

Claude frowned, "You want to live with Martha Stewart, start packin'!"

Earl counted over twenty chicken heads on the floor. The pool of blood was quickly flowing downhill on the uneven floor and heading toward Earl's chair. "I'm gonna get trapped here if you don't stop and clean up."

Claude slammed the axe down hard into the wooden table. Blood splatter flew across the room and landed on Earl's shirt. "I cook. You clean up."

Earl was afraid of Claude when he was in one of his moods. Doctors said he needed to take meds to keep his mind straight. Claude said booze worked just as good. Earl moved from his chair, reached over the pool of blood and grabbed a mop and a bucket. "Let me into the sink there for some water. Best get this 'fore we can't walk."

* * *

Stone Carson rented a modest row house in a quiet neighborhood in Baton Rouge. He put his key in the door, gently kicked it open and stepped to the side of the threshold. No bomb. That wasn't necessarily a good sign. He walked inside and dropped his keys on a small table in the foyer. It had been a few weeks since he had been there. He made his cursory tour of each room noting each of his intruder traps were still in place.

Satisfied he could relax for a while, he turned on the television and searched the news. There was only a brief mention of Senator Dalton's disappearance. Dalton's colleagues suggested he more than likely had gone on a hunting trip somewhere and forgot to follow protocol. After all, he had been under a lot of stress. Authorities stated they have no evidence to suspect foul play. Some critics suggested he was merely hiding to avoid Thursday's vote.

Stone chuckled as he searched his cupboard for something to eat. He couldn't remember the last time something on the news even came close to the truth. He found a box of pretzels and popped open a beer. It wasn't his favorite breakfast, but it would do.

Stone's cell rang, it was Virgil Holmes. "Yes, sir."

"The second half of our problem is still out there. You have until noon Thursday to convince Senator Welsh to vote appropriately or ensure he will not vote at all."

"Understood."

It only took minutes to determine that Senator Welsh's wife and daughters were vacationing in the Bahamas. The eldest daughter had posted all over Facebook her excitement about the trip. By posing as island security, Stone was able to get Senator Welsh's aid to provide the exact hotel and contact numbers for the Senator's wife.

Stone called a fellow contractor in Nassau and arranged the immediate detention of the Senator's family. Within the hour, Stone received the call confirming the women had been abducted and were being held pending Stone's further instructions.

* * *

Acer had stayed in New Orleans at the same hotel as Roger and Paul. There was no reason to leave. Regardless which new employer Acer decided to go with, his assignment would probably be in New Orleans. The federally mandated consent decree ensured a lot of work for people in his business. If law enforcement started to sniff in the wrong corners, people like Acer had to eliminate the smells. Acer's history had been scrubbed fairly well, but new technology could unearth plenty that was supposed to be buried. It wasn't like the good, old days. His safest bet was to assume the FBI would know everything about him by noon. Except for whom he worked.

Acer went to the hotel restaurant for breakfast. He no sooner ordered his food when his cell phone rang. It was his New Orleans contact.

"Acer."

The voice on the other end said, "We owe you an apology."

Acer smiled, "I don't work for you anymore. You assigned Stone to kill me, remember?"

Acer hung up and put his phone in his jacket pocket. He knew they would call back and pay more money.

* * *

CSI had run the prints on the glasses and came up with a hit on Acer in an archived military database. Full name was Acer Noland. Special Ops, retired. Roger thought it sounded scrubbed and forwarded what he had to Mathew Core's email.

Core immediately called Roger back. "I know him. Knew him. Used to be a decent guy. Last I saw him was in France about three years ago. I think he said he was doing some work for the Vatican of all things."

Roger said, "He was having drinks with Stone Carson last night. Seems chummy if Stone tried to kill Acer and Acer tried to set up Stone with the FBI on Dalton's murder. Acer knows the FBI is looking at him now. Everything points to him being the other pilot that dumped the Senator. As far as I know, he is still registered at the hotel across from the casino. I checked this morning. He knows that Paul and I are staying there, too. Guy has some balls."

Core chuckled, "That's an understatement. He took this babe out to dinner a half hour after he…. never mind. Yeah, he's got balls."

163

Roger let the conversation restart. He didn't want to know everything Core knew. "What would happen if you ran into him?"

"One of three things. One: He would know I was tight with the FBI, so he'd clam up. Two: He would assume I was sent to waste him; he would clam up and try to kill me first. Or three: He would assume I had gone straight and he'd feed me bullshit."

Roger asked, "I need to find out what he is up to. I'd like to get him wired. What if he thought you were in New Orleans on a job? Make him dig for it. Could you get close?"

"The old 'birds of a feather' bit? Okay, I'll bite. What job?"

Roger answered, "To kill me."

Core took a moment to answer, "I like it."

* * *

Paul had walked into Roger's office and stood by the desk during the entire conversation. After Roger hung up Paul asked, "Did I just hear you order a hit on yourself?"

Roger slapped his desk, "Damn, I wasn't thinking. I should have made it you!"

They both laughed a minute and Paul said, "I left you alone for ten minutes. Care to bring me up to speed on what inspired this new plan?"

＊ ＊ ＊

Wednesday 8:30 a.m.

Mason Dooley was walking toward his personal vehicle in the cop lot when he heard the voice he had been dreading call him over. He knew this conversation was inevitable.

"Get in the car." The gruff voice of Ward Bromley was a sharp contrast to the sleek, black sedan he was sitting in. Bromley was a Special Investigator for the Department of Justice and worked out of the U.S. Attorney General's office in New Orleans. This title gave him the freedom he needed to make frequent visits to the police station. Dooley was who he used for the dirty work on his special projects.

Dooley sat heavily in the passenger seat and defensively offered, "You don't know what it's like to have to work with idiots!"

"I don't?" Bromley put the car in park and turned to face Dooley. "This cemetery crap is a disaster. The timing couldn't be worse with the FBI beefing up their troops here." Bromley wiped his brow, "The medical examiner has eight new bodies this morning. That includes the judge. These bodies were not supposed to be found until well into next year. That's why we picked the cemetery for God's sake." Bromley snarled, "Tell me exactly how this happened. Don't leave out a single detail."

Dooley started at the beginning. When he finished Bromley looked physically ill.

"You trust these two morons you use not to talk? They actually told you they killed a witch at the cemetery and took her to the swamp? Crap. Do you even know who that was? Who might be looking for her?"

Dooley answered, "It was probably just some crack whore. Who sits around in a cemetery? I've used my morons, as you call them, for eight years now. Never had a problem. They like the money too much. I don't think this is their fault the FBI showed up." Dooley rubbed his temples. "Somebody tipped off the FBI. They came with crowbars."

Bromley moaned. "I'll find out who tipped the FBI. Where's the gun?"

"I got rid of it."

Bromley put the car in gear, "Good. I'll call you on what we do next." Bromley pulled away from the lot. His black sedan eased into traffic and disappeared in the morning rush hour.

Dooley sat in his car and stared at the towel wrapped pistol on his floorboard. Bromley was right. He needed to get rid of the gun. He decided he could clean it well and plant on someone he wanted to get rid of. Once ballistics were run and compared to the cemetery bodies he was off the hook. Bromley only cared about his bosses. Dooley had to protect himself.

Dooley thought about the call from Boggs last night. He had told Boggs he'd stop by today to talk. Hearing that Cat was looking into the Molly Jarvis murder was very bad news. This sounded like something he had better report to his contact.

* * *

Officer Nathan Cottard just finished his shift and sat in his personal car in the police station parking lot. He noticed Dooley exiting Bromley's black sedan in the far corner of the lot. This wasn't the first time he had seen Mason Dooley with Ward Bromley. Dooley looked angry and Bromley's sedan spun out of the lot. Cottard had never really understood Bromley's relationship to the police department other than he seemed to nose around a lot. Cottard knew Dooley's reputation. Cottard started his car and pulled from the lot. His instincts told him he was seeing smoke. Somewhere, there was a fire.

* * *

Stone Carson expected the FBI to conclude that Senator Welsh was in danger. He didn't expect them to figure it out this soon. No matter. Stone saw the black SUV's pull in front of the Senator's home just as he opened the Senator's garage service door. He stood silently in the Senator's kitchen and listened to the Senator talk on his phone. It sounded as if the Senator was being told of Senator Dalton's death and his own danger. Stone passed the doorway of the living room and quietly walked down the hall toward the bedrooms. It would be even more exciting to confront the Senator with the FBI there. The Senator would see for himself, that even the FBI could not protect him.

Senator Welsh hung up from his conversation with the FBI Director and prayed. He couldn't believe that Senator Dalton was dead. He was next. He glanced around the living room and walked over to close his blinds. He felt an uneasy tension in the air, as if he was not alone. Sarah and the girls were vacationing in the Bahamas, thank God. At least he didn't have to put them through this hell.

He turned on the news and didn't even listen until a reporter mentioned the upcoming Senate vote on Thursday. The reporter stated it was expected that Welsh and Dalton would be the deciding votes. In Welsh's opinion, capping the oil company's liabilities and fines was tantamount to offering them a blank check on the environment. The reporter reminded viewers that if both Welsh and Dalton failed to vote on Thursday the measure would pass.

Senator Welsh startled when his phone rang. The caller ID said FBI. "Yes?"

"Senator Welsh? This SSA Roger Dance of the FBI, sir. I have four agents at the perimeter of your home and one waiting to be admitted at your front door. Can you accommodate them now?"

"Thank God. Of course."

Roger continued, "I would like to talk with you. May I come by shortly?"

"Certainly."

Senator Welsh reached over and spread apart the blinds enough to peak out the window. Two black SUVs were stationed at the street in front of his house. They appeared to be empty. The doorbell for the front door chimed.

* * *

We had a little trouble finding the Medical Examiner's office. Once we did, the first thing we did was to turn up our sensor buttons on our watches. The room was filled with vile odors. Large air cleaner fans roared above us. I couldn't imagine how bad it would be if they didn't have those fans.

Mary's face had a fixed expression of disgust. "Mortals have no idea what angels go through to help them."

Linda offered, "Think of the poor mortals that work here. Ugh."

We had to decide who to poke. Linda looked around the room and frowned. "This is not going to be easy. There are at least ten bags on tables and all of these steel lockers."

Teresa asked, "Don't we just need the ones with no toe tags?"

Mary had a toe tag in her hand, "Nope. This tag says Unknown Joe #4317."

Darn, sounded easy for a minute.

Just then we heard the pressure release of a hydraulic door open. Two men walked in wearing white scrubs. The younger man declared he was ready.

The older man walked over to one of the bags and said, "Let's hope there is enough of you left to identify." He unzipped the long bag and a woman's body was exposed. She looked like she was sleeping except her eyes were open. The younger man came over with a camera and started taking pictures. "I'll send this over to missing persons and put her by the window for now."

The older man nodded. "She's pretty fresh. That crypt saved her from the elements. We might just get lucky."

Teresa whooshed in and poked the lady's arm. She looked at us and said, "One down, six to go."

* * *

Ed and Izzy finished breakfast in silence. Izzy put her fork down and wiped her mouth with the paper towel Ed had given her. "I will do up these dishes."

"They can wait a minute and I can help." Ed leaned back and considered his situation. "Izzy, do you have a plan? Do you have family somewhere?"

"Gram was my only family." Izzy stood and carried her plate to the sink. She was clearly done talking. Ed realized he had no idea how to talk to a ten year old girl. He looked through to his living room and the stacks of books that went to the ceiling.

"Do you see all of the books in there?"

Izzy turned and nodded her head. "Have you read all of them?"

Ed smiled, "I've written a couple. When I wasn't invisible, I was a professor at Loyola University."

Izzy slowly walked back to sit at the table. "Then you are very smart. My teacher says I am the smartest child she has taught in a long time." Izzy beamed with pride.

Ed smiled, "Well, then how did two smart people end up having to be invisible?"

Izzy looked thoughtful. "We must have made a mistake?"

Ed shook his head, "You didn't make any mistake. Sometimes people make mistakes, or poor decisions and do have trouble. Sometimes things just happen for no obvious reason. You do realize that you can't survive on your own?"

Izzy stood and looked as if she was going to cry, "You said you would keep my secret."

"I didn't say I was going to break our secret. I asked if you realized the situation you're in. It is much different for a child than for an adult." Ed was afraid of scaring Izzy back into living on the streets. "For now we'll just try to form a plan, okay? I work nights, so I'm going to sleep most of today." Ed pushed a key across the table. "This is a key to this house. You're welcome to come and go as you please and use anything you want. I would suggest you sleep here at night. I'll be gone, but you'll be safe if you lock the door."

Izzy took the key and put it in her velveteen treasure bag. She whispered, "Thank you."

"You are most welcome. I am going to wake up about five and go to Otis's store to get us some food for dinner. If you want to eat here, be home by six. What sounds good for dinner?"

Izzy didn't hesitate with an answer. "Anything but chicken."

Izzy looked past Ed through the front window to Gram's house. That was home. She looked back to Ed, "If I am real quiet, can I stay here while you sleep and look at your books?"

Ed stood and rubbed the hair on top of her head. "Do anything you want. Just don't wake me up. They work me pretty hard on the docks. Washer and dryer are on the back porch if you need them."

Izzy watched Ed yawn as walked down the hall to some room in the back. He was right. A smart person would make a plan.

Izzy walked to the back porch and saw the washer and dryer. They looked like the ones Gram had. She had helped Gram do laundry all the time. Izzy saw two stacks of clothes by the washer. It looked like Ed had sorted them into darks and whites. His whites didn't look so good. Izzy looked in the cupboard for bleach. She knew Gram used bleach and hot water to keep their whites nice. No bleach.

Izzy decided to go to Otis's store and get some. She would surprise Ed when he woke. Gram always said that crisp, white clothes make everything seem better.

* * *

Stone heard the FBI agent assure the Senator that he was safe and to go about his business as if he were alone.

The footsteps of the agent made a soft clicking sound on the highly polished wood floors as he walked down the hall. Stone heard doors opening and softly closing along the way. The agent was checking each room and was nearly to Stone's door.

Stone pulled a hypodermic needle from his pocket, removed the cap and made ready. It was only a token doze and would not cause the agent any permanent harm. As the agent opened the door, Stone pulled him forward, struck his neck with a blow and injected the drug. The agent silently slid to the floor. Stone straightened his own jacket and walked to the living room where the Senator sat watching the news.

Stone sat down across from him.

"You are not the same man that was here a minute ago." Beads of sweat were appearing on the Senator's forehead and his hands were starting to shake. He knew from the cold look in Stone's eyes that he was sitting across from a killer.

Stone leaned forward and placed his hand on the Senator's knee. "No, I am not. I have your wife and daughters. If you vote in favor of the oil liability cap on Thursday, you will have your family back on Thursday evening. If you decide to vote on Thursday to stop the passage of the cap, they will die in a terrible boating accident. That is your choice, Senator."

Stone watched the Senator's eyes move toward the front window. "Yes, the FBI is here. One of them is lying on your guest room floor. You see how effective they are at protection. Do you clearly understand your two options?"

The Senator slowly nodded. "Yes. How do I contact you?"

Stone snickered, "Your vote will be televised."

Stone stood, stepped back, and seemed to vaporize. The Senator slowly turned to look behind him and saw no one. He heard the door from his kitchen to the garage softly close. Then the doorbell rang.

CHAPTER 13

Wednesday 10:30 am

Cat began arranging the file information on Molly's murder to his liking. There were certainly glaring holes in the case. The most obvious was motive. Surely Edward Meyer had heard more scathing complaints on his rhetoric than those of Molly Jarvis. That was the whole motive case. One brief mention by Molly that maybe Ed shouldn't mold young minds.

The evidence was sketchy, too. Even if Cat hadn't seen Reuben's video, it didn't make sense. The police arrested Ed in a stolen car. Ed owned his own car. The gun used was unregistered and reported as missing from an evidence locker three years prior. How would a political science professor obtain a stolen gun from police evidence?

The CSI team reported that the blood found in the stolen car was Molly's and had been smeared on the dash and door. Not transferred from contact. The same for the blood on Ed's clothing. Smeared, not contact. At the murder scene there was an unexplained smear of blood, as if someone started cleaning up.

Ed's personal car was parked a block away from the bar across from Otis Grocery. Ed claimed he received a call from a student requesting to meet him. Ed didn't recall the student giving his name. He wanted to discuss a lecture Ed had given a few days earlier. Ed insisted his students all knew he was available for such discussions.

There was also the preliminary Medical Examiner's report. Time of death had been crossed off and listed as between seven and eleven p.m.. The original time appeared to be listed as between nine and eleven. Between nine and eleven, Ed had been in the bar with over twenty witnesses.

Cat paced the living room and started talking out loud. He was most comfortable pretending he had a jury listening. He decided to play the role of the defense attorney. "So the theory is that Ed stole a car, drove fifteen miles to the Jarvis house and shot Molly three times after she answered the door. He then rubbed her blood on a rag for some reason, rubbed the bloody rag on himself and the dash of the stolen car. He then drove back to town, hid the stolen car with the gun and blood evidence right by the neighborhood bar. Walked back in the bar in his bloody clothes and ate dinner. Left the bar, got back in the stolen car and for some unknown reason drove partially into the alley and parked. Police receive a tip about a drunk parked in the alley and he was caught." It sounded worse out loud than it had in his head.

Cat dialed his office and asked for Steven Marks's extension.

Steven answered, "Hey, Cat. The whole office heard about your bad luck last night. Are you okay?"

"Bruised ego is all. Bunch of punk kids. Hey, I have a history question for you."

"Shoot."

"Molly Jarvis case. How sold were you on Meyer?"

"Jarvis? Jesus, Cat. Why are you digging into that?"

"I'd rather not say. Well? Motive. Did you have more than what is in the files?"

"You're in the files? You're at home, right? Can I pop over in half an hour?"

Cat was surprised at the request. "Sure." Something wasn't being said and they both knew it. "Let me give you my address."

* * *

Claude started chopping chicken heads in slow motion. Finally, he sat at the table to watch Earl mop the blood. Claude was surprised when he glanced at the counter. There were probably thirty chickens stacked. Whatever made him do this? The last he remembered he had been feeding them in the yard. Oh yeah, he sat down and started breaking their necks as they walked over for food. Stupid chickens. Walked right over their dead buddies.

Earl gave a sideways glance at Claude. "Gonna take the better part of the day to get the feathers off 'em."

Claude got up and dug around in the cupboard. He found the medicine the doctor wanted him to take and took two of the pills. "See, I'm takin' the damn drugs. Guess I need 'em today."

Earl stopped mopping. "What if we put four or five of 'em in the fridge there and sell the rest?"

"I don't want to take the feathers off 'em." Claude now looked as remorseful as a guilty child.

Earl sat down, "You know people pay good money for chickens to use as alligator bait."

Claude's eyes danced between the drugs and his good idea. "Let's take 'em out to them Swamp Boat boys. They can sell 'em out there."

"They ain't gonna want thirty chickens with no heads! They take people on rides. They don't hunt alligators." Earl frowned at Claude.

Claude stood and shouted as he raised the axe again, "I say we take 'em to them boys! Let them find alligator people. Not our problem no more."

Earl was afraid to argue. He got a few large, black garbage bags and handed one to Claude. "You want us to take 'em there, we'll take 'em there."

Claude smiled from ear to ear as he dropped the bloody chickens in the bags. "We should get good money for these. We'll clean the rest of this up when we get home. These birds gonna start stinkin' pretty quick." Claude was covered in chicken blood from his neck to his shoes. Pieces of chicken flesh stuck to his shirt and overalls.

Earl suggested Claude wash up some before they leave.

Claude became enraged again, "There ya go with your Martha Stewart crap again. All the hen peckin' I get from you, I should have chopped your head, too!"

Claude quickly wiped a paper towel over his pants and washed his hands in the sink.

"There. You happy now?"

Earl cursed himself again for having sold his house.

* * *

Nathan Cottard caught up with the black sedan about two miles down the road. He took a couple of short cuts and landed right behind Ward Bromley. He wasn't even sure why he was following him.

Bromley turned on Canal Street and parked in the hotel parking lot across from the casino. Cottard eased into a spot down the way and watched. Not five minutes later a man came out of the hotel doors and walked straight over to Bromley's car. Cottard picked up his camera and took about five photos. A tree branch was in his way and he put the car in gear to move closer.

He no sooner stopped and raised his camera again when his passenger door opened and a man sat next to him pointing a pistol.

Cottard dropped the camera and put his hands up, "You're making a big mistake."

Mathew Core answered, "We'll see. Hand me the camera."

Cottard handed the camera over and said, "I'm NOPD. I know you. The SWAT trainer for the FBI."

Core studied his face. Red sweatshirt, Nathan Cottard. Core holstered his gun. "Why are you watching those two?"

Cottard answered, "I'm not sure. That's the truth. The driver is an investigator for the Justice Department. He feels fishy. He's the one I was watching."

Core was more than curious. "I'm watching the other guy."

Acer got out of Bromley's car and walked back in the hotel. Bromley drove off.

Nathan Cottard looked at Core. "Now what?"

* * *

Mathew Core sent a text to Roger: Ward Bromley, Special Investigator for Justice. Might be dirty. Met with Acer in hotel parking lot.

Roger forwarded the text to FBI Special Investigations and the Director.

The Director forwarded the text to the Solicitor General at Justice.

Roger glanced at Paul, "If this guy is clean, we just put a world of hurt on him. Let's get over to Senator Welsh's home."

Paul had been reading the FBI file on Welsh. "Has a wife and two girls: Megan, eight years old and Chelsy who is twelve." Paul stood and grabbed his car keys, "Looks like your standard happy family."

Roger's brow furrowed, "Not anymore."

Senator Welsh's home was a brick, two story colonial in an established, tree lined neighborhood in the Uptown section of New Orleans. Roger pulled in the drive and noticed the obvious presence of his security detail. Paul pointed out that the neighboring homes were all occupied and a reasonable distance away.

Roger was fairly certain Stone would not approach the Senator at his home. Roger rang the doorbell and the Senator himself answered the door.

"Senator Welsh? I am Roger Dance and this is Paul Casey." Roger noticed the Senator's hand shaking as he held the fold of his jacket lapel and stepped back for them to enter.

Roger's eyes darted about the foyer, "Senator, the agent assigned to be indoors with you should answer the door. We want to keep your exposure limited. Where is he?"

The Senator cleared his throat, "There was a man..." The Senator started to collapse and Roger and Paul scrambled to hold him upright. Roger yelled through the still open front door, "Code 4!" The agents that had been stationed at the front of the house ran in.

Roger had guided the Senator to a chair and Paul ran through the house. Paul returned to the living room, speaking on his cell phone, "Officer down. Send an ambulance to 8216 Country Cotton."

Roger's head whipped toward Paul. "What do you have?"

"He's conscious, but not coherent. Drugs? I don't know. He's back in a guest bedroom."

Paul began quickly searching the house, the other agents ran to check the perimeter.

The Senator grabbed Roger's shirt sleeve. "They have Sarah and the girls."

Roger asked, "Who? Who has them?"

Senator Welsh dabbed a tear, "The man said they would be fine if I voted Thursday in favor of the oil bill. He said I either vote appropriately or there will be a boating accident." He looked at Roger with terror in his eyes.

Roger asked, "He was here? In your home?"

"Yes, not five minutes ago." Senator Welsh nodded recognition when Roger showed him a picture of Stone from his phone. "Yes, yes that's him."

Roger signaled Paul to join him across the room. Paul offered, "How did he get past our guys? They've been here half an hour."

Roger looked at Paul. "He got here before we did and waited."

"Why? Why not just deliver his message and leave?"

"It's Stone. The second message was to us, that we can't stop him."

Roger saw a black cat looking at him from the kitchen door. Roger nudged Paul.

Paul said, "Call Kim." Ellen disappeared.

Roger had Paul go sit with Senator Welsh and he walked to the kitchen to call Kim.

"Ellen wanted me to call?"

Kim answered, "Yes. She says that she and the angels are heading for the Bahamas where the Senator's wife and daughters are being held prisoner. She will protect them and send you information as soon as she can. Roger, what is happening?"

Roger answered, "I wish I knew."

The ambulance staff took the injured agent and Roger assigned a replacement. Roger sat across from the Senator. "Are your wife and daughters in the Bahamas right now?"

"Why, yes. How did you know?"

Roger could only imagine the stress the Senator was under at this moment.

"Senator Welsh, I am going to have one of our agents get information from you about your family, locate them and insure their safety. I will keep you posted on my progress. Have you tried to call your wife?"

"No. I haven't yet. That man…"

Roger patted the Senator's arm. "Sir, let's use your phone and try right now."

Roger dialed. The call was answered by a man who had a heavy Spanish accent. "Si?"

Roger asked, "Who am I speaking to?"

The line went dead.

* * *

Roger alerted FBI in the Bahamas about the situation with Senator Welsh's family. He forwarded the information he had and told them to position themselves in Nassau on the island of New Providence. He would send more information as it became available. Roger silently prayed that Ellen and the angels could get him information quickly. There was just no time for any other option to work.

Roger and Paul returned to the field office to await information from Ellen. For the FBI to locate the Senator's wife and daughters in mere hours was impossible. He knew that Ellen and the angels would find them. He prayed he could come up with a way to explain whatever miracle they performed.

Roger's phone rang; his caller ID told him it was Kim. "Ellen called again and said to tell you that a text will come over shortly directing you to an email from Mom, Teresa, Linda and Mary. They went to the Medical Examiner's office and have the identifications and histories on the bodies you found last night in the cemetery. Ellen said to remind you that you can't explain knowing this yet. She told you not to worry about communications. She has it covered."

"Okay. Great."

Roger's phone messaged he had an email. Roger looked at Paul, "Ellen is sending over identifications on the people found in the cemetery last night."

Roger printed off two copies of the email and he and Paul began reading.

Paul exclaimed, "I've never heard of any of these people. Even their bios look clean. Wonder why they were chosen to be murdered?"

Roger said, "I'm going to just think out loud for a minute. We don't know the 'why' yet, but we know the 'when'. We have the actual time of deaths on this list from the angels. The Medical Examiner will only be guessing. We can use this to narrow down who had the opportunity to kill them by crossing cell records." Roger sat back down at his desk. "I'm guessing whoever has been doing this didn't expect them to be found for a while. We can check with the city when those crypts were scheduled to be opened."

"Opened?" Paul looked incredulous.

Roger nodded, "In these above ground cemeteries, a lot of families only purchase a two year permit for their loved ones."

Paul asked, "What happens after that?"

"It depends on the family. Sometimes the remains are bagged and moved. You bring up a good point. People outside of New Orleans wouldn't know about leasing crypt space."

Paul pushed his chin out in his nervous twitch, "Or have access to cemetery records to know which ones are safe for a while. Points to a local killer."

Roger started clicking his pen. "Let's have our forensic techs locate each of our bad guys at these times of death. At least we can get a jump start on this list."

Thor knocked on Roger's open door and said. "I don't like the expression on your face. What's up?"

Roger and Paul brought Thor up-to-date on the situation at Senator Welsh's house and the fact that Stone was in the house when their agents arrived.

Thor frowned, "What is this guy, a ghost? He had to leave the house. Why didn't we see him?"

Roger shook his head, "Stone delivered the message he intended. I doubt he will surface again. It's all about the Thursday vote."

Thor tapped his watch, "That's tomorrow you know."

Roger couldn't believe how fast the week was going. "I must be getting old. Time is getting away from me."

Roger showed Thor the text from Mathew Core about Justice Investigator Ward Bromley being suspected as dirty.

"Shit. I have a meeting with him this afternoon on this consent decree crap. I told Frank Mass I'd take the meeting for him since he doesn't know exactly when he'll get here today."

Roger directed his comment to Thor, "Bromley met with Acer Noland, who we think was Stone Carson's copilot. They met in the parking lot of a hotel less than an hour ago for about ten minutes. Knowing Acer doesn't look good for Mr. Bromley, and puts Bromley on our list."

Thor asked, "What do we have on this Acer guy?"

Roger showed Thor the file on Stone from the ATF. "We have this on Stone, and we know Acer is tight with Stone."

"How the hell did you get this?"

"Interagency co-operation."

Thor looked at the ceiling. "Yeah, right."

Paul chuckled, "Oh, you'll love this, Roger took out a hit on himself with Mathew Core to try to find out what Acer is up to. Core and Acer know each other."

Thor raised his voice, "You don't do anything normal, do you? What the hell? What if this Acer decides to 'help' Core?"

Roger started laughing, "That wouldn't be good. There is a reason he's hanging around and I want to know what it is. Core might be able to find out. We're all staying at the same hotel."

Thor placed the ATF report back on Roger's desk. "Of course you are. How cozy. Any leads on who placed the bomb at the hotel or who it was for?"

Roger answered, "I'm guessing now, I don't think it was Acer that put it there. I think it was meant for Stone."

* * *

Wednesday 11:00 am

Cat looked at his watch. Steven Marks would be there any minute. Cat pulled a card from his wallet. He had taken it from the bar last night. Cat couldn't stop thinking about the little girl that saved him.

Maybe the bartender would know who she was. An answering machine told him the bar didn't open until noon.

Cat looked up the number for Otis Grocery. Toby, the bartender, had said Otis was his brother-in-law. Cat wanted to check out Otis anyway. He seemed to be the only friend Ed Meyer had in the world.

Otis answered the phone, "Otis Grocery."

Cat responded, "This is Sabastian Delacroix. May I ask you a couple of questions?"

Otis walked to the back of the room and motioned for his clerk to take over the counter. "Are you the one they call Catahoula?"

Cat smiled, "Yes. I was attacked last night in the alley across from your store by some punks. It was about eleven o'clock. A young girl, maybe ten, on a pink bicycle stopped to help me. She was able to get adults involved. I am trying to find her to thank her."

Otis knew exactly who Cat was talking about. "Her name is Izzy Dubois. The whole neighborhood is lookin' for her. She was raised by her grandma, got no other family. Dirt poor. Her grandma died a day or so ago. City locked up the house, looters already livin' in it from what I heard."

Cat was astonished, "You mean she is living on the streets?"

Otis answered, "I think she is, yes. She's a smart girl. She probably knows the police are trying to find her though. I guess her grandma told her the state would take her if something ever happened. I would guess she doesn't want to be found."

Cat asked, "What can we do?"

Otis said, "I get most gossip in these parts. I can call you if I hear anything."

Cat gave Otis his contact information. Cat was surprised at the amount of emotion he was feeling. Above all, he felt helpless. How does he find a ten year old child in New Orleans?

Cat's doorbell buzzed.

CHAPTER 14

Cat went to the door and let Steven Marks in. He had met Marks in numerous meetings and saw him occasionally in the elevators. Cat pointed to his table, "Have a seat. Can I get you anything? Sweet tea, coffee?"

Steven waved Cat off, "I can't stay. You know I'm in the fraud division now, right?"

Cat nodded. "I'm more interested in 2005 when you were on Ted's team working the Molly Jarvis case."

Steven stared at Cat and asked, "I need to know where you are coming from on this. Why did you ask me if I was sold on Meyer being the doer?"

"Because I want to know. That's all I can give you at the moment. You're going to have to trust me."

Steven nodded, "I trust you or I wouldn't be here." Steven leaned back and sighed. "Hell, I'm just going to say this and see what you do with it. I was moved to fraud to get me off that case. Nobody actually said that, but I knew. Ted was pissed. He screamed all the way to the top. Hell, past the top. Didn't matter. I kept asking all the wrong questions of all the wrong people. Meyer was set up. I don't know how or who. But I might know why."

Cat leaned forward, "Why?"

Steven said, "We are sharing remember? Your turn now."

Cat turned his computer monitor around and showed Steven the video of Edward Meyer's arrest.

Steven slammed his fist on the table. "I knew it! Where did you get this?"

Cat said, "Not yet. Your turn. Why?"

Steven pushed his chair back and asked, "Did you know that William Jarvis was making noise about running for Governor?"

Cat shook his head. Steven continued, "None of the 'money' people wanted that to happen. They already had their boy in office. There was a bit of panic in some circles that if William actually announced his candidacy, he would take the state by a landslide. The Louisiana good ol' boys didn't want that. National interests didn't want that. There was actually a task force organized to stop him. We're talking genuine panic in political circles. William was by the book. That doesn't play well in these parts."

Cat asked, "What does this have to do with Ed Meyer?"

"This is my version. I have thought about this for eight years. Take it or leave it. Assume that William Jarvis was the real target. If Molly was killed, it would make his suicide seem plausible. Molly was the bait. Ed Meyer just happened to be a noisy academia that Molly had recently commented on. Half of New

Orleans thought Ed was an educated nut. The perfect scapegoat."

Cat leaned forward, "Let's say you are right and eliminating William was the real goal. Who's going to wait around for William to commit suicide? Not exactly an airtight plan."

"You're right, nobody would wait. What if it wasn't suicide?"

Well that thought had never crossed Cat's mind. Cat tried to remember what files there had been on William's death. He couldn't remember much more than a memo. "What do we have on William's suicide?"

Steven answered, "Nothing. Except this." Steven passed a flash drive to Cat, which he inserted into his hard drive. It was a Medical Examiner report stating that the manner of death undetermined. The Medical Examiner noted a curious absence of blood splatter on the back of the shooting hand and trigger finger. His order for a tox screening of William Jarvis had been lost and William's body was transported without proper release. The time of death was very narrow, between nine and eleven o'clock pm.

Cat asked Steven, "Did anyone depose this examiner for more information?"

Steven answered, "He died in an auto accident the same day he sent me this. Actually about an hour after he sent this to me. The death report on record for William Jarvis lists suicide as the manner of death and the time of death between *seven* and eleven o'clock. This may have been the perfect murder. Your turn."

Cat decided Steven had earned the next piece of information. "Edward Meyer is alive."

"Dear Lord."

* * *

Abram stuck his head in the office doorway, "I really need your help. I got two drunk bubbas out here tryin' to sell me three huge bags of dead chickens."

Jackson laughed, "Just tell 'em we don't buy dead chickens."

Abram looked scared, "I told 'em, man. They're not takin' no for an answer. They say we can sell 'em for gator bait. Help me out!"

Jackson chuckled and followed Abram out the door. Jackson about peed his pants when he saw two men leaning against the same ratty old truck he had been following the night before. Betty Sue was still smilin' and flippin' off the world.

Jackson grabbed Abram's shirt sleeve. "That's them! That's the evil Ms. Spicey said were the killers last night."

Abram hissed through unmoving lips, "What the hell we gonna do?"

Jackson's eyes were popping, "We be buyin' them chickens!"

* * *

We finished at the Medical Examiner's office and headed back to Spicey's Voodoo shop. Ellen said Spicey needed us. Sounded fine to me. Anything was better than all those dead bodies. When we arrived at the Voodoo shop, Sasha was locking the doors and turning the signs to say closed.

Sasha frowned, "I want to go over this little plan one more time 'fore we leave here. It sounds too easy to me." Sasha sat heavily on her stool and drummed her fingers on the counter top. Dakin stood off to the side and waited for Spicey to speak.

"The plan is we take us a cab to the end of Betty Sue's driveway. Then we sneak in through the woods there and leave Dakin's Hoodoo tokens on the door step. When they see the tokens they will pick 'em up and Dakin's spell will start working." Spicey nodded and looked at Dakin for confirmation she had it right. Dakin nodded.

Sasha asked, "What supposed to happen to 'em when they pick up the tokens?"

Dakin smiled, "They get real sick, then we call the police."

Sasha started waving her finger in the air, "See? That part right there what gets me. We gonna have to explain how they got sick, ain't we? Don't we have a problem here with trespassin' and poisonin' peoples?"

Spicey tilted her head, "She might have a point." Dakin shrugged.

Mary looked at Teresa, "Do angels just sit by and watch people poison each other?"

Teresa and Linda both shook their heads.

I offered, "This might be a good time to call Ellen."

Mary agreed, so Teresa called and Ellen popped in.

Ellen listened to us explain Spicey's plan. "Hmmm. Nope. That isn't going to happen. How about you gals get Spicey to change the plan? Mambo can probably help. All Mambo will need is something that belongs to Claude and Earl."

That's all? That still means we have to go to Betty Sue's house. Not to mention a trip in the swamp. Dang.

Ellen chuckled. Obviously she was reading my mind. "You're not going to like that house, either." Uh oh.

Ellen disappeared and Teresa said, "We have to get Spicey to look in her crystal ball. She can hear us in the ball."

Linda said, "Why don't we just bring the ball to her?"

Mary shook her head, "That won't work. Sasha will faint."

Teresa concentrated on Spicey seeing us. We could tell from Spicey's expression it worked. Teresa crooked her index finger for Spicey to follow her behind the curtain door. Sasha and Dakin watched Spicey walk real slow out of the room.

Sasha asked, "What's wrong with her?"

Dakin shrugged as she filed her long nails.

Sasha and Dakin peeked behind the curtain and watched Spicey sit at her table and put her hands on the ball. Teresa's face popped into the ball. "Hi. We don't want you to use poison. It's just not cool, ya know? We have another idea. We'll go with you to Betty Sue's house, get something that belongs to these guys and then go see Mambo. She might have a spell that will work. Okay?"

Spicey nodded okay and removed her hands from the ball. She looked at Sasha and Dakin peeking through the curtain. "We can't be using poison. The angels ain't likin' that. We're supposed to go to that house and take somethin' that belongs to them men. Then we're to take it to Mambo's."

Sasha kicked the air, "Dang, dang. I don't like goin' to Mambo's."

Dakin smiled so wide it looked like her spider tattoo on her cheek had crawled up to her eye.

Spicey pleaded to Sasha. "Let's just get this over with."

* * *

Stone Carson's contact at the Chicago Board of Trade called him back.

"You were right. Yesterday New Orleans contact wanted you dead."

Stone repeated, "Yesterday?"

"Yeah. Today they want you back. Real bad. It seems somebody at street level messed up real bad. It's going to take a professional cleanup crew. You and Acer can name your price."

"Interesting."

Stone prepared to shower. He smiled to himself as he thought of Roger Dance. Dance will be furious that he so easily breached the FBI's security at the Senator's house. Stone sang the Beach Boy's 'Key Largo' in the shower. It made him think of the Bahamas. The water from the shower head pounded his face as he imagined the FBI's panic to locate the Senator's family before Thursday's vote. He had contracted very good men. The FBI didn't stand a chance.

* * *

Mason Dooley answered his cell phone and pulled his car over to hear what Bromley was saying. He hoped he had heard wrong. "You want me to shoot who?"

Dooley blurted, "You guys are out of control! You sure you can have me do this shit and keep me out of jail?" Dooley closed his eyes and lowered his voice. "I'm getting worried. You don't give me time to think."

Bromley responded, "You're not being paid to think." Bromley confessed, "Look, I do what I'm told, you have to do the same. Don't make any mistakes on this one. I haven't figured out what we're going to do about the judge yet."

Dooley drove with his portable police light flashing on his personal car. Bromley transferred the GPS locator feed and Dooley quickly located his target's car. Dooley waited until they crossed Highway 90 and pulled the target over to the shoulder. Dooley walked up to the window, asked for registration and shot him as he reached for his glove box.

Dooley returned to his car, removed the police light from his dash and pulled back into traffic. His heart was pounding. He had never just walked up and shot someone before in broad daylight on a busy highway. Especially someone this important. It was surprisingly easy.

Steven Marks, Senior Assistant Attorney General, was fighting for his life in his car alongside Highway 10. The blood from the bullet wound in his head clouded his vision as he dialed 911. His last conscious thought was, of course…. a dirty cop.

* * *

Wednesday 12:30 pm

Roger and Paul discussed Cat while they waited for their lunch order to go was filled.

Paul asked, "Has he ever been married? Kids?"

Roger answered, "Cat told me once that by the time he decided to settle down, all the women he had dated had married other people. I thought a few years ago I'd get an invitation to a wedding but I guess it didn't happen. He's a good lookin' guy so he doesn't have trouble getting women. He probably just hasn't made time for it." Roger paid for their lunches and he and Paul drove toward Cat's house.

Roger added, "You know a lot of people don't know that Cat came from a large family. Seven kids, I think. His mom died in the last childbirth and his dad had a heart attack when Cat was still in high school. Cat was the oldest and basically raised them all." Roger chuckled, "He said that's when he really got his training as a prosecutor, raising his siblings. With seven kids, somebody is always guilty of something. He worked his way through high school, college, and law school. He also helped each of his siblings go to college."

Paul looked out the window, "Sounds like he's earned some time for himself."

"I don't know that he'll ever have the time. He is the top litigator and the Department of Justice considers him to be in his prime. They will use him up if he's not careful."

Paul looked at Roger, "Seems you and I had that conversation a year ago. Now you're with Kim. See how life is?"

Roger smiled, "So what's taking you so long?"
Paul laughed, "I need to grow up first."

Roger and Paul arrived at Cat's and presented him with jambalaya.

Cat moaned as he tasted the first spoonful, "Right here is why I'll never leave New Orleans."

Roger and Paul ate their lunch with him. Paul got up to get something to drink. "You have any tea or anything?"

Cat gingerly got up and Roger noticed some blood spotting on Cat's shirt. "Cat, you're bleeding."

Cat looked down and sighed. "It's just a cut from a boot. Couple of stitches. No big deal."

Roger thought about Cat being beaten by a group of teens with bats. He was lucky to be alive, and lucky he was found. Roger watched Cat help Paul prepare the tea. "You're moving pretty slow. Are you sure you're up for company?"

Paul held up the two cards that were on Cat's counter. "Look at this. He's got phone numbers of two nurses right here."

Cat smiled and walked back, "Yeah, I'm fine. In fact, you're my second set of company today."

Roger's phone went off and he excused himself to the other side of the room. When he came back, Paul could tell from Roger's expression that something was wrong.

Paul asked, "What?"

"That was Thor. He just got word that Steven Marks, from Cat's office, was shot. He's been taken to the hospital."

Cat went pale. "He just left here. Not thirty minutes ago."

* * *

Abram and Jackson watched Betty Sue disappear down the dirt drive. They stood staring at the three large garbage bags of dead chickens. Abram was still shaking with fear. Jackson was physically sick and ran to the edge of the woods to puke.

Jackson walked back, "We already got flies startin' to swarm. Can't believe we paid fifty bucks for this." Jackson kicked one of the bags.

Abram took a deep breath, "That be cheap if we never see those two again. You see the crazy eyes on that Claude? That dude's not right." Abram shivered and offered, "I can call ol' Daryl down the way and see if he wants these chickens. Just give 'em to him?"

Jackson nodded yes. He couldn't get the vision of Claude choppin' all those chickens in his house, out of his mind. Crazy fool said he must have got tired of feedin' 'em. Didn't really know why he did it. Dang, that be a whole new shade of crazy.

Abram interrupted Jackson's thoughts, "Daryl says he'll come by in a bit and get 'em. Thank God."

Jackson and Abram walked back to the office. Jackson mumbled, "Hope the rest of this day goes better than this."

CHAPTER 15

The Director of the FBI saw he had a call waiting from the Solicitor General. He noted that Dan was returning his call quickly, as he had promised. The Director switched his phone to secure mode and answered, "Dan, have you found anything?"

The Solicitor General paused, "I've found out how damn hard it is to get a straight answer around here. Don't worry, I'm not letting this go. Okay, first, Mr. Ward Bromley. Special Investigator for Justice, stationed in New Orleans, twenty three years seniority. I am looking at about four inches of violations and supervisory concerns in his file. For the life of me, I can't figure out why this guy is still with us."

"Secondly, Stone Carson and Acer Noland. Nobody here admits to knowing anything about them. I had security techs put tracers on any incoming inquiries on either of those names. After I asked about them, they each received two hits: one from here and one from the New Orleans U.S. Attorney General's office. Somebody here had to call somebody there and they didn't waste any time."

The Director of the FBI stated the obvious, "Somebody in *your* house wants to know everything you're interested in. You do have a problem."

"Yes, I do."

The FBI Director cleared his throat, "I don't know if this is related or not, but Steven Marks, Senior Assistant Attorney General, Fraud Division, was just shot in his car after visiting with Sabastian Delacroix. My agent tells me Cat is looking into the Jarvis murder case again."

"Cat's looking into what? That case is eight years old. What the hell is going on, Jim?"

The Director of the FBI brought the Solicitor General up to speed on Senator Welsh's situation. Both men agreed that the Senate vote on Thursday at noon was their obvious deadline.

"Like I said, my team is on it. Let's keep these lines open."

"Of course." The Solicitor General hung up and rested his head in his hands. Did he really know so little about his own people? He had a short list of names his IT security man had given him. One of these people was calling the shots for the machine, at least those pertinent to New Orleans.

The Solicitor General called his counterpart at NSA. "These are our people. One of them is bad and we have no time. I want to know who. Look for a New Orleans connection."

* * *

Izzy rode her bike to Otis's Grocery and leaned her bike against the siding. She worried a policeman might drive by and see her. She waited until a woman with two children walked up to the door and she walked in with them. While Otis took their order, Izzy looked for the bleach. Izzy kept glancing toward Otis. She couldn't help herself. Otis looked at her. Izzy's stomach fisted in fear. She should have stayed invisible. She thought of putting the bleach back on the shelf and running out of the store.

The woman and her children left the store. The tinkling of the bells at the door stopped and the big room fell silent. Izzy slowly walked to the counter and took out her treasure bag. Otis said, "Well there is my smart, little friend. How are you today?"

He sounded friendly. Izzy relaxed, just a little, and answered, "Fine. How are you?"

Otis pretended to be troubled. "You know, I've been better. I've too much work to do and nobody to help me. I wish I could find someone to sweep."

Izzy stated, "I sweep real good. Ms. Nelson lets me sweep all the time."

Otis carefully asked, "Are you sure your Grandma would approve of you having a real job? You're very young."

Izzy didn't want to lie to Otis. Her face became very serious. Otis felt his heart breaking. "My grandma says work is good for the soul."

Otis nodded, "Yes, it is. Well, sounds like we have a deal. I'm going to need your address and a phone number, so I can call you when it's time for you to work." Otis held his breath.

Izzy thought for a minute, "I can give you a phone number, but it isn't mine. It belongs to my friend."

Otis put a pen and piece of paper on the counter, "That'll work just as well."

Izzy took out the piece of paper Ed had written his phone number on and copied it down. She put the paper back in her treasure bag and said, "It would best if I didn't start work until tomorrow. I'm very busy today."

"I see you have a big bottle of bleach. You must be cleaning?"

Izzy smiled, "My friend is not so good at laundry."

Izzy paid and left the store. Otis watched her pedal away and looked at the number she had written. It looked familiar. He checked the contacts in his phone. Izzy had given him Ed Meyer's number.

How in the world had those two connected? Otis certainly couldn't call Catahoula and tell him where Izzy was staying. Otis sighed. It seemed he just didn't know Ed anymore. What was Ed thinking?

* * *

Marla waited at the diner, nervously glancing at her watch. Gayla said the food was good and it was close to work. This investigative reporter stuff was nerve-racking. Marla watched Gayla pull her car into a spot right in front and walk in.

Gayla squealed as they hugged, "Girl! You are a sight for sore eyes."

Marla stepped back, "You have lost a lot of weight. You look fantastic."

"Don't I know it. Had to buy all new clothes though. This hasn't been cheap."

Marla lifted a menu and handed one to Gayla, "We better order fast, this place is gettin' busy. Neither one of us gets an hour lunch."

After the waiter took their order, Gayla leaned forward and whispered, "So, who is this mystery cop you've set your eyes on?"

Marla smiled, "Mason Dooley."

All expression left Gayla's face. "You're shittin' me. Of all the men in New Orleans? He's scum, Marla. Good lookin' scum, but scum."

Marla tried to look hurt. "No. Really?"

Gayla snapped her napkin and put it on her lap. "I don't know how he keeps his job. Word is somebody looks out for his butt. I've seen good people get fired for complaining about him! Even the Chief lets him do what he wants. He doesn't answer to anybody."

"You don't say. He must work the night shift. I see him all over in the daytime."

Gayla huffed, "I hear he wants to get top spot on SWAT. All I got to say is look out. You give somebody like him a title like that and a machine gun..." she stuffed a cracker in her mouth. "Last year a woman charged him with rape. It almost got him, too."

Marla asked, "What happened?"

"Poor thing was found dead right in her own house. Home invasion, I think."

Marla twirled her straw in her fingers, "Pretty lucky for Mason."

Gayla looked over her fork, "Yeah. Real lucky."

The waiter brought their bills and Marla grabbed them both, "This is my treat. I asked you to lunch."

Gayla smiled and then quickly frowned, "Oh, no. Speak of the devil." She pointed out the window where Mason Dooley had parked and was standing next to his car.

Suddenly he lifted his long sleeved t-shirt off and tossed it through the driver window. He leaned into the back seat, grabbed another shirt and put it on. Gayla chuckled, "Well, at least we got a show."

Marla nodded and said, "You go on now. We'll have to do this again soon."

Marla watched Gayla pull away and Mason walk into the diner. He sat at the counter and placed an order. Marla kept thinking about that shirt. She wondered if Reuben had Mason's DNA yet?

Marla left a twenty on the table with their bills and walked across the street. She glanced in both directions and then grabbed the shirt lying on Mason's driver's seat. She walked as fast as she could to her car, started it up and pulled away from the curb. It took three blocks before her heart was beating at a normal pace.

Once she parked back at work, she opened the bunched shirt and gasped. There were blood splatters all over the right sleeve and around the neck. Mason didn't look hurt. She had wanted Mason's DNA. She had a sinking feeling she had someone else's DNA, too.

* * *

Mason Dooley took a sip of his coffee when the waiter came over. "Hey, some chick just stole a shirt from your car over there."

Dooley jumped up and ran to the door. He couldn't see anyone on the street, but a blue Prius was darting away. Mason went back in to the waiter, "What'd she look like?"

The waiter was petrified, "Just a lady. Nothin' special."

Dooley grabbed the waiter's shirt at the neck and made a fist, "She pay with a card?"

The waiter shook his head and then said, "She ate with that lady works with you. Gayla."

Dooley slammed a five on the counter and mumbled thanks. He got in his car, saw the shirt was gone and cursed. He slammed his palms on the steering wheel and raced back to the station. That shirt was covered in Steven Marks's blood.

* * *

Dooley stomped over to Gayla's desk and slammed his hand so hard she jumped.

"Who did you have lunch with?" Dooley's veins were throbbing in his neck. Gayla was petrified. Nathan Cottard came around the corner in time to see Dooley push Gala's chair away from her desk, with her on it. He had leaned over her and was pointing his finger an inch from her face.

"I asked who you had lunch with!" Dooley's face was beet red. Some of his buddies started to walk over.

Cottard pushed through the onlookers and grabbed Dooley's shoulder. He pulled Dooley back. "What's your problem? Back off!"

Dooley pulled his arm back. He made a fist and held it. He dropped his arm and said, "This is none of your concern, Cottard. Take a hike."

"I'll take one when you calm down."

Dooley pointed at Gayla. "Her little lunch friend stole a shirt from my car!"

Cottard laughed, "So? They're department issued, get another one."

Dooley scowled, "It was my personal shirt. Doesn't matter, the point is her friend is a thief and I want her name."

Gayla had been wildly trying to come up with a lie that might work. She sure didn't want to unleash Dooley on Marla. Gayla cleared her throat and said, "I sat with a lady at lunch that I didn't know. Women do that. We liked each other's shoes."

Cottard put his hand out. "There. Don't ya feel stupid? You owe Gayla an apology."

Dooley glared at Gayla. He wasn't buyin' it. "You tell this *stranger* lady I'll find her."

Gayla took a deep breath as Dooley stomped off. She thanked Cottard and dialed Marla. "Girl, you got yourself some big trouble."

Dooley drove back to the diner and insisted they give him their security videos for both in the diner and out at the street. He drove home to study them. He had to find that shirt. Dooley sat in front of his monitor waiting for the mystery woman and Gayla to meet. Finally he recognized Gayla walk in the door and hug the mystery woman. Some stranger. Dooley got angrier the longer he watched. They not only knew each other, they appeared to be friends. Gayla had even pointed to Dooley through the front window.

Dooley watched himself from the street video remove his shirt. He watched that woman walk over to his car and take the shirt out. She ran to the blue Prius and took off. Dooley backed up the video, hit stop and wrote down the plate number.

He hissed, "Look out, bitch."

* * *

Stone sent a text to Acer: My source says we are newly loved and wanted.

Acer texted back: I just got asked out again, too.

Stone replied: I'm game. Could be fun.

Acer ended the transmission with: Ditto.

* * *

Ward Bromley looked at the caller ID on his cell phone and cringed. He was about to get another assignment. To his way of thinking, this grand flawless design was unraveling at warp speed and he was snarled in the middle with no way out. The last thing he needed was another problem.

"Bromley."

"Do a full workup on a reporter for the Picayune. Name Reuben Florey. Make it a priority."

"Done."

Bromley returned his phone to his jacket, scratched out a quick note and looked at his watch. He had a meeting with SSA Dan Thor, FBI, in thirty minutes. Mr. Florey was going to have to wait, priority or not. He needed lunch.

* * *

Reuben typed frantically to finish his breaking news story about Senior Assistant Attorney General, Steven Marks, being shot today in his car. Reuben couldn't help but think this guy was lucky. He had been able to call 911 after being shot in the head and an ambulance was actually a half mile away when the call came in. Hospital reports were that he was in surgery fighting for his life.

The press spokesman for the U.S. Attorney General's office had no comment. Reuben glanced over to Marla's desk. She still wasn't back from lunch. Reuben smiled at the memory of Marla teasing him yesterday. She had smacked his arm softly and proclaimed a new found hope they would end up an item. She had told him she decided he must be gay. "After all, how could you pass up this?" She had twirled.

Reuben did have a crush on Marla. He suspected she knew and was confused he never acted on it. He was so consumed with his father's situation that his own life had been on hold. Reuben's phone rang, "I'm in the parking lot downstairs. I just stole a bloody shirt from Mason Dooley's car."

Reuben shook his head quickly and asked, "You did what? When? Why?"

Marla sounded terrified, "Listen to me! The gal I had lunch with just called and said Mason knows I took his shirt and he's mad. Real mad. She called her friend that works at the diner and he said Mason made them give him their security videos. Reuben, he's going to find out who I am!"

Reuben's mind was spinning, "Do you know where I live?"

Marla answered, "Yes."

"Go there and hide. I'll tell Trayer you called in sick. There is a key to the door over the front window. Put your car in the garage. Shit. Bring the shirt in the house. I'll get home about five. Don't leave, you promise?"

Marla promised.

Reuben looked at the ceiling and prayed for some sanity in his life. His prayer was abruptly interrupted by Trayer standing behind him screaming, "Reuben! That story better be on the production desk in five minutes!"

"Yes, sir." Reuben glanced quickly over his text and hit send. Mason Dooley was after Marla over a bloody shirt. What else could possibly happen?

* * *

CHAPTER 16

Wednesday 1:00 pm
The cab driver scowled at the story Spicey had given him. "A scavenger hunt in the marsh is about as safe as knocking on doors in the hood for charitable donations."

He slammed the cab's breaks and dropped us all off in front of the dirt drive to Claude and Earl's house. As angels, we could have just flown there ahead of the cab. It was more fun listening to mortals though. It took being an angel for me to realize the amount of freedom we have as mortals. Just about anything stupid we do we can blame on being mortal. Not so much for 'almost' angels. Heaven has higher expectations. This continues to be a formidable challenge.

Linda and Teresa flew ahead to make sure the house was empty. Mary and I stayed to listen to Spicey, Sasha and Dakin argue about what kind of 'personal' items they would need to steal. Spicey claimed the items should have some DNA. Sasha accused her of spending too much time with cops. Dakin still wanted to poison them.

Linda and Teresa flew back with such speed it created an unexpected gust of wind that sent Sasha's dress straight over her head.

"Well, that be weird." Sasha dug her way out of the folds of fabric.

Teresa looked at Mary and pointed to the house, "There's blood everywhere! Chicken blood."

Linda added, "We saw a whole wastebasket filled with chicken heads."

Mary's nose wrinkled, "I thought people slaughtered animals outside."

Chicken heads? A whole wastebasket full? These guys really like chicken.

Spicey lifted her index finger in the air and pointed ahead. "Okay, let's get this over with."

Sasha and Dakin followed Spicey down the twisted dirt path. The Spanish moss draped so low it was hard to see very far ahead.

Sasha started swiping at the moss, "You know this stuff just crawlin' with bugs and ticks."

They finally hit a widening in the path and saw the dilapidated house hanging on to the porch posts. The center of the roof had years ago given in to the green mounds of moss and vines. Plywood covered all but one window on the front. The door had four sets of hinges. Obviously as one set pulled away from dry rotted wood, another was installed a few inches higher.

A sign was nailed on one porch support that read: Trespassers killed.

Spicey frowned at the sign, "Hmm."

We all covered our eyes as Dakin pulled on the front door. She slowly stepped in followed by Spicey and Sasha. The light from the one window cast eerie shadows on the walls. A single beam of sunlight fought to penetrate the dust and insects in the air.

Sasha scowled, "I'm afraid to breathe in here. Look at all the shit in the air."

Dakin moaned, "My shoes are stickin' to the floor."

They all looked down. As their eyes adjusted to the dim light, they could see pools of blood drying. A crude attempt to mop had ended with a bucket of bloody water flanked by a bloody mop. Their collective gaze moved to a tall trash can filled with chicken heads. A huge axe sat at the ready, imbedded in the center of the table. A lone, live rooster crowed outside of the window. He flapped his wings and created a four foot shadow of his head across the room.

As if orchestrated and practiced for months, they all screamed at precisely the same moment and bolted out the door.

Once outside, no one spoke. They stood silent, panting, staring at each other.

Spicey looked at Sasha, "I can't believe you didn't...." Sasha fainted.

Mary asked, "Well, now what?"

Teresa was flying toward us from the street. She was in a panic and pointed at Spicey. She concentrated on Spicey seeing her. Spicey's jaw dropped and Teresa yelled, "Hide. They're coming back!"

Spicey just tilted her head and then she heard the ratty truck coming.

"Sweet Jesus! Hide! They're back!"

Spicey grabbed Sasha's shirt and started dragging her to the edge of the woods. Sasha's legs started moving as she moaned, "Now what?" She must have heard the truck sounds, too, because she started running. Just as the truck turned the last bend on the drive, Spicey, Sasha and Dakin synchronized a dive into the thick brush.

Teresa stood next to Linda panting. Mary shook her head, "I say we go back in, steal what the girls need and get the heck out of here."

What? Now *we* have to go back in?

* * *

Cat was speechless. His mind swarmed from the news of Steven Marks being shot. His head throbbed, demanding he take his medication. He knew he didn't dare.

Roger and Paul sat quietly waiting for Cat to speak. Finally Roger placed his palms down on the table and looked Cat in the eyes. "You asked for my help. I'm here. Trust me enough to tell me everything."

Cat did.

* * *

Izzy had a little trouble getting Ed's key to unlock the door. Every time she heard a car coming, she stopped and hid behind a large planter of dead flowers. Finally the door opened. Izzy stood in the kitchen and surveyed the situation. It was going to be hard to do a good job cleaning without making any noise.

She carried the bleach to the back porch and started a load of Ed's whites. Her own laundry had been sorted and was sitting in a tiny pile near the door. On the porch she found a few cleaning supplies and a pair of rubber gloves. An old bucket sat by the door with a mop resting against the wall. Izzy turned and looked at the kitchen floor. Yep. She had better mop.

Halfway through her mopping she felt a wave of grief wash over her. Izzy sat at the table, head in hands and prayed. She thanked God for taking care of her Gram and asked for the hole in her heart to heal. Izzy asked God to look after Otis, Ed and the man in the alley. Izzy stood to finish her cleaning. She knew the hole in her heart would be with her for a very long time.

Ed's sleep had been fitful. He woke and looked at his bedside clock. It was only one o'clock in the afternoon. He still needed a few hours of sleep. He heard the sound of water running and tiny noises of footsteps and chairs moving quietly. He guessed that

Izzy was snooping around some. He closed his eyes and fell into a deep sleep.

Izzy caught herself humming. Gram and Izzy always sang when they did their work. Gram said it made the work go faster. Izzy forced herself to stop. She didn't want to wake Ed. Pleased with the way the kitchen looked, she moved to the living room. She didn't think Ed spent much time there except for the reading chair. That was going to be her reward when she finished cleaning. Ed said she could read one of his books.

Izzy stared at the book bindings and read the titles. Many sounded much too hard for her to read. Her eyes wandered to a tattered book titled "The Adventures of Huckleberry Finn". She lifted it from the shelf and opened the cover. There were drawings of young boys playing all through the book.

Izzy laid the book on the reading chair and smiled. If she hurried, she could have time to read about Huckleberry Finn. Izzy giggled. Who would name their child Huckleberry?

* * *

Jeanne volunteered to go to the hospital and personally guard Steven Marks. Jeanne was the most highly trained agent in the office. Thor was reluctant to put her in danger, yet he knew he had no choice.

Obviously, Steven Marks was someone's target. Thor had called Core and asked if Zack could be assigned to assist Jeanne. An assassination attempt on an Assistant Attorney General indicated sophisticated criminals in play. Thor wanted Jeanne's backup to be the best available. Roger was already using Core. Thor also assigned a handful of the new agents to secure other areas of the hospital.

Thor looked at his watch and moaned. DOJ Investigator Ward Bromley was due any minute. Thor heard laughing down the hall and decided to grab a soft drink before his meeting. He walked up to a group of the new agent transfers laughing with DOJ Investigator Ward Bromley.

Ward extended his hand to Thor. "Your boys here were just telling me a Voodoo lady named Spicey gave you the tip on the cemetery."

Thor was not happy. He glared at the other agents, then looked back at Bromley. "You are being hazed by the new boys. Sorry. Heads would roll if someone disclosed our tip sources in this office."

The agents quickly dispersed to other offices. Thor directed Bromley to the conference room. He would deal with these new guys when he finished with Bromley. He was so angry about Spicey's name being dropped that he unintentionally slammed his notebook on the table causing Bromley to jump.

Thor had just started the meeting when his phone went off. It was Roger. Thor looked at Bromley, "Have to take this, sorry." Bromley nodded.

Roger asked if he had started his meeting with Bromley yet. Thor answered, "Yes."

"Any way you can plant a tracer on him and his car?"

"That could happen with some compromise."

"If you're talking about bending rules, do it."

Thor ended the call and asked Bromley, "You want a soft drink or anything?"

Bromley nodded his head, "Yeah. That sounds good."

Thor didn't want Bromley wandering around, so he told him, "Toward the back of that notebook I have some names I want to check out with you before we get started."

Bromley answered, "Sure."

Thor left the conference room and shut the door behind him. He went over to where Nelson and Pablo had been conducting orientation for the new guys and signaled them to the hall.

Thor whispered, "Ward Bromley from DOJ is more than likely dirty. Roger wants his car and his body wired before he leaves. Car is outside, one of you do that. I want a 47t in his watch. I'm thinking we might have to drug him."

Pablo whispered, "There has to be something in evidence."

Thor rubbed his chin. This would get sticky if they got caught.

"Get it. He wants a pop. Give him half a roofy. Line up a 47t. Roger has NSA tracking this guy, but that only gives us conversations on phones. The 47T will give us his conversations in person."

Thor walked back in the conference room. Bromley had quickly shut the notebook. Thor explained the pop machine was stuck. "Got a newbie getting us a pop. Told him to shoot the machine if he had to. We have important company."

Bromley sat up straighter and laughed.

Thirty minutes later he was slouched in his chair, his head lying on the table, drool running from his open mouth. His jacket and watch had been removed and he was snoring.

Thor, Pablo and Nelson stood looking at him. A locator had been quickly hidden in the lining of his jacket. His watch now sported one of the latest model electronic listening device. IT declared it was up and working.

Thor grumbled, "Let's get him dressed. I'll just tell him the meeting went fine and suddenly he fainted. Nelson, call paramedics here. I want Bromley to think we were really worried about him. Don't want him suspicious. You guys perk him up somehow just before the paramedics get here."

Pablo offered, "I saw some speed in evidence." Thor tilted his head for Pablo to get it and a fresh pop. Thor went back in his office to check in with Jeanne and Zack.

"How's Marks doing?"

Jeanne answered, "Hanging on last we heard. We are standing outside of the operating room. The bullet missed his brain and spinal cord, but is lodged in a bad spot. One of the best brain surgeons in the country happened to be in this hospital today meeting with administrators. Can you believe it?"

Thor shook his head, "That guy must have an angel."

Thor walked into the room of newly assigned agents and shut the door. He took a deep breath and tried to control the anger he was feeling. "Who gave up our Voodoo lady?"

A tall guy in the back of the room raised his hand. "I did, I didn't think. I'm sorry."

Thor nodded, "You don't know what this office is working on. That Justice Investigator is knee deep with one of Senator Dalton's hit men."

The tall agent had gone pale. The room was silent.

Thor continued, "He just walked up and asked you, didn't he?"

"Yeah. Asked how we knew to go to the cemetery. I'm really sorry."

Thor had made similar mistakes himself in the past. He knew how easy someone slick could get you to give up information. "I have a problem. Until we figure out this hornet nest, we have to assume that Spicey is now a target."

The tall agent raised his hand, "I volunteer to guard her, sir."

Another agent raised his hand, "I'll help."

Thor looked around the room, "Get two more volunteers on this, twelve hour shifts, and make it around the clock until you are told differently." Thor looked around at the remaining agents in the room. "New Orleans is a criminal sewer. That's why we're here. Federally mandated consent decree. How many of *those* have you worked? How many cities have had to fire or prosecute half their police force, judges and city officials? Assume every tiny detail is connected to a larger story and another case. It is. Don't be impressed with titles. Corruption is the foundation."

Thor pointed to the tall agent, "Spicey will resist you being there. You can only say you are FBI and there to ensure her safety. Nothing else. This is costing me four guys that I need on other assignments. Let's use this as an orientation exercise and learn from it. You have myself, Roger Dance and Paul Casey you can bring information to. Until further notice, that's it. The rest of you guys go find Agents Manigat and Nelson for your assignments."

Thor waited for the tall agent to walk over. "Spicey is a unique lady. You'll probably end up in some situations. I'll pull you guys off this as soon as I can. What's your name?"

"Special Agent Phillip Weaver, sir. Again, I should have known better. I'm very sorry."

Thor actually smiled and said, "By this time tomorrow I'll be saying that to you."

"Sir?"

Thor left the room laughing.

Special Agent Todd Nelson walked up to Weaver and put his arm on his shoulder. "Tough luck there, dude. I spent some time around those Voodoo chicks six months ago. Flyin' snakes, storms that stop mid thunder crack. Found a pile of human bones in the swamp. A couple of live women, too." Nelson's toothpick wiggled at the side of his mouth. "You might meet Mambo, two hundred year old lady lives in a hut behind Honey Island. Little blue flames shooting out of the swamp all around her place. Has an eerie blue glow, ya know?" Nelson nodded his head and chuckled at Weaver's expression. "Make sure you take plenty of ammo."

The agent that had volunteered to help, Douglas Troy, was listening with his mouth open. Weaver looked at him after Nelson walked away. "Shit."

* * *

Wednesday 2:00 pm

Marla was going out of her mind at Reuben's house. She promised she wouldn't leave. She had to do something. She looked around Reuben's house and started picking up. She opened his refrigerator and saw it was empty. Marla calculated Reuben's house was at least three miles from her apartment. Even if Dooley had her address, there would be no reason for him to be over here.

Marla talked herself into risking a quick trip to the grocery down the street. Just run in and get a few things for a dinner. She thought of calling Reuben first and changed her mind. He would tell her no. She checked her cash. She had plenty. With Dooley being a cop she wasn't sure how much information he could get to find her. She knew from television not to use a charge card. Marla tingled with excitement and fear. She pulled out of the garage and inched down the driveway. So, this is what it's been like for Reuben's dad. It's not easy being invisible.

At the grocery, she backed into a parking spot up near the building. Her license plate was not visible. She practically ran through the store throwing items in the cart. Her heart was pounding and she cursed herself for taking the risk. At the checkout she watched a patrol car slowly drive through the lot. It took off, lights flashing moments later. Marla breathed again.

Once back in the garage she felt safe. Reuben would be angry she had taken the risk. Why couldn't she do what she was told, what she had promised? Marla spoke out loud as she hefted the grocery bag into her arms, "What's wrong with me?"

"I was just going to ask that." A man in the shadows stepped forward. It was Reuben.

CHAPTER 17

C laude and Earl stood looking at the disaster they had left in the kitchen. Claude turned to Earl, "I best help with this clean up." They spent half an hour mopping. Earl took out the garbage can of chicken heads to throw in the woods. He walked straight to where Spicey, Sasha and Dakin were hiding behind a clump of briar shrubs. Spicey watched Earl inch closer and squinted her eyes. She heard a loud grunt just before chicken heads, eyes wide open, flew toward them and landed only feet away.

Spicey peeked sideways and saw Sasha roll her eyes back. Spicey hung on to Sasha's arm in a death grip to keep her from falling and making any noise. Spicey was afraid to breathe. Dakin was gripping a turkey foot that hung around her neck on a leather strap.

Claude had walked out of the house and yelled at Earl, "This be good enough. We best find out somethin' about that witch. She best be dead by dark. Don't need no more trouble with Mason."

Earl scowled as he dropped the garbage can by the side of the driveway and walked toward the truck. "How we gonna find her?"

Claude's voice changed to his scary tone, "I bet all them witchy types know each other. We'll just ask at all them Voodoo shops. Somebody knows the lady with a spider on her face." Claude spit in the dirt drive before he hefted himself into the driver's seat. "Throw that big hammer in the back there with Betty Sue. This time we be doin' it right."

As soon as the truck pulled down the driveway, Spicey, Sasha and Dakin climbed out of the brush. They stood picking moss and sticks from each other's clothes and hair. They were wailing about what was going to happen to them.

Spicey cleared her throat and tried to appear strong for the others. "There be a lot of Voodoo shops in New Orleans. We got us some time to make a plan."

Sasha looked at Dakin, "Girl you be getting' a makeover. We gonna cover up that there spider, cut your hair and chop them nails."

Spicey expected a fight, but Dakin agreed.

Linda and Teresa had already gone into the house to find something of Claude and Earl's for Mambo. Mary and I declared we would guard the driveway. I'm pretty sure Linda and Teresa figured out we were avoiding the house. Less than a minute later, Teresa and Linda were back with a cap that said Claude and a mug that said Earl.

Spicey, Sasha and Dakin screamed and ducked as the cap and mug flew toward them. Teresa held them in front of Spicey. Spicey grabbed them both and smiled, "See? We have angels helping us, too."

Dakin was awestruck, "Spicey is the Queen!"

Spicey laughed, "I ain't nothin'. Wait 'til you meet Mambo. Right now, we best get that cab back out here."

$$* * *$$

Roger and Paul had listened to Cat with increasing concern. Steven Marks felt strongly a miscarriage of justice had occurred in the Molly Jarvis murder. The timing of his assassination attempt seemed more than coincidence. If William had been the true target and the murderer had gotten away with it for eight years, Cat was at risk, too.

"Who knew Steven was coming over here?" Roger was worried.

Cat answered, "I have no idea. Steven has been working fraud since he was relieved of the Jarvis case. I think he's kept his suspicions to himself. Actually, I'm sure of it."

Roger wondered out loud, "If someone monitors when case files are accessed, Marks may have triggered something before he left the office."

Cat exclaimed, "I copied all of the case files yesterday to a flash drive. I might have alerted someone."

"That would alert someone to you and him. Why did you call him of all the people that worked that case?"

Cat thought a moment before answering. "He has a reputation as a detail man. A solid evidence type. I reviewed his file notes first for that reason. I couldn't believe he bought the motive on Meyer. I thought he probably had more information than I had found in his file. I just wanted to pick his brain. I didn't know he'd been removed from the case until he told me."

Cat tapped the table with his pen. "He brought a flash drive with him of the original death certificate of William Jarvis. I have it. It differs significantly from the death certificate that was filed. I don't know what computer he kept this on. Wait. It had to be from work. He didn't have time to go home. He must have it buried in his records somewhere."

Roger looked at Cat. "An altered death certificate would support his suspicions. How long was he here?"

"No more than forty five minutes."

Roger looked at Paul, "Cat may have a problem in his building that is greater than just the Jarvis case. Let's step back from this a little. We are monitoring two men that we believe are hit men. There is evidence they are involved in the kidnapping and murder of Senator Dalton. We also have a connection to DOJ. Someone at DOJ kept one of them from prosecution last year."

"Dalton? He's dead?" Cat's voice had raised and his expression was one of grave concern. "He is a surprise witness in a case against a lobbyist our Washington office is prosecuting."

Roger asked, "When was he scheduled to testify?"

"Next month."

"That won't happen. He's in the bottom of the Assumption Parish sinkhole."

"He's where?" Cat stood and walked to his kitchen, "You're giving me a headache." Cat reached in a cupboard and tossed two aspirin into his mouth. "I thought Dalton was on a hunting trip?"

Paul offered, "That's the story until we get more information. We're trying to hold off the press."

Roger continued, "We have connected a Justice Investigator named Ward Bromley to one of Dalton's hit men. Does that name mean anything to you?"

Cat shook his head and then said, "I don't think I have ever dealt with him."

Roger stated, "He's out of your office."

Cat cleared his throat , "Great."

Cat threw his head back and swallowed his aspirin. He looked at his watch and marveled he had only been looking into the Jarvis case for twenty four hours.

Paul was taking notes and now spoke to Roger, "We could have forensics go over the alley video for more tips and the items Ed Meyer has from the dumpster. We are already running what we can on Ward Bromley for our case. We'll just share with Cat."

Roger said, "Add this patrolman, Mason Dooley."

Cat interrupted, "I already asked Thor to check out Dooley for me."

Roger nodded, "Good. Maybe we have something by now."

Cat's cell phone rang, his caller ID said Florey. Cat looked at Roger, "This is Ed Meyer's son, Reuben. I should take it." Cat listened a while and said, "Hang on a minute."

Cat looked at Roger, "I'm not sure how this came down but Reuben's girlfriend stole a shirt from Mason Dooley's car about two hours ago hoping to get his DNA. Seems the shirt is covered in blood. Dooley found out and is looking for her."

Roger asked, "May I?" Cat handed him the phone. "Mr. Florey? This is SSA Roger Dance of the FBI. Do you know where our field office is located?" Roger had paused for an answer. "Okay, where are you now? I am going to send agents there to get you. Reuben, we are working with Cat on your father's case now. Bring the shirt and the bag of items from the dumpster with you."

Roger handed Cat his phone and then retrieved his own from his jacket. "Thor? I need a secure transport of two people to our field office. They may have important evidence in a new twist in our case. Can you send Pablo and Nelson?"

Roger looked at Cat. "I'll get you anything I can to help you make your case. You're the lawyer here. Tell me what you want now."

Cat answered, "I wish I knew what I had. Marks may have been off base. Molly may have been the target. In that case I already have my proof that Ed Meyer probably didn't do it. Case done. If Marks is right, and William was the target I need a couple of big things. I need a court to get what I want now.

"My office will resist getting me what I need. The timing is all wrong. My boss is getting ready to run for Governor. The last thing he'll want is to let me reopen this case and admit we made mistakes eight years ago. Especially since all I have are hunches. I also want to exhume Williams's body."

Roger smiled, "We could bypass your office and make this an FBI case."

Cat smiled.

* * *

Wednesday 3:00 pm

Ward Bromley sat at his office desk. That was the first time in his career he had fainted in a meeting. He had a slight headache, but otherwise felt okay. He blamed the increased stress on Dooley's mistakes. Jesus. He couldn't believe the damn FBI had called paramedics. It took forever to get them to leave him alone. He glanced at his notebook. Shit, he had forgotten to check out this Reuben Florey. Bromley's cell phone rang, it was his contact.

"Bromley."

The voice on the other end asked what he had found out on Florey. Damn.

Bromley slammed a file cabinet drawer shut. "Nothing, so far. I'll keep digging."

He hung up and typed Reuben's name into his databases. There was a weeks' worth of work laying in the morgue, and they want him looking into someone new? An entry from 1982 jumped out at him. Reuben Meyer's legal name had been changed to Reuben Florey by his mother. Father's name was listed as Edward Meyer. Ed Meyer. Why did that name sound familiar? Holy crap! Now he understood the hit order on Steven Marks. Someone was snooping in the Jarvis files.

Bromley quickly searched his other databases and verified Reuben was indeed a journalist for the Times-Picayune in New Orleans. Bromley copied down Reuben's address and closed his notebook. He was reaching for his cell when his contact called again.

"Steven Marks is in surgery."

"That can't be."

The phone went dead.

Bromley's head was exploding with a migraine. How hard is it? Can't anything just be done right?

Bromley pushed his chair back with such force that it toppled. He set it back in place noisily and slammed his office door as he left. Bromley's secretary was on the phone with a co-worker, "Somebody's in big trouble. You should have seen Ward's face just now."

* * *

Thor called Pablo and Nelson to his office. "Roger wants this reporter and his girlfriend escorted here. Evidently they have some evidence this cop Dooley is after."

Todd looked at the address. Nelson handed Thor a file.

"I just printed this stuff off for you on Mason Dooley. I can't believe he's still a cop."

Thor opened the file and glanced at its contents. "This guy is on Cat's radar. Roger and Paul are with Cat. My money says Dooley will end up on our plate." Thor waved the file before he dropped it to his desk. "Be careful."

Thor watched them leave and checked his watch. Steven Marks had been in surgery over two hours now. When a fellow cop goes down, there is a special kind of anger that sets in. It used to make a difference even to the criminals. No more.

Agent Phillip Weaver stuck his head in Thor's office, "Doug and I are heading over to Spicey's place now."

Thor nodded.

Two minutes later there was another knock on Thor's door. Frank Mass stood smiling, holding a cup of coffee. "I don't know how you got my ass back here, but here I am. Get away from my desk!"

Thor moved away and gestured for Frank to take a seat.

"I hope that coffee is strong. I've got a couple of things to review with you on the 'hot' plate."

Mass frowned, "Already? Dance has only been here one day."

Thor chuckled, "I drugged a DOJ Investigator with shit out of an evidence locker about two hours ago in our conference room."

Mass's eyebrows went up. "You did what?"

Thor's toothpick wiggled in the corner of his mouth, "That's the good news."

* * *

Roger expressed his concern for Cat's safety.

Cat returned Roger's serious expression, "Don't go there."

Cat rubbed his left shoulder and sighed, "New topic. There is someone whose safety I'm worried about. The little girl that found me in the alley. I understand she is worried police will make her a ward of the state. She is living on the streets now. She is ten years old and her grandmother passed a couple of days ago. Even if I find her, she won't trust me. What can I do?"

Roger did not expect Cat to be thinking about something like this now with everything else that was going on. Then he remembered, Cat would know how an orphan feels. It pointed out how important it was to Cat for him to mention it now.

Roger answered, "If we can get some basic information on her, we can look for other family members."

Cat nodded. "I know of one man that may be able to get that for us. I'll follow up."

Roger asked, "I'm changing tracks now. The FBI can exhume William Jarvis's body and do the forensics, get you investigative reports on Dooley, Bromley, and our two hit men, and anyone else you want on the QT. If Steven Marks is correct, someone murdered both Molly and William and is embedded deep enough in your office to have hidden for eight years. How do we flush them out?"

Cat shook his head, "I need to meet with Ed Meyer soon. He may be able to shed some more light on his arrest. I need to prepare him for the eventual announcement that I am dropping charges against him."

Roger glanced quickly at Paul then back to Cat, "This is just a thought, what if you announced that first? You could state you have proof he didn't do it and you intend on reopening the case? That should make someone nervous enough to make a mistake, or at least start some conversations we can capture."

"I told you, my boss will have a fit." Cat looked thoughtful for a moment and then smiled, "Unless I got a directive from the FBI requiring I do so." Cat smiled, "Puts the heat on you and keeps important data out of my files."

Paul laughed out loud, "That's nothing new."

Roger smiled, "We know some of these players and already have them wired. If we get lucky, they'll take us back to the rat's nest. If this is an FBI case, you can plead ignorance when it suits you. Let me clear all of this with my Director and get back to you." Roger folded his hands and focused on Cat. "In the meantime, how do we keep you safe?"

Cat thought of Steven being at his table just three hours ago and now in surgery fighting for his life. "I have to act normal if the problem is in my office. I can't have FBI following me around. I can take care of myself."

Paul pushed his chin out in his nervous tick, "Where did you sleep last night?"

Cat laughed, "Point taken."

CHAPTER 18

Wednesday 4:00 pm

Wednesday 4:00 pm
The cab pulled up in front of the Voodoo shop and Spicey, Sasha and Dakin all ran for the shop doors. Once inside, they locked up behind them and headed for Spicey's kitchen. Mary, Teresa, Linda and I just followed.

Spicey pointed Dakin to a chair at her dinette as she quickly moved her bowl of fruit from the table to her counter. "Sasha, you get some clippers and start on those nails. I'm goin' to give our Hoodoo Princess here a haircut."

Sasha ran out of the room on her mission and ran back in one minute later. Her chest was heaving and her face flushed. "We got Men in Black at both our doors!"

Spicey held a lock of Dakin's long hair in her fingers, scissors frozen in the air. "Say what?"

Mary flew past Sasha and came back. "We have backup. We should call Ellen and tell her we can go somewhere else now."

Teresa laughed. "This could get funny. Let's stay and watch."

Sasha stomped her foot. "Men in Black! You know, big spooky government types. The kind that don't smile? Got one at each door out there!"

Spicey laid the scissors down and smoothed the sides of her dress. She exhaled heavily and shook her head, "Probably the damn IRS. I still be protestin' that thirty four dollars. They spent twice that in postage yellin' at me."

Sasha and Dakin followed Spicey to the door. Spicey yelled through the glass and startled the man standing there. "What you want?"

Agent Weaver held his FBI badge up to the glass. Spicey said, "Dang," and unlocked the door. Agent Troy walked around and came into the store front, too. Spicey locked the door behind them. Weaver was prepared for Spicey to resist their presence. Before she could speak he offered, "I am FBI Special Agent Phillip Weaver and this is Special Agent Douglas Troy. We have been assigned to provide you security."

Spicey looked them both up and down. "What took ya so long? We're in the back here. Ain't got time to socialize. Killers be on their way."

Spicey, Sasha and Dakin practically ran back to the kitchen with Weaver and Troy following. Weaver tilted his head as he glanced at Troy's puzzled expression.

Spicey pointed to the extra chairs, "Get comfortable. We be doing a makeover." Sasha left the room and came back with nail clippers. Spicey started combing and clipping Dakin's hair again. Weaver and Troy stared at Dakin's nails and the spider web tattoo that led to the spider on her cheek.

Weaver asked, "If you think killers are coming after you, why are you doing this?"

Spicey had a hair clip in her mouth and tried to talk around it. "Dakin here is a Hoodoo Princess. These two bubbas already killed her once. Well, sort of. Buried her anyway. We just came from the bubba house where there be blood all over and a big ol' axe. Heard 'em talk about lookin' for Dakin again. Checkin' Voodoo shops for who might know her. She be needin' a whole new look."

"One of you can keep an eye out for a rainbow colored truck with a big headed Betty Sue in the back. That be them." Spicey was nodding her head. "Hey. I might have a spell for that there tattoo. Saw it when I was lookin' for somethin' else. Be right back." Spicey ran out of the room and came back with the big tattered book titled, "Truth Seeker".

This was like watching a sitcom for us. We were rolling in laughter at the two agents' expressions. We also were reading their minds. Mary was holding her sides. "This is too funny."

Sasha was on the floor digging in a cupboard. Spicey glanced over, "What you looking for girl?"

Sasha answered, "Where be that electric turkey cuttin' knife? That or a chainsaw. I ain't gonna live long enough to file these nails."

Spicey pointed to a different cupboard. Sasha found the knife, plugged it in and gave its motor a rev. She looked at Dakin, "Give me one of your hands." Dakin held her hand out and Sasha started cutting.

Weaver and Troy kept glancing at each other. This was priceless.

Spicey was reading and shaking her head, "I be needing help." She looked at Weaver. "Just around the corner, by the cash register, is rows of potions in little jars. I'll yell out the names of 'em and you get 'em, okay?"

Weaver just stared at her. Spicey asked, "You deaf?" Spicey looked down at Dakin, "They send a deaf dude?"

Weaver got up and walked around the corner. Spicey was mixing corn starch, eggs, and milk in a large bowl. She yelled out, "I need black egg powder and lizard eyes."

Weaver entered the room with two jars. Spicey waved her hands at him, "Go back, we ain't done."

A minute later Spicey was seated at the table again measuring the black egg powder. She raised her voice, "Okay, now I need dry goat milk, ground beetle and castor root. That ought to do it."

Weaver brought her the remaining ingredients and took his seat again. He and Troy were both mesmerized. Dakin kept looking at herself in a mirror. Spicey had a big wooden spoon and mixed all the potions in the bowl. She quickly finished Dakin's haircut and clipped it back from her face.

Spicey looked at Dakin, "This here facial is supposed to remove tattoos. We leave it on exactly seven minutes."

"Let's do it."

Weaver had to stifle a laugh. There was no way that girl's tattoos were going to disappear. It struck him that the reality of his situation was that he was babysitting a nut.

Dakin sat with the black facial mask on her face and neck. Sasha finished the rough cutting of Dakin's nails with the electric knife. Dakin used a file to smooth the edges. When she finished, Sasha held up the tangled clump of long black nails and asked, "What you want to do with these?"

Dakin grabbed them. "Maybe I can turn them into a necklace?"

Sasha suggested, "Or a wind chime." Dakin was nodding her head. Mary was gasping, she was laughing so hard.

Spicey was looking in her book. She glanced at Dakin and said, "There is a tiny chance of a side effect here in the small print."

Sasha and Dakin said at the same time, "What side effect?"

Spicey cleared her throat, "Says if I use too much black egg might grow hair."

Dakin screamed, "On my face? And neck?"

Spicey shrugged and pointed to the page, "What it says."

Agent Troy thought about his bald spot. Linda cracked up.

Seven minutes passed and Spicey gave Dakin a big bowl of soapy water and a wash cloth. Everyone held their breath as she wiped the black facial goo from her face.

Spicey pointed with pride, "Perfect as a baby's butt. This here shit done saved your life girl!"

Weaver and Troy both walked over to get a closer look. There was no sign Dakin had ever had a tattoo. Weaver shook his head, "That is amazing!"

Spicey looked at her watch. "Dang. We been messin' around too long. Sasha, grab that cap and mug. We gotta get to Mambos." Spicey looked at both agents. "This here might be a good time to call your boss and get another job assignment."

Linda was reading Agent Troy's mind. She punched Mary's arm, "He thinks Dakin is cute."

Agent Troy spoke, "We go where you go." He glanced at Dakin.

Spicey laughed, "Then you be drivin' us to get a swamp boat."

Ellen called Teresa, "Fun's over, gals. Meet me at the FBI field office."

Dang.

* * *

Ellen sat on the desk, her tennis shoe clad feet swinging and said, "This is where we can help Roger, Paul and Cat the most. They have several people they are monitoring or have someone else monitoring for them. The problem is they have not had any time to listen to what has been recorded. Also, they don't have time to sort out what's important and what isn't."

Ellen jumped down from the desk and said, "I know angels aren't supposed to brag, but, our listening systems will help far more than their mortal devices. As soon as Cat announces he is reopening the Jarvis case, our system will go nuts!"

Oh goody. I had this vision of us all sitting around like stenographers with an earpiece, typing out passages we thought were important. Ugh.

Ellen pointed to me and said, "Vicki's got it exactly. Here are your recorders. I'll be back soon." Dang.

Suddenly little boxes with buttons appeared in front of each one of us. There was a little clock on top of each one. I put the earpiece to mine on my head and pushed the first button. I heard Mason Dooly begging Ward Bromley to help him steal evidence from the FBI forensic lab.

I hit stop. "You guys, this really works. I'm listening to Dooley."

Teresa shrugged, 'I don't know who I'm listening to...wait. This is some guy named Stone."

Mary yelled, "I've got Ward Bromley."

Linda was frowning, "My guy hasn't been called a name yet. I don't know who this is, but he talks like he works with the Solicitor General."

Ellen popped back in. "Good, you gals figured it out. Those little clocks will give the actual time stamp those conversations occurred. Be sure to include that for Roger. Call me when you're done."

I looked at Mary, "You should be on the other side of the table. This looks like a classroom and you're the teacher."

Mary moved across the table, "Now pay attention. There's going to be a test."

Linda and Teresa glared at me.

Teresa said, "Thanks."

About thirty minutes later we had transcribed all of the conversations that had been recorded.

Teresa suddenly squealed, "Hey! Ellen says for us to go to the Bahamas! She's going to meet us there on the island of New Providence."

Cool. Finally we get a vacation! Mary changed into a darling bathing suit.

* * *

Nelson and Pablo arrived at the address Thor had given them for Reuben Florey. As soon as they pulled in the driveway a man and a woman ran out of the house and jumped in the back seat. They each carried a paper bag.

Before Pablo could introduce himself, Marla blurted, "How long are we going to be? I put a roast in the oven. Maybe I should take it out?"

Pablo answered, "Let's keep an eye on the clock. It shouldn't take that long."

Reuben leaned forward, "Do you guys know an Agent Dance? He's the one that's helping Catahoula."

Nelson glanced in the rearview mirror, "He's our boss. Roger Dance is one of the best agents the FBI has."

Reuben leaned back, looked at Marla and smiled. Pablo saw her reach over and squeeze Reuben's hand. Huh, new lovers.

A patrol car turned onto the street and drove past them. Marla sunk down in the back seat, "Was that him?"

Nelson answered as he watched in his rearview mirror. "Could be. Slowing down in front of Reuben's house."

Pablo pointed, "Go around the block."

Nelson turned at the corner and sped to the next cross street, turned right again and crawled through the adjoining neighborhood. They saw the back of Reuben's house. They drove a little further and saw the patrol car in Reuben's driveway. Nelson pulled over and parked.

Pablo looked to the back seat. "Stay here. Don't leave the car."

Marla and Reuben both nodded their heads. They looked terrified.

Nelson and Pablo ran through the backyards and found Mason Dooley looking in the tiny window of Reuben's garage.

Pablo raised his voice, "Help you, officer?"

Dooley was clearly startled. He stammered for a minute, "This your house?"

Nelson stepped into view from the side of the garage. "Some reason you're looking in this garage?"

Mason Dooley felt trapped. "Who the hell are you guys? I saw you snooping around."

Pablo chuckled. "You did, huh?"

Nelson recognized Mason from his file and opened his badge. "FBI, Dooley. You've got one minute to answer my question."

Dooley was surprised they knew his name and snarled, "I already did."

Pablo dialed the field office, "Send a unit over here. We have a new guest."

Dooley laughed, "What? You think you're arresting me? I'm a cop."

Neither Pablo nor Nelson said anything. The transport car arrived and Pablo told them to put Dooley in holding until they were ready. One agent drove the patrol car to the field office. The other had directed a very pissed off Mason Dooley to sit in the caged back seat. When the car drove off, Nelson and Pablo walked back to their SUV.

Inside, Marla asked, "Was that him? Was that Mason Dooley at Reuben's house?"

Pablo answered, "Yes, it was, ma'am."

Marla rested her head on Reuben's shoulder. "Good Lord, what have I done?"

* * *

Edward woke, took a shower and walked into the living room. Izzy was deeply engrossed in his collector's copy of Huckleberry Finn. A part of him winced as he watched her lick her finger and turn the page. A bigger part of him was happy.

Izzy looked up, "I already have read over a hundred pages. This is so good."

Ed glanced to the kitchen. It actually sparkled. His laundry was folded and sitting in baskets. He looked at Izzy, "You didn't need to do all of this work. Thank you."

Izzy beamed.

Ed pulled out his money clip. "It is only fair that I pay you for your work."

Izzy looked hurt. "This isn't a job. I cleaned, because you are my friend."

Ed put his money back in his pocket.

Izzy smiled, "Besides, I got a job today at Otis's. He's going to let me sweep. I gave him your phone number. Was that okay?" Izzy looked so proud.

Ed knew he would have some explaining to do with Otis. "I'm going to walk to his store now to get our groceries. Do you want to come with me?"

Izzy rested her index finger where she was reading. "If you need me to help carry, I will."

Ed asked, "Are you in a good part of the book?" Izzy smiled and nodded her head quickly.

Ed rubbed the hair on top of her head. "You stay here and read. I'll be back shortly."

Maybe Otis could figure out what to do. An invisible man didn't need an invisible child.

* * *

Wednesday 5:00 pm

Mathew Core walked in to the bar at Roger's hotel. He hadn't seen Acer leave. Core had placed a tracker and listening device in Acer's car. Core had access to top level equipment. If he installed it properly, it would pick up both sides of any transmitted communication received in the car. Neither device had registered activity all afternoon. Odds were Acer would be looking to get dinner somewhere and would have to pass the hotel bar. Core was sure Acer would recognize him. He needed to make a connection.

Core was on his second drink and pretending to be on a cell call when Acer sat on the stool next to him. Core ended his pretend call with, "I'll get back." Core inhaled deeply and ignored Acer. Core pulled his money clip from his pocket and started to peel off a couple of bills as he stood.

Acer stated, "You didn't really think I didn't make you?"

Core sat heavily back on his stool and showed Acer a fake grin. "One can always hope. How've you been?"

Acer shrugged, "What is it they say? Just livin' the dream."

Core smiled and stood. "Good. See ya around."

Acer grabbed Core's jacket sleeve. "Sit back down a minute. I've got a question."

Core sat. "What?"

"You still a fixer?" Acer took a sip of his drink and smiled.

Core frowned. "Don't know what you're talking about."

Acer grinned, "Fine. I suppose you sell shoes?"

"Sounds about right. How about you?"

Acer nodded, "I'm in the shoe game myself. Big business these days."

Mathew Core smiled to himself. Acer just admitted he was still dirty and believed Core was, too.

Acer leaned forward and lowered his voice, "Couple of FBI staying here right now."

Core took a sip of his drink. "So?"

Acer slapped the edge of the bar. "That's why you're here, isn't it? Which one?"

"Why are you here?"

Acer shrugged, "I'm just waiting for a call." Just then Acer's cell rang. Acer turned away from Core. "Yeah." Acer listened for a minute and hung up. He downed his drink in one gulp. "Duty calls."

Core thought Acer looked tense, maybe even angry. Core said, "Good luck selling those shoes."

Acer glanced back, "You, too."

Core activated his listening and tracker equipment in Acer's car to transmit to his phone. After a few moments he heard Acer talking. "What the hell? This is how you show you're sorry? You hand me a suicide mission?"

Core's device allowed him to hear the voice on the other end say, "I'm confident you can succeed if you hurry. He just got out of surgery. They should still be disorganized and unfamiliar with staff."

Acer had ended the call and cursed. This was so stupid. So cliché. Of course the FBI would be waiting for him. A part of Acer found the idea exciting. It was beyond daring to even attempt. If he succeeded, his services would be invaluable, legendary.

Acer chuckled to himself. Evidently Stone isn't the only egomaniac.

Core dialed Roger, "Do you have someone in a hospital?"

* * *

Steven Marks had been moved to a private intensive care unit room. The surgeon had declared that Steven was a very lucky man and should have a full recovery. The entire medical staff balked at the badges Zack insisted they wear on their left lapels. Jeanne had heard him at the nurses' station, "You will not enter that room without one. I won't give you one without proof of your identity and your need for access to that patient. Period."

The hospital administrator had been called and instructed staff to comply. He also gave Zack a list of those people authorized to care for Steven. Zack walked back to where Jeanne stood flanking Steven Marks's door.

He rolled his eyes and said, "Like we would know who's legit and who isn't."

Jeanne chuckled. "There is a chair over there you can sit down in. I know you worked the gym all morning. You know nothing's going to happen here."

Zack declined and stood on the other side of the door. He looked at Jeanne, "What do you have?"

Jeanne answered, "Glock. Six knives. You?"

Zack answered, "A semi. One knife." Zack's gaze passed Jeanne to a man walking down the hall. He had on blue scrubs and slowed down at Steven's door. He smiled at Jeanne and reached for the doorknob. Jeanne grabbed his arm, Zack pulled his gun and the man stammered, "What the heck?"

Jeanne pushed him to the wall, "Who are you?"

A nurse wearing one of Zack's badges ran down the hall. "Wait. He's okay, he doesn't know."

Evidently the orderly had just reported to work. He had been in the men's room when everyone had gotten Zack's speech, and was just making his rounds. Zack located the man's name on his list and gave him a lapel badge.

The man looked at Jeanne and said, "You guys scared the crap out of me. What did this guy do?"

Zack answered, "He's a good guy, Attorney General's office. We're just security."

The orderly backed up, "No wonder. Hey, I'm sorry. I don't even have to go in there right now." The orderly left and went back to the nurses' station. In minutes he was the center of attention as people shot nervous glances down the hall and spoke in animated whispers.

* * *

We arrived in the Bahamas and spent a little time flying around looking at the beautiful beaches. Suddenly Ellen was flying with us. "Follow me!" She took off, leaving a vapor trail like a jet. Geesh. Ellen landed on the deck of a large yacht. There were two men walking the deck and a man up in the cabin above.

Ellen started down a staircase, "Down here." We followed her down a hall and to a large room in the back. A woman and two girls sat huddled together crying.

Mary whipped around and asked Ellen, "What's the matter with them?"

Ellen answered, "They have been kidnapped. Detained, as the men on the deck would say. That woman is Sarah Welsh. Her husband is a U.S. Senator that is being pressured to vote on a bill tomorrow. The girls are Megan, 8, and Chelsy, 12.

Linda went over and sat by them. We know we can emit calming auras, so Mary followed Linda and put her arms around Megan.

Teresa asked, "Can't we just apply a little ninja angel to these guys and call the coast guard?"

Ellen frowned, "Oh, if it were that easy. We have to let Roger know what we have found out and he has to find a way to send mortal help for them. He can't explain how he knows things we tell him, remember?"

That does complicate this angel class of "Helping Mortals" quite a bit. We can give mortals information, but they have to figure out how to explain knowing things. Never did like that rule.

Just then one of the men threw the door open and stood leering at Chelsy. Chelsy leaned in closer to her mom and Sarah screamed, "Stay away from us! Let us go!"

The man kept sneering and walked up to touch Megan's hair. She started crying and the man laughed and turned to leave. "We can party later." He closed the door and all three women began crying.

Mary had her hands on her hips. "Well, this is not going to happen!"

Ellen sighed, "Gals, you have had over a year of training now. You have been given a great many skills and tools to assist you. I am being told to return to New Orleans and make sure Roger and Cat are receiving all of the communications they need. That means you gals are on your own."

Teresa smiled, "No problem." Uh oh. I know that facial expression of hers and we are definitely going to have problems.

Ellen smiled, "You gals will think of something. Good luck!"

Ellen was gone.

We all were just floating around the room wondering what we should do first. Sarah was trying to comfort the girls. Mary started singing "Oklahoma". Linda joined in. Teresa and I just looked at each other.

When Mary finished, Teresa put her hand up. "What are you doing?"

Mary answered, "Music always makes mortals feel better."

Teresa nodded, "Except they can't hear you."

Mary looked over and a light pink glow was surrounding Sarah and the girls. "Yes, but see the aura? It is helping to calm them." Mary looked at Linda, "Let's keep singing them show tunes while Vicki and Teresa figure something out." Linda started singing, "Oh, What a beautiful morning."

Teresa and I went up to the deck to assess the situation. Teresa had a brilliant idea. "If we could steal one of their cell phones and get it to Sarah…"

"Sarah could call her husband!" Perfect. The man up in the cabin deck had his cell phone lying next to him on the console. We figured he would miss his phone right away, so we flew down to the two men drinking beer on the deck.

We nicknamed one man 'Arnold', he was huge, and the other man 'Einstein' because of his crazy hair. Einstein offered to get fresh beers. We could see his cell phone bulging in his pants pocket.

Teresa said, "We should trip him or something and take his phone."

I thought he looked a tad too big to mess with physically. Too late. He no sooner got up and Teresa had moved his chair to trip him. He was laying on the deck floor laughing.

Arnold threw his head back laughing, "You don't need any more beer!"

I got the cell phone out of his pocket and Teresa and I flew to the stairwell. We could walk right through the door at the bottom. The phone couldn't.

I looked at Teresa, "Now what?" I knew this was too easy.

Teresa smiled at me as she turned the door knob and opened the door. "We could do this the normal way." Oh.

Linda yelled at us, "Stop! Sarah can't just see a phone float over to her. We have to make her think they left it."

Teresa placed the phone on the counter next to her and said, "Make it ring."

We all stood staring at the phone.

Mary squealed, "We have an app for that on our watches!"

Heaven has apps?

Mary hit a couple of buttons on her watch as Linda and Teresa watched. I don't even want to know.

The phone on the counter started making a beeping noise. Sarah jumped up and looked around until she saw the phone. She picked it up and punched in a number. One second later she waved Megan and Chelsy to come stand with her. "Joe? Joe, its Sarah! We're on a boat! Men abducted us from the hotel!"

We listened while Senator Welsh explained to Sarah that the FBI was with him and wanted to trace her call. While they talked, we decided we had better go back to the deck to keep Arnold and Einstein from coming down the stairs.

Mary started singing show tunes again, with Linda joined in for the choruses.

Teresa and I sat on the landing at the top of the stairs.

CHAPTER 19

The Director of the FBI placed a call to the Solicitor General's personal cell phone. The Solicitor General had been waiting for the call and answered, "Your message was received and I have drawn up the documents personally. No one else knows they even exist. I prepared an order for the FBI to exhume the body of William Jarvis and an FBI directive to reopen the Molly Jarvis murder case and drop the charges against Mr. Edward Meyer. You'll have signed copies as soon as you tell me where to send them."

The FBI Director thanked him and gave him a secure e-mail address. "Dan, I really appreciate your cooperation in this. Any idea yet on who is calling the shots at your end?"

The Solicitor General sighed, "I'm still working on that, but have narrowed it down to two people. I have outside people placing equipment tonight. Once this shit of yours hits the fan in the morning, we should know."

* * *

Cat paced his living room reliving what he knew of the Jarvis case. One thing was certain. Someone in his building was monitoring the Jarvis case file access, but why? If William Jarvis had been the real target, practically anyone with a political motive was a suspect and would have benefited. But not just anyone could monitor DOJ case files.

It still seemed more likely that Molly was the target, and William had committed suicide. A crossed out time on a death certificate could easily be explained as an aging Medical Examiner operating under severe stress during the Katrina aftermath. Dillard Boggs certainly benefited from Molly's murder. The class action suit against him had been dropped and all community pressure against his establishments had been buried with Molly. Boggs easily could have a special friend in Cat's office. He would likely pay dearly to keep the Jarvis case buried if he were guilty. He certainly was smart enough to set up Ed. Cat made a note to check the financials the FBI had sent over an hour ago for payoff type transactions.

Senator Dalton's murder was another angle and especially troubling. The timing, the professional aspect of his murder, all suggested people of influence being involved. Dalton's participation as a surprise witness for the Department of Justice was known only to a very few people at the Solicitor

General's office, and a select few in Cat's building. Clearly the common threat was that someone at his office was dirty, and had to be helping whoever was guilty.

Cat sat down and forced himself to focus on what he knew. He had always liked the expression 'the way to eat an elephant is one bite at a time'. Cat twirled his pen and decided to start with Edward Meyer. Cat sent an email to Roger requesting a full data review on Ed. There may not be much available, considering Ed had been declared dead eight years ago and claimed to be living invisible.

Cat was troubled why Ed had waited so long to come forward. He let his son believe he was dead for four years. When he did finally meet with Reuben he discovered that Otis had a video that could prove he had been set up. Why wait another four years? Cat dialed the number Reuben had given him for his father.

Ed saw the caller ID and his heart began pounding. He was halfway to Otis's Grocery. "Yes, Mr. Delacroix?"

"Call me Cat. Ed, I would like to meet with you now. Where are you?"

Ed answered, "I'm on my way to Otis Grocery. I'm almost there. Where do you want me to go?"

"Stay there. I know where it is. I'll be there soon."

Cat put a fresh shirt on. He remembered what the bartender had told him. No suits in the hood. Too bad. Cat strapped on his shoulder holster and checked his gun. He put his jacket on. Roger would not be happy he was heading back to the hood.

* * *

Roger had just taken a call and waved Paul over to join him. "Keep me posted."

Roger smiled, "Somehow the Senator's wife got a hold of one of her abductors cell phones. She called the Senator and we are using the satellite now to locate her. They are on a yacht off the Coast of New Providence Island."

Paul shook his head, "I bet the angels have something to do with this. That was more than lucky."

"Yes, it was."

Roger's cell rang again. It was Core asking if he had someone in the hospital.

Roger answered, "We do. Senior Assistant Attorney General Steven Marks. He was shot three hours ago. He survived surgery. Jeanne and Zack are guarding him. Why?"

Core answered, "Acer just got orders to go to a hospital. Someone fresh out of surgery."

Roger's pulse quickened. "Shit."

Roger ran to Thor's office, Frank Mass was there. Roger asked, "Where's Thor?"

"I think he went to the hospital to relieve Jeanne."

Roger dialed Thor, "Where are you?"

"I'm just about at the hospital. What do you need?"

"Acer is on his way there."

* * *

Paul poked his head in the conference room and told Nelson to take statements from Marla and Reuben and get their items to forensics a.s.a.p. Paul added, "Keep Dooley in holding. We have to leave."

* * *

Zack and Jeanne watched a man in a doctor's jacket walk toward them. His head was down reading. The passing nurses exchanged greetings with him. He had the appropriate lapel pin on. Jeanne noticed he was reviewing a medical chart and a clipboard. Her mind flashed to the photo of Acer that Roger had circulated. She noticed the doctor had the same type of haircut and basic features. She focused on his face as he walked closer. He got within five feet of her and she saw the slightest glint of a pistol emerge from under the clipboard. Acer had wrongly determined Zack was the greater threat. In the instant Jeanne yelled "Gun" Acer dropped the clipboard and shot Zack two times in rapid succession in the chest.

Jeanne kicked the gun from Acer's hand and landed a chop blow to the side of his neck. She pulled a knife from her waistband with her left hand. Acer's eyes were filled with rage as he twisted around and kicked Jeanne's legs from under her. Jeanne had twisted enough that Acer's blow did not cause a break, but she was injured and dropped to the marble tile floor. She rolled, raised her torso, and threw her knife. It stuck deep in Acer's chest.

Acer didn't even pause. He yanked the knife from his chest with a loud growl and raised his arm to throw the knife back at Jeanne. Jeanne had already pulled another knife from her boot and raised her arm to throw. A gunshot sounded from behind her and Jeanne saw a small red dot appear on Acer's forehead. His knife clanged to the floor. Acer slowly folded at his knees and fell forward. Jeanne turned to see Thor advancing with his weapon drawn and screaming for help for Zack. Jeanne crawled over to Zack and placed her hands under his head. "Stay with me. Stay with me!"

Thor and Jeanne backed against the wall and inched their way to a corner to leave room for the swarm of medical staff attending to Zack. One nurse leaned down to check on Acer. Thor yelled, "Let that one rot." Thor squeezed Jeanne's hand and with his arm, pulled her to him. He looked into her eyes. They could read each other's minds as clearly as if they were speaking. Jeanne kissed Thor's cheek and squeezed his hand back. Thor exhaled. It would be hours before his heart quit pounding.

Roger and Paul ran from around the corner. Roger's eyes scanned the mass of people at the end of the hall. Zack was wheeled past him to a nearby operating room. Roger was washed with relief when he saw Thor and Jeanne. Roger didn't try to conceal his concern. He had grown very fond of Zack last year. He knew Core would be devastated.

A bloodcurdling scream filled the air. Roger and Paul ran to help. A nurse was found thrown on an empty bed in a vacant room. Her badge had been taken. That explained how Acer had been wearing a badge. The nurse's neck had been broken. She was dead. Her fellow nurses were sobbing and try-ing to re-establish some sort of order. The PA sys-tem pleaded for all available trauma staff to report to that station.

Roger and Paul joined Thor and Jeanne outside of Marks's room. Thor realized the current chaos could be a cover for a second attempt. He wouldn't move until the area was declared safe.

Core turned the corner in a sprint and saw them standing in a huddle. He ran up to Roger, "Where's Zack?" Even as he asked, he already knew.

The steady beeping from Steven Marks's moni-tor filled the now silent air. Roger touched Core's arm, "Zack's still alive."

* * *

Nelson had one of the new agents drive Reuben and Marla home. Nelson poked his head in the holding room where Dooley sat fuming. "Going to be a while yet. You want a pop or something?"

Dooley hissed, "I want to know why I'm here."

Nelson answered, "Because you wouldn't answer why you were there. At Florey's place."

Dooley slammed his hand on the table, "I saw you guys nosin' around. I was just doin' my job."

Nelson left the room laughing. Dooley threw a chair against the wall. Pablo had been watching through the observation window. "Piece of work, isn't he?"

Frank Mass sprinted down the hall to where Pablo and Nelson were talking. "Just had a shooting at the hospital. One dead and one in surgery."

Mass was struck by Pablo's shocked expression and suddenly remembered that Jeanne was his sister. "Jeanne is okay. Damn, I'm sorry. I forgot she's your sister. Core's guy Zack was shot twice in the chest. Shooter's dead."

Forensics arrived to take the items left by Reuben and Marla. Pablo was on his cell trying to call Jeanne. Nelson told forensics to hurry. Start on the bloody shirt first.

Mass looked at Nelson, "Need you and Pablo to take over for Jeanne and Zack at the hospital. Stay alert."

* * *

Wednesday 6:00 pm

Spicey, Sasha, Dakin and Agents Troy and Weaver arrived at Pete's Swamp Boat Rentals just as

Abram was sweeping off the dock. Last job of the day. Abram was damn glad, too. He had thought about those killer bubbas through three swamp tours.

Jackson had seen the black SUV pull up through his office window. When Spicey got out of the car, he freaked out. "Oh Lordy, no! What she want now?" Jackson went out on the porch of the office and yelled to Abram. Abram glanced over and put his hands on his head.

Jackson walked over to Spicey. He nodded at the men in suits and looked at Spicey, "I ain't glad to see ya and not particularly interested in what you want."

Spicey chuckled and slugged his arm a little too hard. "Funny man. Funny, funny man. Listen here. You be takin' us all to Mambo's."

Jackson thought he was in some kind of nightmare. "First, I don't go that direction in the swamp. Too spooky. Second …well, back to first. Ain't no point in gettin' lost. We only got about an hour daylight. Sane people don't do the swamp in the dark. There. That be two things."

Spicey smiled, "These here be FBI, Jackson. You know, the peoples that gave you the money to buy this here business." Abram had slowly walked up to the group and kept smiling at Dakin. He was now close enough to hear what was being said.

Spicey continued, "We got to take these here items to Mambo to stop them Betty Sue dudes from killin' Dakin here."

Abram looked at Jackson, "Mambo, the Voodoo Queen? For real? You be foolin' now, right?"

Jackson shrugged. "I told you I don't know how to get there. You might as well just turn around and go away." That sounded good to Agents Troy and Weaver. The stench coming up from the swamp was only topped by the creepy noises starting to fill the air.

Spicey started walking toward the docks, "I know how to get there. Go with Willie all the time." Spicey stopped and turned around, her hands on her hips. "Who owns a swamp boat tour place that be afraid of the swamp? Got to get this stuff to Mambo tonight."

Abram pulled his cell phone out. "I done heard a solution in this problem. Let's call Willie."

Sasha shook her head, 'He be at a meetin' for the big Woodstock Reunion. Ain't in town tonight." Sasha turned to the two agents, "Bunch of old folks gonna play it again! Peoples comin' from all over the world. Bands and everything! Got themselves two jars of love potion, too!"

Weaver and Troy glanced at each other.

Jackson rubbed his forehead, cursed and looked at Abram, "Ain't no point arguin' with Ms. Spicey. We be needin' two flat bottom boats. Can't have too much weight or ya sink."

Spicey started walking toward the docks and turned to smile at Jackson. "I knowed you'd do the right thing." She yelled back at the others, "Let's load up. Grab a couple hammers from that there pail 'fore you get on. Case you gotta smack a gator."

Dakin was clapping her hands as she ran past everyone to be the first on a boat. She grabbed a hammer and twirled it in the air as she squealed.

Weaver looked at Troy and hissed under his breath, "Aw, shit."

* * *

Roger and Paul arrived back at the field office from the hospital. Paul went to update Frank Mass. Roger watched Dooley through the observation window of the holding room. A layman would interpret anger and arrogance in Dooley's body language. Roger's profiler training saw fear and guilt. This was a man currently fueled by panic.

Ellen called Kim and reminded her that she was the only mortal that could communicate with Roger for the angels. Kim had remembered and asked, "What do you want me tell him?"

Ellen asked, "Do you remember when we read the minds of some people and repeated it to you, so you could tell Roger while it was happening?"

Kim said, "That time you used the earpiece for Roger?"

Ellen answered, "Yes. I want to do that again."

Kim called Roger. "Hey, handsome. Ellen wants to do the earpiece thing again."

Roger answered, "Good, I'm ready."

An earpiece appeared in Roger's ear and he walked into the holding room where Mason Dooley waited. Roger had Dooley's file and a notebook. Roger took a seat across from Dooley.

"Mr. Dooley, I'm having a bad day. I'm sorry it took so long to get to you. I'll contact your supervisors and explain if necessary."

That was the last thing Dooley wanted. "Why am I being detained?"

Roger laid his pen down, "You were on the private property of someone this office is protecting. When agents asked for an explanation, you lied." Roger opened the file that had been compiled on Dooley. "Your file indicates you've operated for some time without regard to consequences. Before you speak, understand that privilege has ended."

Kim's voice came through the earpiece, "Geesh. I don't believe this. He wants his mom. He also doesn't know what to say. He was looking for Marla."

Roger tapped his pen on the file. "Why were you at Mr. Florey's house?"

Dooley twisted in his chair. "I was looking for Marla. It's personal."

Kim's voice came over Roger's earpiece, "Oh, my God, Roger. Marla has his bloody shirt that will prove he shot Steven Marks."

Roger rubbed his temples. He couldn't explain knowing what Kim had just said. He had Marks's assassin sitting in front of him. Roger had nothing to hold him on.

Roger looked up at Dooley who was leaning back in his chair. Kim's voice told Roger that Dooley thought he was a pushover.

Roger smiled and leaned back in his chair to match Dooley's posture. "Let's approach this from another angle. Since you are here, and you're local, maybe you can help me figure something out. You were at the cemetery last evening, correct?"

"Yes."

Roger twirled his pen and asked, "Why do you think those bodies were put there? The M.E. says they're all pretty fresh."

Dooley shrugged, "Hell if I know."

Kim's voice said, "Liar."

Roger looked thoughtful and then asked, "Do you think these victims may have something in common?"

Kim's voice said, "He's thinking that the only thing they had in common was they were all snitches. He just does what he's told. Oh, my God. Roger. He shot all of them. Even a judge. He still has the gun. A Glock."

Mason Dooley leaned forward, "You know, if you want me to do your job, you should clear it with my boss. I want to leave."

"Who is your boss?"

Kim answered, "Ward Bromley."

Dooley answered, "My Captain. Can I leave now?"

Roger asked, "Who do you think your boss answers to?"

Kim answered, "He doesn't know. Somebody at Justice."

Dooley stood, "This is crazy! Ask my boss who he answers to. I don't even care! I'm leaving."

Roger stood, "Mr. Dooley, I suggest you stay away from Marla. If she wants to resume something personal, she can contact you."

Roger held the door for Dooley to leave, "The keys to your patrol unit are in the ignition. One last question, do you own a Glock?"

Mason's face was expressionless. "No."

Kim's voice said, "Liar."

CHAPTER 20

Wednesday 8:00 pm

Reuben and Marla kicked off their shoes and sat on the couch smiling at each other. Reuben said, "The house smells wonderful. Think that roast is done?"

Marla giggled, "Not yet. About half an hour to go. I'm going to put in some carrots and potatoes."

Reuben made a face, "I don't like carrots."

"How can you not like carrots? Everybody likes carrots. It's like not liking water."

Reuben laughed, "I don't like water, either."

Marla looked at him as if he was crazy. They both burst out laughing. Reuben reached across and grabbed her hand. "Thank you."

"For what?"

Reuben leaned over and kissed her nose. "For everything. You put yourself in danger to help me. And you cooked!"

Marla was actually giddy. "You haven't eaten it yet. I'm going to get those vegetables going." Marla left for the kitchen and Reuben grabbed the remote and turned on the late evening news. The FBI had told them that Dooley would be held as long as possible and warned to stay away from them. Maybe he could actually relax.

Marla finished adding vegetables and found Reuben snoring on the couch. Her visit to the FBI office had restored her faith in law enforcement. Those guys were totally different than the local cops. Marla relaxed knowing that at least for tonight she was safe.

Then she remembered Maddie! My God, how could she have forgotten? Maddie was her baby. An adorable little white and mixed color Shih Tzu. Maddie would be hungry and need to go out. She couldn't leave Maddie alone with Dooley after her. Dooley wouldn't think twice about hurting an animal. Marla decided to run home and bring Maddie back to Reuben's. Dooley was probably still at the FBI office anyway.

She looked at her watch. She didn't want to wake Reuben. She could be back before the vegetables were done. She grabbed her purse and clutched her keys to keep them from making any noise. She left a quick note for Reuben next to the couch. He would understand. He often teased her about all the pictures of Maddie at her work station. Well, now he could meet her.

It was already dark. Marla pressed the accelerator and told herself it wouldn't take more than five minutes to put Maddie in her carrier, grab her dog food and come right back. She didn't want the first meal she made for Reuben to be burnt.

* * *

Dooley couldn't believe his luck. He saw the blue Prius pull into a parking spot. He had almost decided to leave and stake out Reuben's house. Marla ran to the apartment building's front door and went inside. Dooley waited ten minutes. He grabbed the short piece of rope on the passenger seat and walked to the alley next to the parking lot. There was a fire escape going up to the third floor. Her apartment was 301. Just as he placed his foot on the first stair, he heard the buzzer of the apartment building door. He pressed his body against the brick wall of the short alley and listened as soft footsteps came closer. Her heard Marla's car chirp and saw her headlights flash. It was her.

Marla placed Maddie's carrier on the roof of the car and reached for the door handle. A strong hand covered her mouth and a man's arm pulled her backwards. Mason Dooley hissed in her ear, "Gotcha."

Marla nearly fainted. She was terrified and Dooley's eyes looked crazed. He kept his hand over her mouth as he slammed her head against the brick wall in the alley. Marla's vision blurred and it seemed she was spinning.

Dooley hissed, "Where's my shirt?"

Marla made a noise and shook her head as much as she could with Dooley pressing on her.

Dooley hissed, "Is it in your car?"

Marla shook her head, the tears rolled down her cheeks and over Dooley's hand.

"Is it in your apartment?"

Marla was sobbing now and her knees began to buckle as she shook her head. Dooley took his hand off from her mouth to pull her back up by her shoulders. Marla whispered, "The FBI has it."

Dooley's mind crashed. He was blinded with fury and grabbed Marla's neck. He twisted her and threw her to the cobblestones of the alley. He stood looking down at her, furious. He realized she wasn't moving. He pushed on her head with his boot. Her neck rolled freely to the side and Dooley realized it was broken. She was dead.

That damn mutt was yapping. Dooley glanced around for any witnesses and sprinted back to his car. He drove a few blocks and pulled over. His mind raced. He had to get that shirt back. Bromley had to help him. Maybe he knew someone that could steal it back from the FBI.

Dooley dialed Bromley. He had to leave a message. "I need your help. Now."

* * *

Reuben was dreaming he was enjoying a magnificent feast and Marla was dancing for him in a large ballroom. Reuben's eyes opened. He looked at the TV and laughed. The house sure smelled good. He rolled his neck and saw the note from Marla.

I'll be right back. I have to get Maddie! Marla

She shouldn't have left his house. Maybe it was okay. Dooley was probably still at the FBI office. There was no way to know for sure. Reuben was annoyed as he called her cell phone. No answer. He went in the kitchen, turned off the oven and removed the pot roast. No carrots. He smiled. He picked a piece of beef from the roast and savored it as he dialed Marla again. Still no answer. Now he was worried. It was just like her to run back to get that dog. Reuben smiled. Her love for that dog was actually one of things that had attracted him to her. Her face lit up every time she talked about her Maddie.

A loud pounding on his door startled him and he dropped the lid to the pot roast on the floor. Holy crap. He hoped it wasn't Dooley. Reuben ran in the living room and looked out the side window to his front door stoop. A man in a black suit knocked again.

Reuben opened the door. "Yes?"

"Mr. Florey? I'm Agent Williams with the FBI. I'm afraid I have bad news, sir."

Reuben's heart sank, he was sure something had happened to his dad. Reuben invited Agent Williams in the house and noticed he was holding a pet carrier. Reuben saw big brown eyes peeking through tufts of white, brown and slightly golden fur. It was a tiny dog, a Shih Tzu. It was Maddie.

Reuben's puzzled expression prompted Agent Williams to say, "Agent Dance thought you might be willing to take her."

"Take her?" Reuben was suddenly struck with a thought too horrific to verbalize.

Agent Williams put his hand on Reuben's shoulder. "I'm so sorry. Marla was found murdered by her car only minutes ago. Agent Dance is at the scene and asked that I come here right away."

Reuben couldn't speak. He sat in a chair and looked at Maddie. Maddie softly barked two times. She looked so sad. Reuben reached over and opened the carrier. Maddie glanced around the room, jumped in Reuben's lap and curled herself up tightly. She looked up at Reuben and whimpered.

Reuben swallowed and then looked up at Agent Williams. "What exactly happened to Marla?"

* * *

Cat had driven around the blocks surrounding Otis's store. He was acutely aware of the darkness settling in and the small gangs of young men huddled on every corner. His eyes were searching for that little pink bike. The thought of Izzy living on the streets with no one to protect her was haunting him. He rehearsed in his mind different ways he might approach her.

Cat finally parked in front of the Otis Grocery and looked at the alley across the street where Izzy had found him. What had brought her to the alley? The dumpster. Was she scavenging for food?

Cat locked his car, walked in the alley and looked behind the dumpster. Nothing. A door opened from the back of the bar building and Toby, the bartender, walked out with a bag of trash.

"Man, you just don't learn, do ya?"

Cat smiled, "I was looking for that little girl from last night."

"Ain't seen her."

Cat handed Toby a card. "Call me if you do."

Toby read the card. United States Attorney General Prosecutor, Sabastian Delacroix.

Toby pushed out his lower lip and said, "Dang. You're that dude they call Catahoula."

Cat nodded.

Toby put the card in his pocket and watched Cat walk across to Otis's place. Wonder what was going on over there?

Cat heard the tinkle of bells at the door announce he was in the store. Otis stood at the counter and waited. A man stood next to Otis and put his hand out, "Mr. Delacroix? I'm Edward Meyer." Otis suggested they could talk privately in his back room. Otis walked to the door, flipped the sign to closed and turned out the light.

Otis asked Cat, "Do you want me to wait out here?"

Cat looked at Ed who shrugged. Cat answered, "I probably need you both."

* * *

Ward Bromley assumed Dooley was calling because he saw his missed call list. Bromley had tried to reach him at least four times in the last hour. Bromley tried to keep his voice calm. He was infuriated at the problems he was facing because of Dooley's screw ups. "Why haven't you answered my calls?"

Dooley glanced at his phone and realized Bromley had been calling him. Dooley figured he better find out what Ward wanted first. "I was busy. Didn't notice. What did you want?"

Bromley laid it all out. "You didn't take care of our little job this afternoon. Steven Marks lived. We just lost a man trying to clean up your mess."

Dooley leaned his head back against his car's headrest. Marks was alive?

Bromley's voice boomed, "Did you hear me, Dooley?"

Dooley quietly answered, "Yes."

Bromley asked, "Did Marks see your face?"

"Yes. I shot him in the damn head. He's probably a vegetable. We've got one more problem to fix."

Bromley screamed, "What the hell now?"

Dooley told him about Marla stealing his bloody shirt, and taking it to the FBI. Dooley added, "I killed her. I didn't mean to. I just wanted the shirt back."

Bromley was silent. He felt like he was falling in a sinkhole.

Dooley pleaded, "Come on. You can get somebody to steal it back, can't you? They can't do anything without evidence."

Bromley realized Dooley quite possibly had just sealed both of their fates.

Bromley quietly said, "Let's think a minute. The FBI uses their own lab for forensics here in New Orleans. The shirt is probably already there being worked on. We would probably have to find some way to steal it from there."

Dooley sounded hopeful, "I can do it! Just tell me what to do."

Bromley shouted, "You know what I want you to do? Quit killing people! Any way you left any evidence where you killed this girl tonight?"

"No. I'm sure. They'll suspect me though."

"Then you'll need to get an airtight alibi. Get one! I'll call you when I figure this out."

Bromley ended the call and dialed his contact. There was little point making excuses for Mason Dooley. They all knew what he was, a common street level fixer. Some snags were to be expected. Some would be excused. Some wouldn't.

His contact listened and promised to call back soon. Bromley knew if that call didn't come, he was next.

* * *

Abram had Agent Weaver and Spicey in his boat.

Jackson had Agent Troy, Sasha and Dakin in his.

Jackson yelled over to Abram, "Look out for this creepy ass moss hanging up here. Got bugs and shit."

It was now pitch black under the moss canopy. The sounds of the marsh and swamp were deafening. In this part of the swamp, the only boats that could get through were the shallow, flat bottom boats that were guided with long poles. Motors couldn't function with the grasses and rotting debris.

Abram screamed, "Gator, gator!" and started slapping the water with his long pole.

Spicey yelled, "Stop. You leave 'em be, they won't hurt ya. You piss 'em off and they attack! Dang, some swamp man. They get too close just thunk 'em with a hammer."

Everyone in both boats raised their hammers and started watching the black water for red eyes.

Spicey yelled to Jackson whose boat was in the lead. "See that bent over cypress tree there? Duck down and go under it, there be a left turn right there."

Jackson looked back. "You be crazy. Don't look like nothin' there but land."

Sasha, Dakin and Agent Troy all ducked down low as Jackson guided their boat under the low hanging branches. Sure enough, a waterway appeared. Jackson could see a blue glow peeking through the trees far ahead of them.

Jackson turned and asked Spicey, "What's that blue glow up yonder?"

Spicey answered, "That be Mambo's place. See? I told you I knew how to get there."

Jackson looked puzzled, "She has electricity out here?"

Spicey answered, "That FBI lady Jeanne and Jeremiah brought her a generator last year. That's for running her fridge and heater though. Them blue lights be natural. The swamp gasses make little blue flames shoot up through the water and poof. Most them flames be at Mambo's."

Jackson was mumbling to himself that there wasn't nothin' natural about any of this.

Spicey added, "You just follow the blue lights from here on."

Spicey looked at Agent Weaver. "You know folks come from all over the world to study this swamp. Scientist types, people of learnin'. Got lots of folks think a whole tribe of Rugaru be living out here."

Agent Weaver knew he was going to regret asking, but did anyway. "What's a Rugaru?"

Spicey answered, "Sort of the Louisiana answer to Big Foot. 'Cept ours is part man and part wolf." Spicey looked thoughtful, "Rugaru said to eat humans, lives in this here swamp. Don't think Big Foot eats humans though. Rugaru climbs trees, too."

Weaver and Troy looked up at the overhanging branches. Weaver remembered Nelson telling him to bring lots of ammo. Suddenly they heard several large splashes in the water and saw brown animals the size of big raccoons dropping from the branches above.

Spicey screamed, "River rats! Shoot 'em! They attack!"

The water was filled with luminescent yellow eyes wildly swimming toward them. The splashing continued and Weaver and Troy were shooting in all directions.

Jackson screamed, "Don't shoot the boat!"

Spicey, Sasha and Dakin were flat on the deck. Abram clutched the pole and squatted down as low as he could. He peaked over the edge of the boat. A huge rat nose topped with glowing yellow eyes looked right at him. The rat opened its mouth and hissed, exposing long yellow fangs.

Agent Troy yelled, "Freeze!" to Abram and shot the rat as its long nailed fingers grabbed the edge of the boat and lifted itself from the water. Jackson was beating the water with his pole, while screaming. There must have been twenty dead rats floating on the water. Yellow eyes watched from the shore as Jackson and Abram quickly pushed away from the narrow inlet to more open waters.

Jackson yelled to Abram, "'Til we seen them rats, I was thinking it was safer to stay by shore."

Abram yelled back, "I was just thinkin' be safer not to be here at all!"

Spicey looked at Agent Weaver, "I think Jeremiah told me the rats live in little colonies. We must just looked like a little second line parade comin' down the street. Reminded 'em they be hungry."

Agent Troy rolled his eyes and put a new clip in his gun. He looked down at his suit pants and realized no dry cleaner on earth could ever save them. Dakin and Sasha were sitting, huddled in the center of the boat.

Dakin looked up at Troy, "You're so brave."

Sasha rolled her eyes.

* * *

The man on the top deck yelled down to the other guys, "Check on the broads! This isn't a vacation!"

Uh oh. I looked at Teresa. "You have a plan I hope?"

The men were both walking toward us. Teresa smiled, "Remember when you turned into a monkey?"

"You want me to turn into a monkey and do what?"

Suddenly Teresa was a huge tiger. She sat at the top of the stairs and roared at the men.

Einstein took out his gun and shot her! Teresa started slowly walking toward him. He shot until his gun was empty and kept backing up. He and Arnold were screaming and pressed against the deck rail. Teresa lay down and started licking her paws.

The man on the upper deck started shooting her. Arnold and Einstein screamed for him to stop. It wasn't working anyway and they were worried he would shoot them. All in all, it was brilliant. The men stayed plastered against the rail and the other man stayed on the top deck. Teresa took a nap. Linda and Mary kept singing show tunes. I played a game of solitare.

Ellen sent a message to Linda's watch that the FBI had located the boat and the Coast Guard, with FBI, was on its way. Cool.

* * *

Dooley walked in to the Dirty Secret and saw Dillard Boggs sitting at his favorite booth. Dooley order a drink from a passing waitress and sat down. Dooley watched the stripper on stage until Boggs spoke.

Boggs' eyes darted about the room, "Were you followed?"

"What? Who would follow me?" Dooley had forgotten how crazy Boggs could get.

Boggs sat his drink down and leaned his body as far forward as his bulk would allow. "What did you find out? Why are they lookin' to pin this Jarvis thing on me? Hey, I know you're connected, give it to me straight." Boggs looked very nervous and in a very bad mood. He slammed back his drink and whistled loudly for another.

Dooley had his own problems to worry about but he didn't need to get on the bad side of Boggs. "I don't know why Cat is snoopin' in the Jarvis case. I do know he wouldn't be wastin' his time for no reason."

"Thanks. That helps a lot. I'll be sure to think kindly of your help when I'm rottin' in prison." Boggs' beady eyes glared at Dooley.

"What makes you think you'll go to prison?" Boggs was a known coke head and paranoid as hell.

"That Catahoula dude wants my alibi for that night. Eight friggin' years ago! Can you believe it? Who the hell knows what they were doin' eight years ago?"

Dooley got an idea. "I've got a problem myself right now. I need an airtight alibi for tonight from about 7 to 9 p.m....... Any thoughts?"

Boggs displayed a big toothy grin, "Yeah, I got one."

CHAPTER 21

Cat, Otis and Ed took seats at a big round table in the back room of the grocery store. Otis offered soft drinks and handed out yellow legal pads and pens. He sat in his seat and waited for Cat to begin.

Cat leaned forward and asked Otis, "Have you heard any more about Izzy?"

Ed answered, "She's at my house." Ed explained how he found her sleeping in the dog house of neighbors and invited her to his house. "She spooks real easy. She is scared to death of becoming a ward of the state. I don't know what to do. I can see her taking off. She's a smart kid, thinks she can raise herself."

Cat offered, "I have a friend at the FBI that said if I could get him information on her, he would look for family members."

Both Ed and Otis scoffed. Otis said, "Her momma died in childbirth. Nobody knows anything about her daddy. Her Gram raised her from a baby on nothin'. I heard from Ms. Nelson that after rent,

289

those two only had two hundred dollars a month for utilities and food."

Cat's heart was breaking. He asked, "Do you think if you introduced me as your friend, she would talk to me?"

"I don't know. She's waitin' on me now to bring home some dinner. She cleaned my house, did laundry and is reading Huckleberry Finn right now." Ed paused, "I have to leave for work in a couple of hours. I'm working at the docks for cash."

Cat looked at Ed. "What is your financial situation?"

Otis chuckled, "He has more money than God. Bought this store from me and let me keep it. Paid me four times what it was worth."

Ed smiled, "I've always earned well and saved. Otis saved my life having that video. Working at the docks has allowed me to stay invisible."

Cat focused on Ed, "One thing about you bothers me, Ed. Why did you wait eight years to come forward?" Cat's penetrating gaze unnerved Ed. He felt a chill go down his spine.

Ed shrugged, "You may not believe this, but up until recently it hasn't been that bad. I guess I worried if I came forward and you couldn't help me, I'd go to jail for murder. It felt safer to stay invisible."

"What changed? You're no safer now than you were eight years ago."

Ed smiled, "I guess I got lonely. I want to be with people again. I guess I'm willing to risk it now."

Cat asked, "Risk what?"

"Risk you would be willing to help me."

Cat responded, "You could have asked me eight years ago. Four years ago. Otis had the tape."

Ed shook his head, "Man, you're definitely a prosecutor. Maybe I don't have a good reason for 'why now'. I just got lonely."

Cat leaned forward, "Most people afraid of being arrested, declared dead, would assume a new identity and make new friends. Plus, you also still had Reuben and Otis. That didn't take care of lonely?"

Ed was becoming flustered, "Maybe it's my ego, my career. I don't want to just survive as *someone*; I want my own life back."

Cat nodded, Ed's last response seemed closer to the truth. It still didn't answer the eight year wait. "The FBI is officially reopening the Jarvis case. I will be dropping all charges against you. You can have your life back. When I figure this out, you can have your good name back."

Ed started to tear up. He couldn't help it. It had been such a long time in hiding.

Otis grabbed a box of tissues from a shelf and shoved it towards Ed. "Don't start blubbering, damn it!"

Cat leaned back in his chair, "I'm asking both of you to keep private what we say here tonight. I want to prove who did kill Molly Jarvis. There is a theory that her husband William was the real target and his death was not a suicide. The FBI is also exhuming his body."

Ed nodded his head. "Never could figure out why anyone wanted Molly dead. You always think of the husband, but he's dead, too. What motive theory are you working with for killing William?"

Cat answered, "He made some noise he was going to run for Governor."

Ed slapped the table. "That's the missing piece. Of course!" Ed started laughing. "William Jarvis as Governor would have been disastrous!"

Cat was offended. "William Jarvis was a very brilliant, principled man."

Ed stood and began pacing.

Otis rolled his eyes, "There he goes."

Ed pointed at Cat, "Exactly. That is precisely why he had to be stopped. The machine liked the incumbent." Ed kept pacing, "Brilliant, principled men are not welcome in politics. REAL money will use unlimited resources to ensure weak, greedy, power crazed morons are elected." Ed looked at Cat, "You may be on to something!"

Cat exhaled. He didn't want to listen to Ed rant politics.

Ed sat down, "Why haven't you run for some office?"

Cat had never even considered it. "I find politics distasteful."

Ed nodded his head, "Look at your credentials. You are known nationally. You also have eight years with the Attorney General's office. I will *guarantee* that you have never been asked. Never."

Cat hadn't thought about it. "No. I've never been asked."

Ed asked, "Why do you think that is? On the surface, you are perfect. A shoe in with the public.

Especially the women! Look at you. I can see the posters now."

Otis actually laughed.

Ed had Cat thinking. "So, you think William was killed so he would never run. Your theory doesn't explain why William would want to run."

Ed pushed his notebook around and said, "Oh, a few strays actually gain office against the odds. These few strays, I believe, are actually men of principle that feel an obligation to serve the greater good." Ed leaned his chair back, "You have to feel sorry for them, though. The machine has unlimited resources. Honest men face dirty tricks around every corner. The machine is relentless. Eventually they are all brought down. Look at the shit that's been thrown at Senator Dalton lately. He's one of the last good guys out there."

Cat was shocked that Ed mentioned Senator Dalton. Wait until he hears Dalton's been murdered. Cat asked, "This 'machine' you talk about looks for people they can manipulate?"

Ed threw his hands in the air, "More than manipulate. If you're going to take their money for any position of power, you just sold your soul to the devil *and* proved you were worthy. They're going to own you."

Cat frowned, "Now you lost me."

"Lessons we learned from the Watergate tapes. Everyone knew Nixon was dirty, that wasn't the news. The real story was the workings of the machine. We got to hear how they think, how far they're willing to go. That was really what had the Senate in a panic.

Until the Watergate tapes, they only suspected the machine would get that dirty. Now they had proof and voices. That was over four decades ago! The machine learned a lot from Watergate, too. They learned they had better own some people at Justice and in the Senate. Now, it's like the mob making you prove your bones. You pay up front with leverage they can use against you, to keep you in line. *Then* they buy you an office."

Cat observed, "That's a pretty dismal view of our political system."

Ed shrugged, "How else could the real decision makers operate unobstructed and invisible?"

Cat said, "Let's pick this up from here tomorrow. Get food for you and Izzy and I'll give you a lift home. You may want to rethink going to work tonight. Your days of hiding are almost over."

Cat dropped Ed off at his modest bungalow. Through the curtain he could see a little girl curled in a chair, reading. Cat was so relieved that Izzy was not on the street that he almost didn't hear his cell ring. It was Roger.

"Where are you? Reuben Florey's girlfriend has just been found dead. 74 Marmot Street. This one belongs to Dooley."

"I'll be right there." Cat turned his car around and sped to the scene. Cat's mind raced. Reuben's girlfriend had a bloody shirt she stole from Dooley's car, hours ago, and now she's dead. Who's blood was on that shirt? Cat didn't know why, but he thought of Steven Marks.

* * *

Agents Weaver and Troy waited with Jackson and Abram in the boats while Dakin, Spicey and Sasha went into Mambo's hut. Jackson watched the shoreline for rats and snakes. Abram watched the water for gators.

Jackson finally asked, "What's the FBI want with Spicey?"

Agent Weaver answered, "We've been assigned to protect her."

Abram rubbed his chin and looked at Jackson, "I bet it's those two chicken bubbas."

Jackson nodded and looked at Agent Weaver. "Case you ain't been told they drive a ratty old truck painted every color you can think of. Some huge picture of a lady's head on the tailgate says 'Betty Sue'. Oh yeah, she's flippin' the bird."

Agent Troy just started laughing. "You talk like that is an everyday sight here."

Abram pushed out his lower lip, "Ain't that unusual."

The gals ran back to the boats all excited about their visit with Mambo. Spicey was smiling from ear to ear. "We did it. We got Mambo to put a curse on them bubbas."

Jackson asked, "What kind of curse?"

Sasha laughed, "Mambo wouldn't tell us! Guess we just wait an' see."

Dakin slapped her knees. "Mambo gave me an amulet. I met Mambo! I can't believe this."

Jackson and Abram guided the boats back toward the Swamp Boat Rental docks. Abram kept pointing to different landmarks in the swamp and saying, "Last time I'm ever seein' you. Creepy damn place."

Spicey started singing Cajun folk songs and everyone joined in. Once Weaver and Troy learned the words, they added harmony.

Abram looked up at the moon when they hit open water. "Look at that moon! All full and yellow. Sounds of joy on the swamp tonight."

Dakin raised her hands to the moon and began chanting. In the distance a series of long, unnatural, haunting howls pierced the air and echoed through the swamp. Dakin stopped.

Spicey looked at Agent Weaver. "There be the sounds your Rugaru makes."

Suddenly loud crunching and mashing sounds emerged from the marsh bank about fifty yards away. It sounded like something huge stomping on the undergrowth. Everyone in the boats got silent and Agents Weaver and Troy pulled out their guns. Then there was a huge splash.

Spicey pulled a gun from her purse and started waving it around, "You best not be a Rugaru or I'll shoot your ass!"

Agent Weaver hissed, "Put that gun away! What's wrong with you?" He continued to stare at the area just to the left of them under a clump of cypress trees.

Agent Troy whispered, "I think I see something just off that point of that peninsula."

Out of the swamp water a hairy figure rose and slowly dredged toward the shore. It was dragging something behind it. The hairy figure made it onto the shore and turned to face Jackson's boat.

Abram shouted, "Sweet Jesus, what that be?"

Sasha fainted. Agent Weaver stepped over her as he moved to get closer. He shot a warning shot in the air and the huge animal dropped to the ground. They heard rustling like it was crawling away.

Weaver said, "I couldn't have shot it. I shot straight up."

The swamp air exploded with the sound of a shotgun blast from the shore.

Jackson's paddle had been hit. He looked at the hole, dropped the paddle and flattened himself on the deck of the boat. "Shit, shit, shit."

Agent Weaver yelled, "FBI. Stop shooting! Identify yourself."

A moment of silence was broken by a human, male voice on the shore, "Abram? That be your boat?"

Abram peeked over the edge of the boat and yelled, "Who I talkin' to?"

"Daryl. What you be doing out here? Almost got yourself shot!"

Agent Weaver holstered his gun and told Jackson to get their boat closer to the shore. They got up close enough that Agent Weaver could see a very large, hairy man that had an alligator lying next to him.

Weaver asked, "What are you doing out here?"

Daryl pointed at Abram, "I'm catchin' gators with their chickens! What you doin' out here?"

* * *

Wednesday 10:00 pm

Steven Marks was still unconscious. His doctor has said that his brain waves looked good. It was the nature of his injury to need extra time.

Zack was slowly waking up in the recovery room. His eyes opened tiny slits. He saw Roger and Core sitting in chairs across the room. Zack raised his hand and they both walked over.

"Jeanne?"

Roger assured Zack that Jeanne was fine, Acer was dead and Steven Marks was safe.

Zack smiled and shook his head slightly. He motioned for his water and Core passed him the glass with the straw and held it for him.

Zack pointed at Roger and smiled. "Every time you come to town something happens to me."

Roger answered, "As if I don't feel bad enough."

Zack looked at the clock across the room. "Go home. I need sleep." Zack closed his eyes.

Roger and Core left the room feeling relieved. Mass sent an agent to guard Zack's room also.

In the hall, Core exhaled, "That was too close."

Roger said, "Look. You need your rest. The FBI is opening the Molly Jarvis case tomorrow and exhuming William Jarvis's body. We are running a shadow case for Catahoula. Steven Marks is just the beginning of the fallout we can expect."

Core looked at his watch. "I remember the Jarvis murder. That was a big case. Call when you need me."

Roger nodded. "Our friend, Ward Bromley, is up to his neck in this. Bromley will find out tomorrow morning that the Jarvis case is being re-opened and that William Jarvis's body has been exhumed. Hopefully that will spur cell calls we can monitor and find out who else is in this. Breaking this case is going to happen through communications. We need to get them talking and identifying themselves."

* * *

Izzy and Ed were both reading in the living room. Ed had made cheeseburgers and Izzy had cleaned up. Izzy looked at Ed. "I thought you had to go to work."

Ed was prepared for the question. "I quit my job. In a few days, I won't have to be invisible anymore. I can get a better job."

Izzy's face fell. "Do I have to stop being invisible, too?"

Ed laid his book down. "The secret to stop being invisible is to do it the smart way. I'm thinking that I can help you do that. I am working on a plan for you."

Izzy raised her voice, "I don't want to be a ward of the state!"

"I know that. I have a lot of friends that are very smart. We can figure something out. I will promise you that if you don't like the plan we come up with, we'll keep making plans 'til you do. Deal?"

Izzy nodded her head. "I'm on page two hundred and four. What page are you on?"

Ed pretended to be worried, "Oh, no. You're ahead of me!"

Izzy giggled and went back to reading.

Ed laid his book down. "You need to go to bed soon. You've had a long day. That first door down the hall is for guests. You can use that as your room."

Izzy jumped up and ran to the door and opened it. "It has a bed and everything! All for me?"

Ed answered yes.

Izzy ran over and kissed his cheek. "I've never had my own bed before. I wish you had known my Gram." Izzy smiled, "Gram would have loved you, too." She grabbed Huckleberry Finn and ran to her room.

Tears ran down Ed's cheeks. If only he could go back in time. Lord, save this child.

* * *

Reuben was devastated. He was sure that he and Marla had been on the verge of something wonderful. He blamed himself for getting her involved. He knew the FBI and Catahoula would make Dooley pay. That wouldn't bring Marla back. Reuben wiped his tears and decided to go to bed. He turned to shut off the kitchen light and saw the bag of carrots Marla had bought sitting on the counter. He walked over and put them in the fridge. He smiled remembering Marla's shock that he didn't eat carrots. He would from now on.

Maddie stood in the middle of the hall and barked so loud it made her little body move backwards. Reuben smiled at her. "Well, little gal, I guess we'll take this one day at a time. Come on, let's go to bed."

Reuben removed all his clothes but his boxers and collapsed on his bed. He stared at the dark ceiling and thought of Marla. Soon he felt his blankets compressing from Maddie moving up toward his pillow. She nuzzled into his armpit and laid her head on his chest. Reuben looked down at her big brown eyes and thought he felt Marla in the room. Maddie raised her head, barked once at the dark corner at the end of the bed and laid her head back down on Reuben's chest.

* * *

Roger was notified the Coast Guard had rescued Sarah and the girls. They were being flown home. The agents that made the arrest stated that they were met with no resistance. The three men arrested were in a frenzied state. They claimed a tiger had been on board the yacht. They also said they had shot it and it wouldn't die. It didn't even seem wounded. When the Coast Guard showed up, the men claimed the tiger just disappeared. The agents that arrested the men attributed their story to possible drug and alcohol consumption.

Roger chuckled to himself. He knew the 'tiger' had probably been one of his angels. He imagined the encounter with a tiger could be quite a sobering experience. Roger called Senator Welsh as a courtesy follow up.

Senator Welsh had a smile in his voice. "The FBI has been outstanding in this. Locating my family so quickly seems impossible. My God you have only had hours! I have spoken with my family and we are in agreement about tomorrow. I have a favor to ask, Agent Dance."

"Certainly, sir."

"Just being cautious, could you arrange for my transportation to the Senate, so I may place my vote tomorrow?"

"It would be an honor, sir."

* * *

Cat prepared to go to sleep and noticed his phone had a message. The call must have come in when he was in the shower. Cat listened to the voice of Dillard Boggs.

"Yeah, sorry to call so late Mr. Delacroix, been hours and hours goin' through my old records here. On the night Molly Jarvis was murdered, I was training my new security guy at the Dirty Secret. Off duty cops are what we use to keep it legal and all. Name's Mason Dooley. You check with him. He was here all night right by my side. You have a good night now, ya hear?"

Mason Dooley was hardly an alibi since he was on video in the alley. Dillard Boggs had moved quickly to provide an alibi that he thought would be airtight. Guilty people scramble. Cat made a mental note to concentrate his efforts in the morning, on the information the FBI had sent over on Boggs. Cat wondered if Boggs hadn't hired Dooley for the dirty deed. It fit, if Molly was the target.

CHAPTER 22

Thursday 8:00 am
As Cat exited the elevator on his floor in the Justice building, he could see Martha sitting high in her perch. Her eyes were narrowed at seeing him, and her head slightly tilted. Cat smiled, "Morning, Martha." He winked and opened his door. His desk was free of files for the moment. He sat twisting in his chair and waited.

Martha appeared in his doorway, "Sabastian Delacroix. What are you doing back at work already? You can't be feeling that much better."

Cat booted up his computer and glanced over to her. "It was your soup! It was delicious."

Cat had a mischievous grin on his face. "Have you instructed the new guys on your office rules?"

Martha chuckled, "Darn right, I did. Told 'em to leave you alone, too." Martha left his office to return to her desk. Cat watched her lightly dust her monitor, straighten her stack of files and throw her shoulders back. Cat was fairly certain he wouldn't have many interruptions this morning.

He leaned back in his chair and called Roger from his cell phone. "Do you have any idea when my mail will be arriving?"

Roger answered, "I just sent it by courier ten minutes ago. Is your boss there yet?"

Cat leaned forward and saw Ted talking to James Mulley, a transfer attorney from the Virginia office. "He's here."

"I have it addressed to you, since you are Senior in the office. I thought you might want to break this to Ted yourself."

Cat rolled his neck and winced at the still present soreness in his shoulders. "Yeah, I do. This isn't going to be easy. He just cleared his calendar to start working on his campaign."

Cat hung up from his call and watched Ted in the hall. He was going to make a good Governor. Maybe too good. Cat kept remembering Meyer's words, "A few strays actually gain office against the odds. Dedicated men who do this for the greater good. They don't stand a chance over the long haul. Not with dirty tricks. *Always* get stopped." Cat thought about Senator Dalton.

Cat was answering his emails from being out of the office all day yesterday. He opened an email from Judge Ingle. Cat couldn't remember ever getting an email from the judge.

The email read : My messages to your office have not been answered. Have important information for you. Urgent attention required. Please contact me.

Cat buzzed Martha. "Have I received any messages from Judge Ingle?"

Martha responded, "Not that I've seen."

Cat remembered the Judge's bailiff complaining the judge was getting forgetful. Maybe that was it. The timing was certainly suspect, the email had been sent Tuesday evening, when Judge Ingle had been murdered.

His next task was going to be reviewing what the FBI had on Boggs and Dooley. A quick knock on his opened door made him look up to see Ted.

Ted was shaking his head as he walked in and took a seat. "Heard you have a bit of a black eye. How's the rest of you?" Ted laid some files on the desk and leaned back waiting for an answer.

Cat smiled, "Let's just say I don't want to do that again for a while."

"What the hell were you doing over there at night anyway?" Ted's brow furrowed in concern.

"I went for hamburgers." Cat shrugged.

Ted reached over and pushed the door shut. "Look. I'm your friend more than anything else. People go to that neighborhood for one thing. If you have a problem, I can help you. Nobody needs to know."

It took Cat a moment to figure out what Ted was implying. "You think I went there for drugs?"

Ted shrugged. "Makes more sense than hamburgers."

Cat decided to start warming Ted up for the news. "Okay. Listen, I went there to follow up on a rumor I heard about the Jarvis case."

Ted leaned forward, "The Jarvis case? What kind of rumor?"

Cat lied, "A friend of mine at the FBI says they have a video of Edward Meyer being set up for his arrest. I guess the video shows him being drugged and placed in that stolen car. Exactly like he claimed it happened. I wanted to see the alley for myself."

Ted stood and began pacing, "A video? Where has this video been for eight years? Where did it come from? I thought the surveillance cams weren't working there." Ted sat and twirled his pen in his fingers. "The motive was always weak. Marks screamed about that all along. But it's the only thing we had." Ted leaned back in the chair, "FBI? Wonder how they got this?"

Cat didn't say anymore. He saw Martha arguing with a courier outside his office. Ted was deep in troubled thought. Cat hit his intercom, "Martha, if that is for me or Ted, it's fine."

Martha answered, "You're the winner. Has to be a hand- to- hand delivery." Her disapproval was evident in her tone. "It isn't good enough for me to give it to you when you have a minute."

Cat chuckled and stood. He looked at Ted and pointed outside of the office. "Just a second, Ted. Let me get this and we can continue." Cat signed for the delivery and brought the envelope to his desk. The return address was FBI. Cat tapped on the address, "FBI. Person –to– person." Cat took his letter opener and opened the file. He pulled the documents out and began reading.

Cat moaned, "Oh, brother."

Ted put out his hand, "What?"

Cat handed Ted the order from the Solicitor General to the FBI authorizing the reopening of the Molly Jarvis case and dropping the charges on Edward Meyer. Cat read the second order, "What the hell? They are exhuming the body of William Jarvis." Cat hoped his acting skills would pass.

Ted stood. "Give me that!" He grabbed the papers with such force Cat was expecting them to tear. Cat glanced out his window to Martha's desk and saw that she was mesmerized by the animated conversation that was happening.

Ted dropped to his chair, "Who at the FBI sent these?"

Cat pretended to have to search for a name, "Roger Dance."

Ted's jaw set, "Never heard of him." Ted hit Cat's intercom for Martha. "Martha, see if Steven Marks can come up here. He's in fraud, downstairs."

There was a pause and Martha answered, "Steven Marks was shot yesterday. I think he's in the hospital."

Ted was stunned, "What? When? By who?"

Martha answered she didn't know, but she would call the hospital and get an update for them.

Ted looked at Cat, "Did you know Steven Marks was *shot* yesterday?"

Cat searched his mind for an answer that wasn't a bald face lie. "I was home yesterday eating Martha's soup."

Ted lifted his chin toward the ceiling and closed his eyes. He mumbled, "I was in meetings in Virginia all day. Damn finance crap for the campaign." Ted leaned forward, "I can't think of a worst time to reopen a case this big." He looked at Cat, "You know the FBI will have us do all of the legal on this or they wouldn't have sent us a copy. I wonder why they went to the Solicitor General instead of just filing it here."

Cat clicked his pen, "Would you have allowed these to be filed if they had asked you?"

Ted shrugged, "Hell, I don't know. One thing's for sure, I can't run a campaign and work on this too."

Cat replied, "I can do this. You run your campaign."

Ted stood and snickered, "They may not want me if I charged the wrong man in the biggest murder case in the last decade."

Cat decided to push, "Why do you think they are exhuming William?"

"Someone thinks it wasn't suicide."

"Is there any chance of that?"

Ted's voice had gotten louder and he waved the papers for effect. "The medical examiner ruled a suicide. What the hell do I know? It doesn't matter. By the time the FBI agrees, my campaign will be in the toilet."

Cat considered Ted falling victim to dirty tricks already.

Cat asked, "Who found his body?"

"Cleaning lady." Ted spat out the words as he left Cat's office.

Cat watched Ted walk to his office with the orders from the Solicitor General clutched tightly in his hand and close his door. It certainly was bad timing for the Jarvis case to surface now. But that would mean that Reuben and Edward coming forward now was part of some devious plan. That didn't seem likely. Someone other than Ed killed Molly and Mason Dooley was in the middle of it.

Cat walked out to Martha's desk and met her raised eyebrows with a shrug. "I'm going to leave for a couple of hours. Could you check around and find out where the evidence boxes are being stored in the Molly Jarvis case and have them brought here?"

Martha didn't even try to hide her surprise. "That's what's going on? Dear Lord."

Cat nodded and took a mint from a bowl on her desk. He knew they were just for Martha and him. He had seen her slap other people away. He took the wrapper off it and she held her hand out.

Martha dropped the cellophane paper in her basket and asked, "Who started this?"

Cat answered, "FBI."

Cat walked to the elevator and noticed Martha was already on her phone hunting down the evidence. Cat dialed Roger as soon as the elevator door closed.

Cat asked, "When is William's body being exhumed?"

Roger answered, "They did it last night. Listen, I had an idea last night about your little friend, Izzy. Well, truthfully the idea was from my fiancée, Kim. I took the liberty of asking Ed to bring her here at ten this morning. Kim thought if she saw the FBI office and met some officers, she wouldn't be as afraid of them."

"Mathew Core's wife has agreed to bring their daughter, Jamie, and offer to take Izzy with them on a shopping trip. If Izzy goes for it, Ed will be available for us to plan how we move this thing forward. None of us will be worrying what Izzy is doing."

Cat caught himself sighing with relief. He had been very worried that Izzy would get spooked by Ed's 'coming out' and run. Cat answered, "Tell your fiancée she is a genius."

* * *

Ed fried some sausage hoping the smell would bring Izzy from her room. Breakfast was ready and still no Izzy. Ed walked down the hall and knocked on her door. "Hey, gal. You hungry?" Ed waited for a response and then opened the door. Izzy was gone.

Ed noticed the bed had been neatly made and he didn't see any of Izzy's things. The Huckleberry Finn book lay on the nightstand. Ed felt sick. Did he scare her somehow? Maybe it had been too soon to talk about her making a plan.

He thought he heard his front door open. Ed walked to the end of the hall where Izzy stood with a grin from ear to ear. She brought her arm from behind her back to expose a huge bouquet of flowers.

She put her finger in the air to stop him from talking. "I didn't steal these. Gram and I planted them last year. Aren't they beautiful?"

Ed reached out, "May I?" He held the bouquet under his nose and took a long deep breath. "I believe these are the most beautiful flowers I have ever seen. We should put them in water."

Izzy ran to the kitchen and grabbed an old iced tea pitcher that had been under the sink. Ed noticed it now sparkled. Izzy put her hands out, "Let me show you Gram's trick." Ed handed her the flowers and Izzy searched in his silverware drawer for a small knife. She laid each stem flat on the counter and made an angular cut at the bottom of each stem. "See? If you cut the stem at an angle, more water can get to the flower face. Do you have some sugar?"

Ed reached in the cupboard and brought down a small sugar bowl. Izzy carefully put a level teaspoon of sugar in the pitcher of water and then looked at him. "You mustn't waste sugar. One teaspoon is plenty." Her jaw was firmly set as she carefully stirred the sugar with a wooden spoon. She arranged each flower until the bouquet was complete.

Izzy turned to Ed and held out the arrangement. Her face beamed with expectation and pride. A look only a child could portray. "Do you like it?"

Ed wiped a tear. "Izzy, it's the most beautiful thing anyone has done for me in a very long time. Thank you."

Ed sat the pitcher in the center of the table. "Let's eat some breakfast. I have a field trip to go on today. I would like you to join me."

They were nearly done with breakfast. Ed was very aware he had to carefully choose his words or he would alarm Izzy. "Do you know what the FBI is?"

Izzy put her fork down and stared at Ed. "They are very important police."

Ed took a bite of his eggs and nodded. "Very important, yes. They are helping me to not be invisible anymore. They have a smart plan for me and want me to visit them this morning."

Izzy stared at Ed and didn't speak.

Ed continued, "I was thinking if you came with me, we could go to the library afterwards and look for some books."

Izzy tilted her head. "You don't need more books."

Ed chuckled, "I don't, but you do. Huckleberry Finn will be read soon and I don't have many children books here. Wouldn't you like to see the other books that author wrote?"

Izzy frowned, "You could go to your meeting and then come back to get me. Or I could find the library and meet you."

Ed realized there was no point in trying to trick her into going. "Remember when we talked about how smart people sometimes still ended up in situations?" Izzy nodded. Ed put his napkin on his plate. "We are both smart people. So are the FBI. You don't want to spend your whole life afraid of police, because you think they want to make you a ward of the state. That's not smart."

Izzy's face was turning red. Ed quickly added. "I just want you to meet them. I promise you are coming home with me after the meeting. Nobody there will try to take you."

Ed's promise had made the difference. He could see her body relax and she smiled. Izzy put her hand across the table. Her arm barley reached to halfway. "Pinky swear?"

Ed wrapped her pinky finger in his and said, "Pinky swear."

* * *

Cat stood outside the observation window of the Medical Examiner's office. There was a row of six bodies lined up with white sheets covering them. Cat surmised these were the people found in the crypts awaiting someone to identify them. He assumed they were presentable or they wouldn't be in front of the window.

Cat hit the visitor buzzer and was greeted by Dr. Ames, himself. Seventy four years old and still working. Clumps of uneven white hair topped his pink face. He handed Cat a scrub robe and pointed to the autopsy room. "Who are you here for?"

Cat answered, "I wish I knew." Cat pointed to the row of bodies. "Our crypt people?"

Dr. Ames nodded. "All but one. Finishin' him up now. Judge has already been picked up by the funeral home."

Cat asked, "All shot?"

"Yep and I'm bettin' with the same gun."

Dr. Ames crooked his index finger for Cat to follow him. "Found one unusual substance on every single one of them."

Cat asked, "What's that?"

Dr. Ames held up a small glass sample slide. "Moonshine. The real crude stuff." Dr. Ames walked over to his microscope and said, "I'm no forensic genius, but I also see the same two sets of fingerprints all over the clothes of these people. You have the same two people touching all of these clothes."

Cat asked where Dr. Ames's reports would be sent when he completed them. "To your place, I would assume. You have another idea?"

"Yes. Send a duplicate report to the local FBI office to the attention of Roger Dance."

Dr. Ames frowned and walked over to his desk. "Say that again." The doctor wrote the information on his pad.

Cat had a thought. "Doctor, did you work here during Katrina?"

"On and off some. Officially, I was still in Baton Rouge. I tried to help Guzzy when I could get away. He was gettin' on in years and totally overwhelmed."

"Guzzy?"

Dr. Ames started laughing, "Dr. Orlick. We called him Guzzy. Don't know who started that or why. Probably don't want to know. Why are you asking?"

"I have heard that the post mortem samples from William Jarvis's autopsy, his personal effects and his tox screen reports all came up missing. Most people blamed Katrina."

"They aren't missing. I have them." Dr. Ames looked dumbfounded. "Why would they be missing? We didn't flood down here."

Cat couldn't believe his ears. "How did you get them?"

"I always had them. Guzzy said they were too important to leave here. All the mess after Katrina, I suppose. Sent them back to Baton Rouge with me the day he died. I never even looked in the box. Always wondered why nobody asked for them though. Jarvis being such an important man and all."

Cat asked, "Wasn't that unusual? Sending evidence samples to an outside office?"

Dr. Ames nodded his head, "Yeah, well...My office is as secure as this one. That whole day was unusual. Guzzy got more pissed every time the phone rang. All about that Jarvis body, people were rushin' him maybe. He shoved that box at me and told me to go back to Baton Rouge. He said he'd get with me about it later. Never did, rest his soul."

Cat dialed Roger, "Can you send someone from your Baton Rouge office to the Medical Examiner's office there? Dr. Ames claims the reports and samples from William Jarvis are in their storage."

Roger couldn't believe what he was hearing. He asked to speak with Dr. Ames himself to find out specifically where the items were. Roger also told Dr. Ames that he was not to let anyone know the FBI was coming for the box.

Dr. Ames hung up from the call and stared at Cat. "I'm no genius, but I think I just stepped in somethin'."

Cat said, "You might have just become a hero. I'm going to ask you for a favor."

Dr. Ames raised a bushy, white eyebrow and asked, "What favor?"

"Keep this our secret. Hey, I also want to be the first to know these IDs on the cemetery people."

Dr. Ames answered, "That's two favors."

* * *

Sasha walked up to the front door of the Voodoo shop and stared at the man in the black suit guarding the door. More men in black. She leaned out and saw there was a second man standing at the other front door.

Sasha smiled, "You best both step inside right fast. That city water truck be coming around the corner any minute."

The Agent looked confused. Sasha sighed, "They come by here every morning and spray down sidewalks and streets with lemon scented water. 'Bout one hour in this heat and the whole place will smell like lemon puke. You, too, if you don't move it."

The Agent looked around the corner and yelled, "Carl. Get inside."

They no sooner entered the store and what looked like a huge Zamboni turned the corner and sprayed water up to the windows.

Spicey had heard voices and came from her apartment in the back into the store front. She was wearing a long flowing dress with bright colored flowers and a beaded scarf wrapped around her head. A large turkey foot was pinned in the center of her headpiece to rise above the folds of bright fabric. The turkey foot was surrounded by feathers and had two small bells that dangled onto Spicey's forehead. Spicey's bracelets crawled up from her wrist to nearly her elbows. Around her neck were a variety of leather straps with amulets and long gold chains with charms. All of them seeking refuse in her deep cleavage.

Sasha stood looking at her with her mouth open.

Spicey held her arms out, "What? Too much?"

Dakin entered the room looking like a college co-ed. Blue jeans, an old t-shirt and a pink stripe in her hair. She had put on some of Spicey's makeup and fixed her newly cropped hair to have a whimsical shaggy look. She was beautiful.

Sasha mouth stayed open. Finally she spoke, "Can't believe how good a job we did."

One of the agents looked at Sasha and said, "I'm Agent Thompson, FBI. This is Agent Cross. We're here to protect you today."

Sasha giggled, "You ain't here for me. It's the Hoodoo Princess everybody tryin' to kill."

Agent Thompson walked over and extended his hand to Spicey. "So sorry, my mistake."

Spicey frowned, "I ain't Hoodoo! I be Voodoo. Big difference."

319

Spicey pointed at Dakin, "That be your Hoodoo Princess."

Dakin wiggled her fingers in a wave.

CHAPTER 23

Thursday 10:00 am
Ellen had us meet her back at the FBI field office. "Good job in the Bahamas, gals! Sarah, Megan and Chelsy are on a flight home right now. We need to finish sorting out these communications for Roger and Cat. I just sent your transcripts from yesterday to Roger. This morning is going to be very busy with these calls. All the bad guys are just now finding out that the Jarvis case is being reopened. We can't miss a single call. And we can't make any mistakes."

Ellen looked at me.

"What?"

Ellen said, "I want you to listen to this."

She played a piece of Bromley talking to Dooley: "You need an air tight alibi."

I looked at her, "Yeah, so?"

"This is what you wrote down: You need an air flight to Uruguay."

"Close?" Dang. Wish I could hear. I smiled, "Did you fix it?" I had visions of Roger sending a team of FBI agents to the airport. I *thought* Uruguay was a strange place to go.

"I fixed it. Just be careful. If you aren't sure of something, put a question mark next to it, okay?"

Teresa said, "That's how I ended up in Iraq. Won't they see our machines at this table?"

Ellen answered, "No. These are for your benefit. Mortals won't know you're here. They plan on having a meeting soon and I wanted you guys to listen in on that, too."

Mary said, "I like meetings with mortals. My mortal mind still misses them."

Linda nodded agreement and we all had a melancholy moment remembering life before we became angels. I still felt a little guilty that Heaven arranged for Kim to be able to see and hear all of us. Linda, Mary and Teresa didn't have that kind of connection left with their loved ones.

Linda must have been reading my mind. "I go visit Bob and the boys all the time. I leave them little hints I'm still around."

Teresa laughed, "I do that, too! I love picking on Sheila!" Sheila is Teresa's little sister.

Mary looked at Ellen, "I have a feeling that Roger, Paul and Cat might get enough information from these transcripts to piece this mess together."

Ellen shrugged, "It's hard to know what is really helpful and what's just noise. That's really one reason you gals have been so successful. You can still think like mortals."

I didn't want to seem argumentative, but it seemed as if every time I thought like a mortal I got in trouble as an angel.

Ellen pointed at me and smiled, "It's called moderation. That was a term that proved a challenge even before you were an angel." True.

Just then Roger and Paul walked into the conference room and placed files and notebooks on the table. Paul walked over to a large whiteboard and began drawing a chart. "I don't want to completely fill this in until we are done with Ed."

Roger added, "I have a call in to Ed's son, Reuben. I think Cat wants to go public on Ed this afternoon. Reuben should be the one to break the story but after Marla being killed last night, I don't know how he is doing."

I looked at Linda, "Marla was killed? Who's Marla?" Linda shrugged.

Edward Meyer walked in the room with Izzy. "Gentlemen, I would like you to meet my friend, Izzy."

We all went, "Aww."

Mary's eyes twinkled and the elementary school teacher in her beamed. "I bet she's smart, too!"

* * *

Stone listened to his New Orleans contact with disbelief. Finally he said, "It was a suicide mission you gave Acer. Do any of you read or watch TV? They always try to kill the guy in the hospital with a hit man dressed as a doctor. Who's in charge over there?"

The contact responded, "That is precisely why we thought he could succeed. It is so cliché, it would be unexpected. Mr. Marks had only been out of surgery and in his room a few minutes; there was no time for the security people to get into place. Let alone identify who was authorized and who wasn't."

Stone shouted, "Do you hear yourself? Obviously they were prepared or Acer wouldn't be dead. You are dangerously underestimating the FBI." Stone didn't care at this point if he pissed them off. Virgil Holmes was his real boss now.

The contact interrupted Stone's thinking. "Federal evidence storage is a block building on Parish Rd. 42 in Jefferson Parish. I'll forward you the exact location. Many boxes from other facilities were moved there after Katrina for safe keeping. The evidence we need retrieved can be found in the more organized section. I need you to enter the building and subdue the guard. Do you have any G190?"

Stone answered, "Of course."

The contact continued, "Fine. Spray the guard, do not injure him. When he comes to, he won't remember anything. We can't alert anyone that the security there has been compromised. I'll be available, so wear your earpiece. There is only one small box to be retrieved, but I have to obtain the ID number. I'll have it by the time you are in position."

Stone couldn't believe they were going to pay his price for something this menial. "Ordinary evidence storage? I should be insulted. Just send your cop."

The contact paused before answering, "He is no longer an option. This may sound menial, but it is vital. This evidence belongs to 'us' not authorities. It has been purposefully mislabeled and concealed. Authorities will be combing that building sometime today for other items. We cannot risk ours being found. Do you understand?"

Stone considered not taking the assignment at all. It seemed things were heating up for the machine. That wouldn't bear well for him. "Pay me double. I want half transferred before I go. The last half when I turn it over."

"Your demand will be met. Notify me when you are in position."

Stone called Virgil and relayed the assignment given him by the New Orleans contact.

Virgil sounded troubled, "Obviously there is another new problem in New Orleans that I have not been made aware of. Retrieve that evidence box, but get it to me."

* * *

Linda shouted, "This is important! Hello? What do I do?"

Mary looked at Roger talking to Ed and Izzy. She saw Cat and Thor outside the door talking in the hall. Mathew Core was walking into the conference room. Mary went to the white board and guided Paul's hand to write…get Roger to call Kim, hurry.

Paul stared at his hand as it was writing. He knew he wasn't moving it. Paul looked at the board and then Roger. "Uh, Roger? You are supposed to call Kim, now."

"What?" Roger saw what Paul was pointing to on the board. Paul shrugged, erased the board and shook his hand out by his side. Paul was creeped out even though he knew it was angels touching him.

Roger excused himself and called Kim from the other room. "I'm supposed to call you?"

Kim answered, "Yes, Linda has a recording that just came through. She said both you and Cat have to listen to it right now. They are going to send the audio to your computer for you. Roger? Ellen says there will be a lot of audio communications that Cat has to listen to. Ellen says Cat can only piece this together from the angel technology, not yours."

Roger told Kim thanks and turned to his monitor. He wasn't sure how he could convince everyone at the field office and Cat, that the FBI truly was able to capture audio transmissions from both sides of encrypted calls. Out of the corner of his eye he saw Cat in the hall. "Cat, come here a minute. I need you to listen to something."

Roger hit play and they both listened. When it was over Cat asked him to play it again. Roger said,

"I recognize the one voice is Stone Carson. He's one of the hit men we think killed Senator Dalton. I don't know the other two voices."

Cat stood, "I know one of the voices. The other I'm not sure, but it sounds like Virgil Holmes. He's in the National Security Division of the Solicitor General's office. That would certainly explain a couple of things. Can we set a trap at the evidence storage building? I need that box."

Cat asked Roger, "Do you mind if I just work from here for a few? I want to hear what you get and I want to see this evidence the minute it arrives."

Roger nodded yes. Cat wasn't disclosing the identity of the other voice he recognized. Roger had seen that look on Cat's face before. He was on to something. His steel blue eyes now glared with intensity. Roger could almost see Cat's keen mind scheming. Roger thought that for once, the press had gotten something right.

Cat was pacing, "When will we have the Medical Examiner box?"

Roger answered, "Within the hour."

Roger found it fascinating to watch Cat's process. He was sure Cat didn't realize how intense he had become. His body language was purposeful, stealth, cautious. Cat excused himself to make a few calls while he waited for the evidence to arrive. Cat had two theories playing in his mind each dependent on the target, Molly or William. Roger's technology was getting him conversations almost as they were happening. Each conversation seemed to point to a different target.

Mathew Core stuck his head in Roger's office. "Lisa and Jamie should be here any minute. Hope this works for Izzy. Jamie is beside herself to have a playmate."

Roger smiled, "You and your family are being very kind Mathew."

Core chuckled, "I didn't have to sell Lisa at all. Just mention a kid that doesn't have family, and she's all in. It should be fine."

Roger played the message about the evidence locker for Core.

Core asked, "Do you want me to stop Stone and get the box?"

Roger's expression was serious, "I do, but Stone is a high level threat. I want you safe."

Core said, "I'm down a guy with Zack out. There is a guy from the PD I think would do. Can you get him for me?"

"You could have anyone you want from here. Are you sure you want PD?"

Core nodded, "He's SWAT trained and shows promise. Besides, I could probably take Stone alone."

Roger asked, "I'm sure you could. I just don't want to take unnecessary risks. This is a very important box. What's this guy's name?"

Core answered, "Nathan Cottard. You'd be smart to grab him for the FBI."

Roger placed the call to the Police Chief and was assured Nathan would report to the field office shortly. Roger stood and invited everyone to the conference room. "Let's see if we can get Izzy comfortable with Lisa and Jamie."

In the conference room, Jamie and Izzy were already paired off in the corner. Cat paced by the door. He noticed Izzy showing Jamie how to make some origami animals. Cat cautiously walked over to the girls and took a seat across the table from them. Izzy's body immediately stiffened.

Cat smiled, "Izzy, you saved me in the alley a couple of nights ago. Do you remember?"

Izzy nodded her head and stared straight into Cat's eyes.

Cat put his hand out. "Would you allow me to shake your hand and thank you?"

Izzy relaxed and smiled. She put her hand across the table and Cat gently shook it and held it for a minute. Cat looked in Izzy's eyes and said, "You are my friend. You are a very special little girl, Izzy. I want you to call me if you ever need anything."

Izzy asked, "What's your name?"

Cat answered, "Sabastian Delacroix, but my friends call me Cat."

"Cat?" Izzy started to giggle. "That's as funny as Izzy!"

Cat laughed, "Yes it is. Here is a card with my phone number on it. I want you to call me anytime you need *anything*. Even just to talk. We are friends now, do you understand?"

Izzy took the card and put it in her treasure bag. She looked at Cat, "Does your head hurt?" Cat nodded. Izzy asked, "Would you like a hug to make it better?" Cat nodded.

Roger looked over to the corner and saw Izzy walk over to where Cat was sitting and give him a hug. He saw Cat wipe his cheek, stand and walk back out to the hall.

Lisa waved and smiled as the men entered the room. Core walked up to her, kissed her cheek and whispered in her ear. Roger saw Lisa walk over to the girls.

Lisa bent down and spoke in a whisper, "I'd rather go to the mall than stay here. How about you girls? Izzy, you're welcome to come with us."

Izzy was smiling at first and then asked, "My friend, Ed, promised I could go back to his house when his meeting is done."

Lisa asked, "Let's get his approval of our plan then, okay?"

Izzy nodded and Lisa motioned for Ed to come over. When Ed arrived Izzy said, "I have been invited to go to the mall with Jamie. I want to make sure it's the *smart* thing to do."

Ed almost laughed out loud. Izzy certainly knew how to convey her point. Ed whispered, "That will be a lot more fun than this meeting. You have my phone number that you can call when you're ready to come to my house. How's that?"

Izzy stuck out her pinky. Ed curled his pinky around hers.

* * *

Nathan Cottard sat opposite from Gayla in the station house and tried to offer her some comfort. "There's nothing you could have done, Gayla. This isn't your fault."

Gayla blew her nose, tossed that tissue and grabbed another. "Marla wouldn't hurt a fly. I know Dooley did this, Nathan. I know it!"

Mason Dooley entered the room and walked to the water cooler. He glanced at Gayla's desk and saw Nathan sitting with her. Dooley walked over. Nathan muttered, "There's no end to this guy."

Dooley took a drink from his water and smirked. "I hear your little 'stranger' lady got herself killed last night. That couldn't be what you're crying about though, is it? You didn't even know her, remember?" Dooley rapped his knuckles on Gayla's desk twice and walked away.

Gayla looked at Nathan with fear in her eyes. "He knows I lied."

The Department Chief belted from across the room, "Cottard. Get in here."

Nathan patted Gayla's back and walked away. Once inside the Chief's office, he asked, "Sir?"

Chief smiled, "Someone at the FBI likes you. Do you know a Mathew Core?"

Nathan remembered Core was his self-defense instructor and caught him spying on Justice Inspector Ward Bromley. "I know who he is, sir."

"He is requesting you assist him in an FBI assignment."

Nathan beamed, "Really? When, sir?"

"Now." The Chief pointed at him, "You play your cards right this could be a career play for you. The FBI boys in town right now are some of their best. I'm proud you've made this impression for us. Heaven knows we need it."

Nathan thanked the Chief and walked toward the exit door. He couldn't wait to report to the field office and Mathew Core. Someone grabbed his right arm and turned him halfway around.

It was Mason Dooley. "Get your ass in some trouble there, Cottard?" Dooley was grinning.

Nathan yanked his arm free. "Get lost, Dooley." Nathan took a couple of steps, turned and walked back. "And stay away from Gayla."

* * *

CHAPTER 24

Thursday 11:00 am

Agents Thompson and Cross stood inside, near the doors of the Voodoo shop and watched customers come and go. People were lined around the corner to have Ms. Spicey tell them their fortune. Sasha rang up the sales and Dakin had set up a small table where she was wrapping turkey feet, feathers and buffalo hair together with leather straps.

Agent Thompson waited until there were no customers immediately near and asked, "What are those things supposed to do?"

Dakin smiled and said, "These are protectors for anyone who has one. I'm going to give you each one. I want you to take Agents Weaver and Troy each one, too."

Agent Thompson curled his lip a little and flared his nose. "They sort of…stink."

Dakin laughed, "That's just because they're fresh. That will go away after a while and the toes will close in together." She reached in her blouse and pulled a turkey foot on a strap from her cleavage.

She pushed in the center of the turkey foot and the toes separated displaying the long claw nails. "See?"

Agent Thompson nodded slowly, "Yeah, I see."

Agent Cross was snickering across the room. Dakin frowned. Spicey walked out from the back room. "You ain't gonna believe this. My Spirit lady just told me Mambo didn't really put any curse on them bubbas. Said it wasn't necessary, that Dakin be safe now." Spicey looked at the two agents. "You might as well go back to the office. Mambo says we be safe, we be safe."

Dakin looked distressed, "Mambo lied to us?"

Spicey held her finger in the air, "You watch that, girl! We have us a Hoodoo / Voodoo match right here and now! Mambo didn't lie. If you remember, she said she would do what was appropriate. We *assumed* that meant she would put a curse on 'em."

Dakin stood and came within inches of Spicey's face. "Mambo lied. You want a piece of Hoodoo? I can make you fart flames!"

Spicey put her finger up to Dakin's face. "I can turn you into a toad!"

Dakin screamed, "I can fill your face with purple warts!"

Spicey said, "I'll make your nose hairs so long you gotta braid 'em!"

Dakin thought a minute, "You can do that?"

They both started laughing and then hugged each other. Agents Thompson and Cross had been listening in terror. They never had to break up a fight between Hoodoo and Voodoo before.

Sasha laughed at their expressions, "You Men in Black ain't used to Cajun women fights, are ya?" She slapped her knee. "I best go outside and thin that crowd. We ain't wantin' to work through lunch time."

Sasha had only been gone a few minutes when she ran back through the door screaming. "Them bubbas be parkin' down the street. We be only two Voodoo shops away from 'em comin' here."

Sasha looked at the agents, "Get your guns ready! It's gonna get Nawlens nasty!"

* * *

The whisper microphone was barely visible in Stone's ear, hidden by tufts of his light brown hair. Naked bulbs hung from long wires. They illuminated three foot spots of light down the center of the long, dark hall. On either side of the walkway stood tall metal cages stacked with evidence boxes and secured with industrial padlocks. Stone needed to locate the guard and neutralize him in order to properly search for the box.

The voice of Stone's New Orleans contact came over his earpiece. "Can you see the guard?"

Stone whispered, "No."

Stone made his way to the end of one long aisle and grimaced at the length of the building.

He was hoping to find the guard asleep in a chair somewhere. He only needed a few seconds to spray him to guarantee at least thirty minutes of uninterrupted search time. Stone froze in position, the hairs on his neck signaled danger. He turned his head to look behind him. Searing pain flashed across the back of his neck and the world went black.

Mathew Core reached down to retrieve the earpiece and whispered, "Guard down."

A slight pause was followed with, "F 496."

Core whispered, "Copy."

Core removed the earpiece, pried the back off and flipped a round chip from the tiny chamber. Core cuffed Stone to the iron fencing of the evidence locker. He removed Stone's weapon and saw the G190 spray and called Cottard over.

"See this? Gives you a half hour while they sleep. When they wake up they don't remember anything. They didn't want anyone to know they had been here."

He turned to Nathan, "Check him for a cuff key. He has one. He'll only be out for a minute."

Core left to search for the evidence box. Cottard found the cuff key and put it in his pocket.

Stone stayed on the floor and waited until Core's footsteps were some distance away. Stone pulled the second cuff key from where it was taped to the center of his back. He unlocked the cuffs and watched Cottard through a narrow slit of his closed eyes. Cottard had nervously moved to the side and stared down the long hall after Core.

Stone landed a blow to the back of Cottard's neck, and went after Core.

Core had located the box. He dialed Roger.

Roger answered, "You have Stone?"

"Got him, and I have the box."

Roger had asked Thor and Jeanne to wait near the site and assist in transport once Stone was caught. Roger called Thor, "They have him."

Core sensed Stone before he saw him. His training kicked in and he was on automatic pilot. Core tossed the box across the room, crouched and spun around. Stone was leaping toward him with a lethal kick aimed at Core's head.

Core let the kick pass through and quickly leaped behind Stone and landed a crushing blow on Stone's neck and then on Stone's right forearm. Stone grimaced and came back at Core with a series of blows to Core's upper body. Core wasn't expecting Stone to switch out techniques and it nearly took him down. Stone was extremely strong and fought with a warrior's fierceness.

Core stopped Stone's next punch and pushed back on Stone's fist to twist Stone against the wall. Core's forearm was pressing against Stone's neck. Core could feel Stone's torso twisting and he knew Stone's left arm would soon be free. Stone did a full body twist and landed Core against the wall. Now Stone's forearm was on Core's neck.

Suddenly Stone pulled away, stepped back, his hands in the air.

Core was panting, looked around Stone to see Nathan Cottard with a gun pointed on the back of Stone's neck.

Core leaned forward and spit on the concrete floor, "What the hell took you so long?"

Stone spun turned around to face Cottard. Core yelled, "Shit!" the very instance Stone took the gun away from Cottard and fired.

The gun had jammed.

Jeanne's voice came from the side, "Drop it, Stone."

* * *

Cat marveled at the technology the FBI apparently had now. He was reviewing transcripts and listening to captured cell conversations. Both sides of the conversations on burn phones with encrypted SIM cards. Amazing. He had taken over a small office at the FBI field office, so he would be there when the evidence boxes arrived from the medical examiner and from the evidence storage locker.

Cat had spent the last hour scouring the financial records of Dillard Boggs. He did find several sizable payments to Mason Dooley for services rendered. One was for ten thousand dollars and a month prior to Molly's murder. It became obvious fairly quickly that Boggs ran several sets of books designed to obscure the true nature of his transactions. It was looking like Boggs may have hired Dooley to kill Molly. Dooley may have just decided on his own to set up the first guy he came across that night. It just happened to be Ed.

Roger knocked lightly on the door and walked in. "I have a couple of new transcripts and audios for you."

Cat said, "I want to hear the audio first."

Roger watched Cat's expressions as he listened. "I can tell that you are piecing this together. It still has me stumped what half of these conversations have to do with the Jarvis case. This is your baby. I'm going to feed you information and do what you ask of me."

Cat smiled, "I appreciate that." Cat stood and began pacing again. "I'm still missing a part. Obviously, the machine, as Ed would put it, is done with Dooley. That was a pretty clear hit order to Ward Bromley. It sounds like he's being told to do it personally."

Roger agreed, "I think you're right and I don't think it's normally Bromley's job to get that dirty."

"Agreed."

Roger said, "We have enough to arrest Dooley now. Forensics came back on that shirt. We have Steven Marks blood all over it."

Cat spoke through his hands as he messaged his temples. "How do people end up this callous?"

Roger stood to leave, "I don't know how callous Dooley really is. He actually mumbled he wanted his mom when he was in holding last night. I think the thought of going to prison terrifies him. I think this group he's mixed up with terrifies him."

Roger left the room and Cat started clicking his pen. Cat entered the public records data base, entered a few names to the search engine and waited. His index finger rested on his upper lip as he narrowed the dates on his search even further. Finally he saw proof of what he suspected. Cat stood and looked out the window to the bustling traffic below.

Steven Marks had been right all along. *William* had been the target. Cat and Steven looking at the Jarvis files is what started all of these conversations. Roger's case on Senator Dalton and Senator Welsh shared some common players. Ed's manifesto crept back into Cat's mind.

Mathew Core and Nathan Cottard walked past Cat's door heading for Roger. They were carrying a small box. Behind them an FBI courier carried a larger box. Cat followed them all to Roger's office. For Cat, this was it. This would be the moment of truth.

Roger knew Cat wanted to review the items first. Roger signaled for Core and Cottard to follow him to the conference room. Roger handed Core a piece of paper. "Raise your right hand and read that."

Core did. Roger swore him in as a representative of the FBI.

"This is the arrest warrant for Mason Dooley. We have proof he was the shooter of Steven Marks."

Nathan's jaw dropped. Roger looked at Nathan, "Do you have a problem arresting a fellow officer?"

Nathan put his shoulders back, "Not this one, sir."

Core and Cottard left.

Roger signaled Paul and they joined Cat in Roger's office. Cat was sitting at the desk with a very serious expression on his face.

Roger asked, "Anything there that helps you?"

Cat glanced over to Roger, "Oh, yes. Tox report on William Jarvis shows extremely elevated levels of insulin. The box has post mortem tissue and blood samples."

Roger asked, "Was he diabetic?"

Cat answered, "Not according to his medical history. The Medical Examiner also saved a skin graft of the needle injection site from Williams's neck."

Paul declared, "Neck? Then it was murder."

Cat nodded, "Yes."

Cat pointed to the small box that he had opened. In that box was a hypodermic needle and a piece of paper. The piece of paper was a confession for both murders of Molly and William Jarvis. It was signed. The guilty party acknowledged Williams DNA would be found on the needle in addition to the confessor's fingerprints. Cat handed the paper to Roger.

Roger read it and handed it to Paul. Paul sighed, "Dear Lord."

Cat looked at Roger, "Now I'm ready."

* * *

Ed had just hung up from talking to Izzy. She was having a blast at the mall and asked if she could stay with Lisa and Jamie longer. Lisa had told Ed she was going to go grocery shopping and let the girls make cookies. She also suggested that Izzy was welcome to spend the night if she wanted. Ed had been so happy listening to Lisa describe how well Izzy and Jamie got along, he had forgotten about his own life.

Reuben placed a call to his dad. "Dad? The FBI says we can go public now about you being alive and innocent. They asked we wait until this afternoon. Dad? Did you hear?"

"Today? This is great." Ed's sat down and took a deep breath. This was the last big step. Reuben sounded so happy for him. Ed remembered what Roger had said about Marla. "Son, are you okay? I heard about your friend, Marla. I'm so sorry. I feel guilty about getting you involved in all of this…"

"Dad, stop it. Marla is, was, a wonderful person. She had a mind of her own. I'm going to miss her. She was becoming very special…" Reuben's voice broke, "to me. We have waited four years for this day for you. You can have your life back. Don't be thinking about me, I want you to enjoy this."

Ed felt a pang of guilt. He didn't deserve a son like Reuben. Ed tried to lighten the mood. "I hear you have a roommate now?"

Reuben chuckled, "Dang dog got in the shower with me this morning. Loves water! Kept nippin' at the spray. Scared me to death I was going to get bit."

* * *

Agent Thompson looked at Dakin, "Did you file a police report when these two attacked you?"

Dakin shook her head and said, "I haven't had time."

Thompson looked at Cross, "All she has to do is point them out and we can arrest them. Let's do this outside."

Sasha was hopping up and down. "Spicey, Mambo was right! We don't need no curse, we got Men in Black!"

Agent Cross shook his head. "You gals walk with us to where these guys are and point them out. We'll take it from there."

Spicey turned around, grabbed something and dropped it in her pocket.

Claude and Earl were just leaving the Voodoo shop next door to Spicey's and walking toward them. Dakin pointed, "That's them!" Dakin quickly jumped behind Sasha and grabbed the back of Sasha's dress.

Sasha waved her arms trying to shoo Dakin away. "Don't you be hidin' yourself behind me."

Claude and Earl looked at each other and then at Agents Thompson and Cross. Agent Thompson walked up to Earl. "Put your hands behind your back."

Claude and Earl both stepped back and stared at Dakin's face peeking from behind Sasha's dress.

Claude pointed at Dakin, "What does she mean, 'that's them'? I ain't never seen that girl in my whole life!"

Spicey stepped forward and dangled the wind chime Dakin had made from her long contorted black nails. "This here spurt your memory?"

Earl moaned, "Uh, oh."

Claude spun around and started running. He was nearly to Betty Sue when Agent Cross yelled, "Stop or I'll shoot." Claude opened the truck door, jumped in and Betty Sue let out a loud cough. Then the motor started. Claude pulled a shotgun from the floorboard and put Betty Sue in reverse.

Agent Cross jumped out the way. Claude pointed the gun at him and pumped the slide to load. "You drop that gun, pretty boy."

Agent Cross let his gun drop to the pavement and put his hands up. Agent Thompson had his gun drawn and yelled for everyone on the sidewalk to get back. Spicey grabbed Sasha before she could faint. Earl started to run toward the truck. Spicey grabbed his overalls and tossed him to the sidewalk. She sat squarely on his back and yelled for Sasha to come help. Sasha walked over; her eyes rolled back and she fainted. Her midsection landed right next to Spicey on Earl's back.

Spicey shrugged, "Weren't too graceful, but that'll work."

Dakin ran into the center of the street, right past Agent Thompson and right in front of Agent Cross. She put her hands out in front of her and began chanting and hissing at Claude.

Claude screamed, "Get away from me, you crazy witch."

He was mesmerized by her chanting that got louder and faster. His gun barrel began to shake.

Claude didn't notice Agent Thompson approach the truck from the passenger side. Thompson whistled. Claude turned his head to see Thompson's gun pointing at his head. Agent Cross grabbed the shotgun when Claude turned.

Claude was dragged from the truck, cuffed and sat on the pavement waiting for a patrol unit to respond. Earl had been released by Spicey and Sasha, cuffed and placed next to Claude. Sasha had assigned herself to do crowd control and Spicey was handing out business cards. Thompson saw the patrol unit approaching and moved toward the tailgate. He looked at Betty Sue's face and marveled that someone would actually do their truck that way.

He glanced past Betty Sue and noticed a wallet lying in the bed of the truck. He carefully climbed up, retrieved the wallet and opened it. There was no money, but the driver's license was for Judge Ingle. That name he knew. Looked like the bubbas had a lot of explaining to do.

* * *

Mathew Core let Nathan Cottard walk into the police station first. Core told Nathan on the way over he could make the arrest. Gayla noticed Cottard walk in and she gave a little wave. Core and Cottard walked over to her desk and Cottard asked, "Where's Dooley?"

A voice from across the room belted, "Over here. What do you want?"

Mason Dooley was leaning against the water cooler. A few of his friends stood near him.

Cottard walked over and stood in front of him. "Turn around and put your hands behind your back. I have an FBI warrant. You are under arrest for the attempted murder of Senior Assistant Attorney General, Steven Marks."

Dooley shouted, "This is bullshit! You're not arresting me."

Cottard squared his shoulders, "Please resist."

Dooley's friends started moving toward Cottard. Core stepped forward. "You men step back." Core's expression left no doubt they should listen.

The group looked at Core and looked at the determination on Cottard's face. They stepped back. Dooley pushed Cottard's chest and screamed, "You're gonna have to earn it boy."

Cottard flipped Dooley to the floor, placed his knee on the back of Dooley's neck and started cuffing him. Dooley tried to flip over, Cottard put his other knee on the small of Dooley's back and yanked Dooley's arm towards his shoulder blades. "I wouldn't go there."

Dooley stopped resisting and Cottard yanked him to his feet. "Let's go."

The Department Chief stepped out of his office and smiled. He had been watching from his observation window. Roger had alerted him to the arrest warrant and the Chief had agreed to keep Dooley at the station until they got there. The Chief beamed with pride at how professional Cottard handled the arrest. Yep, he had a good one there.

Gayla jumped up from her chair and cheered. She couldn't contain it any longer. She yelled at Dooley through tears, "They're gonna get you for Marla, too!"

Nathan Cottard looked at Gayla and smiled.

CHAPTER 25

Ellen had us chase down Ward Bromley. We found him sitting in his car in the police station parking lot. He was parked next to Dooley's car and on his cell phone. The transmitter Thor placed in Bromley's watch was picking up both sides of the conversation. Teresa shouted, "He's being told to shoot Dooley now. Right in the middle of his arrest!"

Mary hit the alert button on her watch to send live transmissions directly to Roger's cell phone. Roger saw the alert and listened. Roger heard Ward Bromley say, "I don't kill people. You know what? I'm done."

Bromley looked in the rearview mirror at his refection. He had done a lot of illegal things for the machine, but he was not a murderer. They would either protect him because of what he knew, or not.

Roger called Core. "You have Bromley in the parking lot. He was just ordered to shoot Dooley, but he probably won't do it. I want Bromley too, since he's there. We have plenty on him."

Core couldn't figure out how Roger knew the things he did, but he learned a long time ago not to question it. Core looked at Cottard. "We're going out the back door. Grab keys to a cruiser."

One of Cottard's fellow officers had been listening and threw a set of keys at him. "Take mine. It's right at the back door."

Core looked at the other officer, "Go with him." Core looked at Cottard, "I'm getting Bromley."

Core looked out a side window of the station and saw Bromley in his car. There wasn't any way to sneak up on him. He had backed into a space and parked along a fence row. Linda said, "I'm reading Mathew Core's mind. He knows Bromley is here. He's not sure how to get to him."

I had an idea, "Remember when we turned into animals? Maybe we could just turn into monkeys and take Bromley's gun away."

Linda looked at me. "He will shoot us."

Mary said, "We're already dead. Nobody will see us except him if we do this right."

Teresa asked, "Why do we have to turn into monkeys? Can't we just take his gun away?"

Hmmm. Monkeys would be more fun. Teresa is just too practical.

I was trying to come up with a good answer when Teresa yelled from Bromley's car. "He's not going to do it."

Bromley was sitting in his car with his hands up.

Linda said, "Mathew Core is watching him."

Bromley threw his gun out the window. Core went to the driver door, threw it open and stated, "You're under arrest!"

Bromley stepped out of the car and put his hands behind his back. Core cuffed him and walked him back to Core's car. Core cuffed him to the cage in the back, and grabbed the gun from the pavement.

Core looked to the back seat through his rearview mirror as his car left the parking lot. "Seems to me you'd be curious what I'm arresting you for."

Bromley answered, "Does it matter? It won't stick."

Core chuckled, "Do you know who wants you arrested?"

Bromley shrugged, "I'm telling you it doesn't matter. Do you know who I am?"

Core shrugged, "Yes. A cockroach. When you're gone, a thousand more will replace you."

* * *

Nathan knocked lightly on Roger's door. Roger looked up. "Good, you're back. Where's Core?"

Cottard answered, "He's bringing in Ward Bromley. They should be here any minute, sir."

Cottard stood silent a moment.

Roger asked, "Was there something else?"

Cottard asked, "Could there be a place for me with the FBI, sir?"

Roger opened a desk drawer and took out three pages stapled together. "Here. I have already filled out the sponsor section. Mathew Core said you would ask for it. Your application for internship is now sponsored. Have someone here help you fill out the rest. This would start you in the program. There are extensive educational requirements. You can satisfy them while working an intern position. Read all of this carefully, it takes a long time and it's a lot of work. If you decide to proceed, we would be honored to have you, Nathan."

Roger stood and extended his hand. Nathan Cottard shook it aggressively, "Thank you, sir. Thank you." He backed out of the office and Roger heard him let out a yelp down the hall.

Paul stuck his head in the office doorway, "Remember when we thought this was fun?"

Roger smiled, "Bromley here?"

"Yep."

Roger called Cat. "Bromley and Dooley are in holding if you want them."

Cat answered, "I do. Say, Dillard Boggs says his alibi for the night Molly Jarvis was murdered is Mason Dooley. He claims Dooley was by his side all night at the nightclub. Since we know that is a lie, I want Boggs to make a formal written statement so we can charge him later for lying. No big deal, but I think Molly would like it."

* * *

Thursday 3:00 pm

Cat spent ten minutes asking Ward Bromley questions he wouldn't answer. Roger knocked on the observation window. Cat excused himself and joined Roger. Roger handed Cat a recorder.

Roger smiled, "I have the conversations you wanted recorded in the order you wanted. Your Solicitor General has arrested a member of his National Security staff as the contact in his office. The Solicitor General negotiated a deal with him that includes anonymity and witness protection in exchange for names and testimony. You were correct about it being Virgil Holmes. Here are your names for the New Orleans people."

Cat winced at the names on the paper. "This time I was hoping to be wrong."

Cat walked into the room with Bromley again and stated, "I'm going to write down two names. You confirm your relationship to them and their involvement in the death of William and Molly Jarvis. If you cooperate, we may be able to deal."

Cat took out his recorder. "Before you decide, let me enlighten you to today's FBI technology. Were you aware that secure, encrypted SIM cards on burn phones could actually be recorded? Amazing. Both sides of the conversation, too."

Roger listened from the observation room and hoped that was really true somewhere in their intelligence network. Right now Cat was using angel technology.

Cat clicked off the recorder. Bromley was pale after listening. "Would you like to hear the one about the cemetery bodies or the dead girl named Marla? Maybe you'd like the one where you encouraged Acer to stay on point with the machine, forgive them for the bomb at the hotel. I like that one. Machine. Sounds unstoppable, doesn't it?"

Bromley dropped his chin and looked up to Cat's eyes. "What kind of deal are we talking?"

"I'm afraid it's not a very good one. Oh, I forgot to show you the names." Cat slipped the piece of paper across to Bromley.

Bromley read the names and looked up. "So, now you know."

* * *

Roger played Mason Dooley the tape of the hit being ordered on him. Dooley pushed his chair back and stood. "That's a lie. That's a trick. That would never happen!" Roger played it again. Dooley had his head in his hands.

Dooley sat back down and looked up, "Can I deal?"

Roger shrugged, "You know, I doubt it. It's not up to me though. We have you cold for attempted murder of Steven Marks, the murder of Marla Wilson, Judge Ingle, six bodies in the cemetery and who knows how many more? We have you, Dooley. Why would we deal?"

Roger left Dooley in holding and joined Paul in the hall. "I think Cat is close to wrapping up."

Cat walked up to Paul and Roger. "I have all I need. I need you guys to follow me."

Roger answered, "Our pleasure. We'll wait in your lobby for the call. Give me a time frame for the TV station."

Cat answered, "An hour?"

Roger watched Cat leave the room and slap open the double doors to the outside. Cat's body language told Roger that Cat was troubled by what he was about to do.

Paul looked at Roger, "There goes a man with a lot on his mind. How do you think he'll handle it?"

"Cat's going in for the kill."

* * *

Reuben and Ed sat on the set of the news station. The station manager was beside himself. "Reuben, can't you at least give me a hint what this is about? For God's sake, the FBI called me to arrange this thing. It must be huge!"

Reuben smiled at his dad and whispered, "Should we tell him?"

Ed nodded. Reuben crooked his index finger for the station manager to come close. "Swear you'll keep this secret? This is my dad, Edward Meyer. Federal authorities are announcing all charges have been dropped against him for the murder of Molly Jarvis. They are going to announce a new arrest today, too. Let me guest anchor this part of the six o'clock news and your station can have it first."

The station manager stood with his mouth open. "Edward Meyer? You're dead."

Ed smiled, "Evidently not."

The station manager looked at Reuben. "Hell yes you can guest anchor!"

CHAPTER 26

C at arrived at his office at exactly four thirty pm. He glanced around to see who was there. The addition of the new attorneys and their staffs had certainly increased the amount of activity. Martha frowned at him. "You told me this morning you'd be out a couple of hours." Martha tapped her watch face.

Cat remembered. "I guess you could say I got sidetracked. Sorry." He winked at her and she shook her head. "You know the stack of messages on your desk is in two piles now. Urgent and he better call me now or else."

Cat laughed. He could only imagine the number of rumors circulating by now. Jarvis case reopened, Steven Marks's assassination attempt, William Jarvis's body exhumed and Mason Dooley and their investigator, Ward Bromley, arrested. Quite a day and it wasn't over.

Ted walked out of his office, "Thank God, you're back. Can I talk to you for a minute?"

Ted didn't look very happy. Cat tilted his head toward his office, "Sure."

Cat sat down and Ted opened a file folder. "I just received this request for representation from Investigator Ward Bromley. He works out of this office, Cat. Evidently he has been arrested by the FBI."

Cat nodded, "Yes, he has."

Ted sat back, "You're not surprised? What did he do?"

Cat frowned, "Not as much as you."

"Pardon me?"

Cat hit the buzzer, "Martha, could you join us, please?"

Ted looked puzzled. Martha came in and took a seat in the corner, flipped her notebook and nodded she was ready. She assumed Cat wanted her to take notes.

"Ted, I'm not going to bother to Mirandize you. The FBI will do that in a few minutes. I just want a record of exactly what I am going to say." Cat held up a recorder. "I'm recording, Martha, I just want you to hear this." Cat smiled at her. Martha was in an obvious state of shock at what she was hearing.

Cat looked at Ted. "This is what happened the night Molly Jarvis died. You picked up a car that had been stolen by Mason Dooley and left in a pre-arranged spot. You drove to the Jarvis house, shot Molly three times and wiped some of her blood on a rag. You returned the stolen car to where you picked it up. Left the bloody rag and gun in the car. Dooley drove the car to the alley where he injected Ed Meyer, wiped blood on him and the car, and put Meyer's fingerprints on the gun."

Ted laughed, "You've gone mad." Ted nervously glanced at Martha.

Cat continued, "Once Molly was buried, you nurtured William's grief to gain his trust. On the night he died, you drove to his house and injected him with a fatal dose of insulin. Then you took his hand, placed it on the revolver and pulled the trigger. You know what really gets me? I have a seven a.m., time stamped photo, of your car parked in William's parking spot. It's in this building, the morning his body was discovered. You knew he wasn't coming in, and you wanted that spot. Still have it, don't you?"

Ted stood. "You *are* mad. Why in the world would I kill William?"

Cat pointed to Martha, "Because she told you to."

Ted sat down and Martha stood up. "What?"

Cat frowned at her and raised his voice, "Sit!"

Martha sat down.

"I can prove everything I'm saying with enough evidence that a first year trial attorney could win these cases. I want to do this myself though."

Cat looked at Martha, "Your own son. Mason Dooley. You ordered a hit on him less than two hours ago. Don't bother denying it. We have it recorded. Your 'secret contact' at the Solicitor General's office, Ward Bromley, and your baby boy will testify to everything you've done."

Martha's facial expression began to change to a sneer. Her brows pushed forward and she snarled, "You have no idea what you're up against."

Cat leaned back in his chair and looked at his watch. "Darn! Toss me that remote."

Martha tossed him the remote and looked at him as if he was mad.

Cat turned on the TV to the interview. "Remember that guy? It was actually his crazy political rants that solved this case."

Ted went pale. "That's Edward Meyer. How...?"

On the TV the voices of Reuben and Edward filled Cat's office:

Reuben asked Ed the question, "Why do you think you were chosen as the scape goat in this plan?"

Ed had a thoughtful look on his face and answered, "I could do a two hour lecture of how a complacent society allows injustices. The real reason I was chosen was because I dared to challenge conventional thinking." Ed looked in the camera and pointed his finger. "Conventional thinking is simply the palatable term for the machine's design. Nurtured, bought and paid for." Ed looked at Reuben, "Ask the tough questions until you get a logical answer."

Reuben smiled, "Give me an example of an unanswered tough question." He knew his dad had baited him.

Ed smiled. "That's easy. Look in the sky at the sun. Then ask yourself why we drill our earth. Then think of who benefits from not answering that question."

Cat shut the TV off. "Martha, your job has been to watch me. Not watch out for me. Ted, you thought the machine would never let you down. You waited eight years for this Governorship and you proved you earned it. Remember the evidence they insisted you give them? The insulin needle with your fingerprints and William's DNA? Pretty good stuff. I have it now."

Martha went pale. Cat pushed a button on his cell phone. "Guess we're ready."

Ted leaned forward, "Cat. You have to listen. They made me do it. Let's deal."

Martha frowned at Ted, "Stupid coward. Shut your mouth."

Cat looked at Ted. "I don't deal, remember? I'm the office litigator, Ted. We go to court."

Cat looked at Martha, "Know when I first thought of you? The night you brought food to my apartment, I checked my activity log in the morning and guess what? My computer had been on while I was in the hospital. Only one person other than me knows my passcode. You have obviously operated under the premise you were protected from consequences." Cat pushed his chair back and sighed. Martha's contorted facial expression revealed her true personality.

Cat was staring at pure evil. "I actually lost track of how many murders you have ordered. The arrogance of power. Or was it the money? You have accumulated a nice little nest egg of that, too. In your maiden name, of course. Stupid mistake for such a smart lady. But hey, you make great soup. You should be real popular in the prison kitchen."

Roger and Paul appeared in the door and Paul started reading Ted and Martha their rights. Cat twisted in his chair and laid his pen down. He felt used and betrayed. Ted and Martha had been his work family for almost eight years. Cat's entire adult life was about bringing justice to the guilty, and some measure of closure to the victims. As good as it felt to see Ted and Martha arrested he knew they would never pay a just price for all of the pain they had caused. He also knew there were more where they had come from.

Roger knocked on the door to get Cat's attention. "Moving on?"

Cat nodded. He listened to the elevator close down the hall and looked out to Martha's empty desk. Damn it. She had been the best secretary he ever had. It sent a chill down his spine that she had watched his every move for eight years. Eight years of making sure he stayed wrapped up in litigation and insulated from the real workings of her partners. Cat wadded up the list of points he had prepared, rolled his chair away from his desk and tossed the paper wad into the wastebasket across the room.

Nailed it!

* * *

Cat looked at his watch. He had to hurry. He arrived at the TV station just as Reuben and Ed finished their segment. Cat walked over and congratulated Ed on his coming out.

"Say, if you have a minute, I'd like to talk to you." Cat pointed toward an empty office that was used as a waiting room.

Ed said, "Sure. Should Reuben stay, too?"

Cat shrugged, "It's up to you."

Reuben announced he wanted to get back to the Times-Picayune office and prepare his story about his dad being alive.

Ed and Cat sat across from each other at a small, round table. Cat shook his head. "Well, thanks to you,we have William's murderer." Ed smiled. Cat continued. "You know, I kept asking myself why a man as smart as you would agree to become invisible. Then, it hit me. Money, of course." Cat pulled out a bank statement from his briefcase. He looked up at Ed, "Lots of money. From what I can see about eight million dollars. Original deposit date one week before your arrest."

Ed started to squirm in his seat. "What is that? You have my bank statement? What are you getting at?"

Cat leaned back in his chair, "It was your idea! You were the one that understood how the machine really worked. You were going to beat them at their own game. You figured out how to earn eight million dollars from them and set them up to take the fall. All you had to do was wait until they were ready to put Ted in office."

"You approached Ted with a foolproof plan to end up the Governor. You told him he would have to 'make his bones', your words. You also knew he was a weakling and would need you as a partner to stay on task.

"You've watched the local machine for years, closely, and knew exactly who to approach. You offered up a U.S. Attorney General that would do what they wanted and you got rid of William, who they feared. At next election, in eight years, the machine would have a Governor they had murder evidence on. Ted was a sitting duck. He would have no choice but to do anything they asked of him. And you got paid eight million dollars for a month in jail and your willingness to be set up for Molly's murder.

"You had to plan your way out through this whole thing. You put yourself in that alley. You made sure Dooley parked where it would be 'caught' on Otis's video. Of course, they had to promise you that you would escape soon, somehow. That was the weak link wasn't it? Getting out of prison and not being killed by the machine. Katrina was a blessing! You could become dead. All you had to do was stay invisible until Ted ran for office. There are still fourteen prisoners missing from that transfer during Katrina. It was perfect."

Cat rearranged himself in his chair. "I can't believe you convinced Ted he had to give them proof he killed Molly and William. I'm sure they sent someone with Ted to make sure he really did it and collect the evidence. At that moment, Ted became *your* patsy. Then you could play it exactly the way you did. Bravo."

Cat wasn't smiling, his eyes focused like lasers on Ed's. As much as he had hoped Ed was innocent, he knew that Molly and William Jarvis died as pawns in Ed's ego driven plot.

Ed looked spent, "It was almost brilliant, wasn't it? I can see where I made one mistake though. I assumed you couldn't figure it out, the part about me. What gave me away?"

"You did, Ed. The way you think, the scheme of things. Ted isn't that smart. Just now in your interview you said, 'Ask the tough questions until you get a logical answer'. You were the only one bright enough to have pulled this off. You are the logical answer."

Ed shrugged, "The irony is I hated them so much I became one of them."

Cat shook his head, "The irony is you traded everything you had for nothing. You used everyone that cared about you, especially Reuben. He had to believe, didn't he? You let him think you were dead for four years. You couldn't stand it anymore, you needed attention. You needed someone to know you weren't invisible. You felt sorry for yourself even though it was all your own doing. You could have stopped right there. For you, it was still more important to take down a piece of the machine. You had to push it to the end. You would have gotten away with eight million dollars if you had stayed invisible."

Ed actually chuckled, "You had me go on national TV. Brilliant. You had *me* prove I was alive."

Cat shrugged, "I can't prosecute a dead man."

Cat pushed the cell button to call Roger, "We're ready now."

Cat looked at Ed, "You might consider calling Izzy."

Ed winced, "I'll do that right now."

Cat was impressed with how Ed handled the situation. He was truthful and told Izzy he wasn't as smart as he thought he was. He confessed to her that he had done something very wrong years ago. He asked Izzy to give the FBI and Mathew, Lisa and Jamie time to help her with a plan.

Ed hung up, "That may have been the worse part of this."

Cat reminded Ed he still had to talk to Reuben.

Ed talked to Reuben for a few minutes and then handed the phone to Cat. "He hung up. I think I have disappointed him beyond repair."

Cat said, "I'll make a point of meeting with Reuben soon. Not for you, for him."

Roger had Paul cuff Ed and lead him from the building.

Roger shook his head, "How did you ever piece together that it was Ed's plan?"

Cat answered, "I had his help all the way."

CHAPTER 27

The Solicitor General placed a call to Virgil Holmes's office.

Virgil answered, "Yes, sir?"

The Solicitor General stated, "There are two armed security agents that will arrive at your office shortly to escort you to my office. I respectfully request that you comply with their orders."

"Sir?"

"You're done."

The Solicitor General leaned back in his chair and smiled. It wasn't often enough his job proved this satisfying.

* * *

Thursday 6:00 pm

The six o'clock news led with the story of Theodore Dupre, U.S. Attorney General, arrested for the 2005 murders of Mary and William Jarvis. FBI spokesperson Supervisory Special Agent Frank Mass, confirmed that several other officials at Justice were also facing charges.

"In other news, the Senate failed to pass a bill that would have capped the liabilities of entities guilty of causing environmental damage. Given credit for the bill's failure to pass was Senator Welsh of Louisiana. He was quoted as saying, "It was the right thing to do." The Senator's critics have promised he will face a fierce uphill battle in his next election."

The TV anchor holding the microphone for the six o'clock news was Reuben Florey, reporter for the Times-Picayune. Reuben looked in the camera and stated, "Mr. Edward Meyers, my father, announced today he is alive and no longer a suspect in the murder of Molly Jarvis. He will, however, be facing a number of federal charges stemming from that incident. My father corrupted himself in his fight against corruption. Suspended New Orleans police officer, Mason Dooley, is being charged with the attempted murder of Senior Assistant Attorney General, Steven Marks, and is under investigation for the murder of Marla Wilson. Marla was a very dear friend of this reporter."

The camera man signaled they were off the air and then stated, "Man, that had to be hard to report."

Reuben sighed, "About my dad? I think a part of me always knew."

* * *

Roger and Paul had stopped at the diner near the field office for jambalaya. Thor, Jeanne, Nelson and Pablo had joined them. Pablo held up his glass for a toast. "Another well played team effort."

Everyone raised their glasses. Thor looked at Roger, "I didn't realize our technology had come so far in the last year."

Roger glanced at Paul and then answered, "I think it is one of those things that will continue to evolve. We probably don't know the half of it when it comes to surveillance. It helps to have the right contacts."

Paul pushed his chin out in his nervous twitch.

Jeanne reached over and squeezed Pablo's hand. "Stay safe, you leaving tonight?"

Pablo nodded.

Nelson looked at Thor and Jeanne. "That's what I want. Right there."

Jeanne blushed. Thor nodded. "*This* is livin' the dream." Jeanne kissed his cheek.

Roger was so inspired he called Kim right from the table, "I'm coming home tonight. Love you."

Paul looked around the room, "Damn, guess I gotta quit horsin' around."

Thor signaled another toast.

* * *

Thursday 8:00 pm

Reuben stood outside waiting for Maddie to do her business. Instead she barked at him and scuffed at the grass. "What do you want? I don't know dog talk." Reuben had picked up a leash at the grocery store when he had stopped to get dog food. Exercise really wasn't his thing, but he knew dogs had to be walked. "I don't know how you figured out what this is, but come here."

Reuben had decided that his father's crimes belonged to his father. He was tired of lies. What he was determined to have was a fresh start.

Maddie wiggled up to him and he attached the hook on the leash. Maddie took off running down the sidewalk. Reuben had missed grabbing her leash and was frantic. Traffic was heavy and he saw Maddie turn the corner way ahead.

"Damn it all." Reuben turned the corner at full speed and ran into a pretty woman holding Maddie. Maddie was licking her chin.

"Hi. I seem to have your dog. She just jumped into my arms." The lady handed the end of the leash to Reuben and lowered Maddie on the sidewalk.

Reuben smiled, "Thank you. She got away from me."

The lady held out her hand, "My name is Diane. You must be taking her to the dog park?"

Reuben shrugged, "Where's that?"

Diane smiled, "Just down the way a block or so. I'll walk with you if you want?"

Reuben smiled, "Sure."

Maddie stopped, looked back at him and barked twice.

Reuben looked at Diane, "I think she is telling me to hurry up."

They walked about a block when Diane said, "You know I lost a very dear friend yesterday. She had a dog just like yours."

Reuben stopped, "Marla?"

Diane gasped. "Yes!"

* * *

Core stopped by the hospital to visit Zack. Zack was sitting in the bed with a food tray in front of him. His chest was heavily bandaged and he had IV's in both arms. A wall of monitors beeped along at a steady pace.

Core walked over, "You going to eat the pudding?"

Zack shook his head, "Help yourself."

Core asked, "Taking two in the chest messed up your day didn't it?"

Zack answered, "The doctors thought a paid month or two in the Bahamas was probably the best medicine." They both laughed and Core brought Zack up on the events of the day.

"That's all?" It hurt Zack to laugh, but he did anyway. "I'm telling you, whenever Roger Dance comes to town I want to know ahead of time. We should both leave. Deal?"

Core smiled, "Deal."

* * *

Core shut the door quietly behind him. It was ten o'clock. Lisa and Jamie would be asleep. He opened the spring latch wall cavity and placed his gun inside. The snap of the quick release lock told him the gun was secured and not a risk to Jamie. After his disclosure last year to Lisa about his real employment, there were many new house rules. Core chuckled to himself remembering the thirty page document that Lisa and Jamie had presented to him.

Seven year old Jamie had given him her sternest look when she said, "These are the new rules, Dad. You have to sign these and promise to behave."

Core would have done anything to keep his family, and gladly signed all thirty pages. He walked into the kitchen and found Lisa sitting on a stool at the island nursing a cup of tea.

Core kissed the top of her head as he passed behind her to grab an apple from the basket on the counter. Lisa said, "I took the girls shopping this afternoon."

Core sat on the stool across from her. "How did I know this little temporary situation was going to cost me money?" He took a big bite of the apple and grinned.

Lisa's big brown eyes were filled with tears as she looked at him, "Mathew, Izzy has *nothing*. She has never been to a mall. The child cried when I told her to pick out some new socks. She tried to pay me." Lisa shook her head and then pushed her tea cup away. "You know her grandma taught her well. She has wonderful manners and is a brilliant child. She and Jamie played computer games for an hour! The Apple store man said he never saw kids pick up the concepts so fast."

Core nodded. "I'm glad this hasn't been too much for you. Roger says they are still looking for some family members. So maybe by the end of the weekend...."

Lisa had stood and grabbed a rag from the sink. She began to feverishly wipe the counter where she had been sitting. "Where were these family members when Izzy needed them? Where were they when she and Gram had to share an *orange* for dinner?" Lisa started crying and Core stood to hug her. He knew what was coming next.

"I want to keep her, Mathew."

"She's not a puppy." Core sighed. "With my history I don't know if we could, Lisa."

Lisa pulled away from his hug and stared at him. "Can't we try?"

Core nodded, "Of course, we'll try."

Lisa squeezed Mathew's hand. "Ed called Izzy. I think she understands, but she's only ten years old. Adults keep leaving her one way or another. It breaks my heart."

Mathew sighed, "All we can do is hope she gives us a chance."

They walked upstairs to go to bed. Lisa wanted to peek in on Izzy and quietly opened the guest room door. Lisa gasped. "She's gone!" She flipped the light on and tossed the blankets from the bed.

"Mathew, she left us. She's out there in the streets at night! You have to find her!"

Core walked down to Jamie's room, opened the door and crooked his finger for Lisa to come over. He put his finger on his lip to signal her to be quiet. Lisa looked in and Izzy and Jamie were both in Jamie's bed. They were one big tangle of hair, feet and stuffed animals.

CATAHOULA
List of Characters

U.S. Attorney General's office, Louisiana Eastern Division, New Orleans

1. Sabastian Delacroix, Catahoula (Cat)
2. Theodore 'Ted' Dupre, Louisiana U.S. Attorney General, Cat's boss, going to run for Governor
3. William and Molly Jarvis, ex-Louisiana U.S. Attorney General committed suicide after wife, Molly, murdered
4. Steven Marks, Senior Asst. Attorney General, Fraud Division
5. Ward Bromley, Special Investigator – Criminal Division
6. Martha Wells, Cat's secretary
7. Virgil Holmes, Asst. Director, National Security Division of Solicitor General's office, DOJ

Local characters, New Orleans

1. Otis, owns small grocery store
2. Izzy Dubois, 10 yr. old girl, left orphan after grandmother's death
3. Reuben Florey, reporter, son of Edward J. Meyer
4. Marla Wilson, works with Reuben at Times-Picayune
5. Edward J. Meyer, accused murderer of Molly Jarvis
6. Abram Davis, half owner of Pete's Swamp Boat Rentals

7. Jackson Moore, half owner of Pete's Swamp Boat Rentals
8. Spicey, Voodoo shop owner, has some limited real abilities
9. Sasha, friend and co-worker with Spicey
10. Dakin, Hoodoo princess, seeking Spicey's help
11. Claude and Earl Pegan, brothers hired to dispose of bodies for Dooley
12. Mason Dooley, bad cop
13. Lisa Core, Mathew Core's wife
14. Jamie Core, Mathew Core's seven year old daughter
15. Dillard Boggs, owner of chain of strip clubs

FBI

1. Supervisory Special Agent Roger Dance, lead agent brought to New Orleans
2. Supervisory Special Agent Paul Casey, teams up with Roger for tough cases
3. Supervisory Special Agent Dan Thor, senior agent New Orleans field office
4. Special Agent Jeanne Manigat, assigned New Orleans office, relationship with Thor
5. Special Agent Pablo Manigat, brought to New Orleans for case, twin brother of Jeanne
6. Special Agent Todd Nelson, brought to New Orleans for case
7. Misc. agents: Thompson, Cross, Weaver and Troy assigned to protect Spicey

Other important players

1. Mathew Core, owner of security firm in New Orleans, works exclusively for FBI
2. Zack, former ATF, works for Mathew Core and owns gym used only by FBI
3. Stone Carson, hired hit man
4. Acer Noland, Stone's counterpart, same employer, hit man
5. Nathan Cottard, New Orleans Police, good cop
6. Senator Joe Welsh and family; wife Sarah, daughters Megan and Chelsy

Angels

Mary, Linda, Teresa and Vicki are four friends that decided to take a Hawaiian vacation together. On the way to the airport they were killed in a car accident. Heaven welcomed them as angels, but decided to keep them together as a group, and let them retain some of their mortal thoughts in addition to their angel thoughts. The premise of this decision was that angels that could still think like mortals would have an advantage in helping mortals do good.

The flaw in this premise is that mortal thinking isn't always 'angelic'. Heaven assigned angel trainers to the gals that would appear familiar and likeable. One angel trainer looks and acts like Betty White, and the other, Ellen DeGeneres. Heaven also has developed a number of tools available to the angels to assist them in their assignments. Vicki's daughter, Kim, was given the ability to see and communicate with the gals. This assists greatly in communicating with mortals in need of their services, but unaware the angels exist.

Betty primarily assists the gals when further training is required. Ellen, being more energetic, directly assists in assignments and serves to direct the gals in an efficient order.

Shallow End Gals
About the Authors: Teresa Duncan, Vicki Graybosch,
Linda McGregor, Kimberly Troutman
The staff at the bar gave us the nickname, 'The
Shallow End Gals.' This stems from our choice to
always sit at the short 'L' of the bar at lunch time.
We think the name refers to the fact that there are
fewer stools at this end. The full group meets two or
three times a week. The conversations often resemble some bizarre internet search engine. The facts
that some of us don't hear as well as we used to,
and I have my own language called 'Vicki Speak',
are contributors to this phenomenon. After several
people suggested we should write a book, or seek
professional help, we decided to try the former. We
hope readers will enjoy spending a little time with
us and we welcome you to the Shallow End.

DEDICATIONS

Billie Jo McMullen, my mother, Vicki Graybosch

My husband, Bob, Linda McGregor

Steven Phelps, my father, in loving memory,
Kimberly Troutman

Kenneth W. Duncan, my father
Mary V. Duncan, my mother
Sheila M. Varner, my sister
Jennifer Unger, my niece, Teresa Duncan

Mary Hale, in loving memory, all of us